RUAIRÍ, THE GREY HORSE

Ruairí raised his face and looked over the room. "I want to be in your service, Anraí. And I am valuable; there is no better horseman remaining on the whole island than I."

Anraí blinked thoughtfully. "I believe that, if you're half so good riding as being ridden. And what in return, my lad? Are you a devil, that you have a fancy for my soul? Or is it my lovely wife you covet."

Ruairí laughed in his nose and put a foolish hand through his hair. "I could scarcely do better than Áine, it's true, but I doubt I have force of arms to tear her away from her old man. And I have no interest in your soul, Anraí. What I need of you is the protection of your name and of your establishment."

The small man pulled himself up onto the pile of pillows. "The . . . the protection of my what?"

"I must convince Seán Standún of the ships th̶̶ ̶m a respectable man, so that he will give me h̶̶

Bantam Spectra Books by R. A. MacAvoy
Ask your bookseller for the titles you have missed

THE BOOK OF KELLS
DAMIANO
DAMIANO'S LUTE
THE GREY HORSE
RAPHAEL
TEA WITH THE BLACK DRAGON
TWISTING THE ROPE

THE GREY HORSE

R. A. MacAvoy

BANTAM BOOKS
TORONTO · NEW YORK · LONDON · SYDNEY · AUCKLAND

To the people of Carraroe

THE GREY HORSE
A Bantam Spectra Book / May 1987

All rights reserved.
Copyright © 1987 by R. A. MacAvoy.
Cover art copyright © 1987 by Charles DeMar.
This book may not be reproduced in whole or in part, by
mimeograph or any other means, without permission.
For information address: Bantam Books, Inc.

ISBN 0-553-26557-1

Published simultaneously in the United States and Canada

Bantam Books are published by Bantam Books, Inc. Its trademark, consisting of the
words "Bantam Books" and the portrayal of a rooster, is Registered in U.S. Patent and
Trademark Office and in other countries. Marca Registrada. Bantam Books, Inc.,
666 Fifth Avenue, New York, New York 10103.

PRINTED IN THE UNITED STATES OF AMERICA

O   0 9 8 7 6 5 4 3 2 1

NAMES OF THE PEOPLE

Anraí Ó Reachtaire – Henry Raftery, sometimes called Anraí
   Thurlaigh, or Henry, son of Turlough, after his father

Áine NíAnluain – Anne Raftery, his wife

Seosamh Ó Reachtaire – Joe Raftery, their son

Ruairí MacEibhir – Rory MacEever

Eibhear, pronounced "Eever" – Granite: Ruairí's father

Gaoth, pronounced "Gwee" – Wind: Ruairí's mother

Donncha MacSiadhail – Donald MacSheel

Máire NíStandún – Mary Stanton

Eibhlín NíStandún – Eileen Stanton, her sister

Seán Standún – John Stanton, their father

Tadhg Ó Murchú – Tim Murphy, priest of the parish

Diarmuid Ó Cadhain – Dermitt Cain

I went from door to door in Carraroe, with an introduction from Peig Bean Uí Cheallaigh and accompanied by one of the Ó Ceallaigh boys, trying to find out the history of the place. Everyone told me there had been none: that the great events of the last century and more in Ireland had passed that parish cleanly by.

At last, in the parlor of the rectory, I discovered one fact: that in the early years of the Land League, a group of Carraroe women had held off an eviction by their combined strength. Around this one bit of history I have woven a great deal of fiction.

None of my characters are based on real people of the time. Tadhg Ó Murchú was not priest of the parish. I expect there was always more than one. There are many Ó Reachtaires in Connaught, none of them related to Anraí, the trainer. Standún, or Stanton, is another common name.

MacEibhir is a name I made up.

I am indebted to the Ó Ceallaigh family of An Sruthán for their hospitality to a stranger and for the "protection of their name" all the time I was with them. And I am indebted to Dr. Peadar MacanIomaire for his support in an effort he may have thought a little bit mad. I feel a great debt to all the people of the Cois Fhairrge area of Connemara, because folk such as they are the hope of the world.

CHAPTER ONE

An Sruthán, or The Eddies

The sky was full of the grey scum of a soup kettle on the boil. The wind blew from the east, or the north, or south from Galway Bay; it was always changing. Anraí Ó Reachtaire came along the Cois Fhairrge Road holding his hand up against his forehead as a sort of makeshift hatbrim, equally ineffective against the pinching hail and the unexpected flashes of sunlight that made his eyes water.

Anraí's hair was thin on top, and the wind was doing its best to thin it further. It might have been that years of leaving his hat behind in places as far from home as Dublin and London had worked the damage, but the weathers of Connemara were enough cause for baldness by themselves. He was a man of approximately seventy years and had never been noted for either grace of body or beauty of feature: not even in his coming-up years. His pride in those early days had always been the length of time passed (once, five years, and another time, seven) since a horse had unseated him. At this time in his life Anraí was wary of that subject, and it was his study to get the better of the animals that were his occupation without undue risk. He always carried a rope halter concealed under his shirt, to save trips to the stable.

He had come this route last night, delivering a yearling filly to a man at Doleen Harbor, but his own mount had begun the day lame, and Anraí had decided to walk until he could catch a ride on some passing wagon. There had been no wagons and a lot of weather.

Anraí stopped to breathe, for the way from here to Carraroe was uphill, and he let the wind turn his face toward the water. He braced his feet and locked his knees.

So much activity in the air and on the ruffled water, and even grass sods being blown, root, dirt, and all, over the road . . . Only the granite of the hills was safe from it. Anraí found himself wishing he himself had a few more of the characteristics of stone, but as the eroded clods blew over the toes of his boots it struck him with some satisfaction that even the earth could not keep its hair on. He laughed out loud in a social fashion, as though he'd have been glad for someone to hear him.

There was someone to hear and to answer him. Anraí saw a movement of grey against grey and he heard a surprised throaty sound. He shifted his head and received a spatter of hail across his nose.

There was a bare, round hillock of stone, with sparks of quartz shining in the wet. It was thirty feet high, and the road went unambitiously around it. Anraí put his face into a squint and made out the shape of a horse or pony at the top of the hill.

A horse on a hill was as common a thing as a dog on a front stoop, but Anraí, being who he was, could never have left it alone; it was necessary he go up and see what horse it was.

The slope was slippery and gave him a twinge in the lower back. The horse looked down upon Anraí's slow progress. There was something laughable in the position of the man: hair in his face, and hands as much as booted feet scrabbling over the bright stone and oozing mud. There was also something undecided about him, for Anraí was neither looking at the beast nor approaching it directly. Despite the effort he was expending, it did not seem the man had any interest in the horse at all, but instead only wanted the small increase in view the elevation would give him.

And perhaps because of this inconsequentiality, the horse stood and allowed Anraí to scuffle up beside him, and even to use his untrimmed mane as a handhold when he painfully straightened his back. All this—the air of inconsequentiality and seeming purposelessness—was Anraí's art and the study of his lifetime, for a man cannot catch and hold a horse by main force.

There was room at the top of the hill for six legs, and Anraí leaned against the animal's dirty white side and waited for his heart to stop banging him. With the horse he looked out over four stone cottages—one of which had a slate roof—thirteen granite-piled low fences, and the little pier of An Sruthán, where one of Seán Standún's fishing hookers was tied.

It was a beautiful boat, high fronted and slim, and it rocked against the bags full of kelp that padded its contact with the stones of the pier. A man in a black guernsey and a very dirty tam was handing out fish in a wooden bucket to Seán's big, dark daughter, who took the bucket over her arm like a handbag and turned back away from the water, the weight thumping against her hip.

"It's beyond me what you find to keep you here, my lad," said Anraí, who had no maritime interest whatsoever, and he put his arm companionably over the broad back. The horse turned a huge, mild eye upon him—mild, but ironical about the furry edges—and in that instant the hail and wind gave up its work and the sun struck silver out of the horse's coat. Anraí lifted his eyes in astonishment to a sky gone mostly blue.

The boat was green and gold above a brilliance of water that hurt to see. Máire Standún was carrying enamelwork fishes set in with diamonds and rubies and other stones Anraí couldn't name. Her bored, sullen face lit as the sun touched it, in such a manner that Anraí did not know whether it had been a trick of light or of her own mood. The sailor put both arms to his head and tore his tam off. He shouted something Anraí could not make out, but certainly expressed enthusiasm.

"Well," said Anraí, thumping the dirty fur. "Pretty picture, isn't it? Certainly that was worth some puffing and blowing. In the winter, too." Then, having established rapport and communality of interest with the horse, he dared turn to look it straight on.

"God bless you, I don't know you at all, and if you'll take no offense by it, I'd like to have a good look now."

The horse shifted its very small ears, as though to say that no offense had been taken so far, and Anraí let his resting arm slip over the horse's withers and down the point of the brawny shoulder, for it was Anraí's habit, with winter-coated horses, to look with his hands.

It was a laudably straight and clean foreleg he felt, free from swelling or splints. The fetlock was hard and the pastern remarkably well angled and long, considering the animal's solidity. None of its other legs seemed a whit worse, and when Anraí, using a little shove and pinch, unweighted and lifted a foot, the ragged-edged hoof was as healthy and symmetrical as that of any of the ponies of Connemara. Which is to say, as perfect as can be.

His neck was long and his chest oval, and beneath a beard that might have concealed as well the head of a camel as that of a horse, he had the platter jaw and delicate face of a mountain pony. He gazed blandly at Anraí and sighed at the liberties the man was taking.

Anraí Ó Reachtaire walked a circle around the grey horse, one hand always on the beast's body, mumbling to himself. An excitement almost painful was growing on him. His heart, which had its problems, had not settled from the effort of the climb and now beat drumrolls down his legs and arms, but he did not care greatly.

It was important to him that he find something wrong with this beast, or else he felt he might die here, on top of this little mammary dome, and never see Áine or his own barns again. It had been years . . .

He pulled firmly on the tail of the horse, walking behind, because it was common belief that a horse would not kick one in that position. Anraí did not believe this horse had such an ungenerous intention, and he *had* been kicked by horses whose tails he'd been holding, but still he pulled as he stepped behind. It did no harm.

What he saw, standing behind the horse, was not a fault exactly, but it did change the complexion of the matter. This was a stallion standing alone on the hill, without hobble or halter.

There were stallions enough roaming the hills to the north, certainly. Little stallions. It was easier and far cheaper to allow it so than to try to control the breeding, for a stallion was less use and more trouble than his board was worth.

But they weren't welcome in society, as it were, and the

man owning a "better" class of mare was their sworn enemy. The stallions of the improved lines were kept on straw and under roof: Thoroughbreds, Hackneys, Welsh Cobs—and any man who desired a profitable foal took his mares to one of these.

This was a native horse, thought Anraí. As certain as he was a native man. A very perfect native horse, he thought further, and did not continue the analogy. Anraí bred Thoroughbreds and half-breds, for a man must make a living, and he understood and respected the blood horse. But as he stroked the muddy hindquarters and the very yellow tail of the horse on the hilltop, he was very glad that its perfection was clearly not due to any influx of imported blood.

"You're a fine horse," whispered Anraí. "Please God, there's nothing wrong to say about you. And if you were with *me*, I'd feed you as much oats as was good for you!"

The horse cocked a listening ear, and his brown eye was warm in the sunlight. At the word "oats" he nodded his head forcefully, as a horse does when it tastes something sweet.

Anraí laughed at him. "Oats," he said once more, experimentally, and the animal gave a low rumble in its chest. "Indeed, you're no wild animal; you have the flavor of Irish speech too well. Can you speak English, too, I wonder?" He gave him the word in English as well, but the horse merely stared.

Anraí pulled on its mane in a teasing manner. "That was wasted breath. Only a Gael would keep a horse like you. You're not leggy enough for the exalted tastes of the English. You've too much brain, I bet, and not enough temperament by half!"

The sun went in at this, as though it could not endure the force of Anraí's criticism, and the grey horse (suddenly dim) took a step away from him. It occurred to Anraí that he did not, in fact, own this horse, and that he had forgotten his hat. Slipping and scuffing, he headed down the hill.

The horse stood and watched him, its head turned on its long neck and its tail swishing in an unsettled manner. As Anraí reached the road, groaned, and rubbed his spine, the horse let out a shrill, commanding whinny.

The old man had to stop and look, and he turned just in time to see the horse launch itself from the top of the hill. It jumped like a cat, with back bent and its nose between its knees, and landed in a controlled skid on the granite. Another pounce and it was on the road behind Anraí, who stood with mouth open and hand over heart. The horse danced toward him, quite conscious of the effect of its performance. Its neck was arched and its head at the vertical. With every step, it made proud little gestures with its forefeet.

"God be praised," said Anraí, on the intake of breath. But as the horse grew closer, Anraí's manner changed completely and his dry old face wrinkled in anger. "That's the way to break your feet, my lad, and when your coffin bones have come out the bottoms of your blood-red and crushed foot soles, then what use will you be, to yourself or to living man?"

Taken aback, the horse halted three paces away. It gave a disgusted snort and pounded its near forefoot against the stone of the roadway. Anraí saw that foot in the air and feared the worst. He closed the gap between them and demanded the hoof. Obediently, the horse gave it.

Anraí took a pick out of his pocket and poked the perfect horse foot with it. He squeezed and prodded, but to his surprise and secret satisfaction it seemed quite sound. "You haven't taken yourself to the knackers this time, lad," he said, and dropped the foot.

It seemed he had dropped the whole horse with it, for there was the great beast, on its front knee on the road. It looked up at him and grunted, nodding its head impatiently. Anraí blinked, but he was wary.

As a lad, he had trained a horse to bow for a lady. Once. He had vowed after that never to teach such a demeaning trick to a noble animal. A lady that couldn't mount with a block and the aid of a groom's hand might as well stay withindoors. It had been many years since he had come across a beast taught in this manner.

Still the horse knelt and nodded. Anraí rubbed his hand over the bristle of his chin. "Are you soliciting me, my boy? Have you so much regard for my grey hairs that you'd sooner carry me down the road than see me walk?" He grinned at the idea, especially since the horse was at least as grey as the man. "Or is it that you want to take me at a disadvantage, and as soon as I'm up you'll fling yourself into the bay and drown me, as Other Folk do to Christian souls?"

The horse looked away. It bit a fly on its knee, lost interest in the matter, rose, and walked away, ahead of Anraí, who felt he'd been rather impolite. It took him a few minutes to catch up with the beast (without seeming to chase it) and offer a full apology.

"You see, it's a hard world, lad, and one gets more used to a neighbor's opposition than his help. It's rarely enough that one's fellow creature offers charity, and I should not have scorned you so. But you must remember that the stories are . . ."

As though it had been shot, the horse dropped again on the road, where it knelt, nodding. The force of Anraí's grin tickled his ears. "Well, I can't in conscience refuse again, after that, can I?" He pulled out the scapular from around his neck, kissed it, reached for the rope halter, and stepped onto the horse.

A little moment later, as the horse was rising up (very fast, as though on springs) it occurred to Anraí that the thing to have done was to put the halter on the horse before climbing on. Simple mistake. Because now that the animal had bounded off, striking sparks from the road in its flight, there really would be no opportunity to do so.

The twin hills receded, and the bare hooves pounded over the bridge of the stream itself. Anraí sat the wild gallop of the wild horse with his hands on his lap, thinking to himself that he had done a very silly thing, for an old man.

The horse ran with his head forward and low, in relaxed fashion, and his gait was very easy to sit. For Anraí, there was nothing very disturbing in being run away with, for he was as at ease on horseback as he was on foot: more so, for on horseback his back did not hurt him, and his wind did not suffer. If the animal had a brain in its head—if it were a Connemara horse, let's say—it would take care of the rider as part and parcel of taking care of itself. There was the rare animal that would purposely slam its side into a wall or a tree to do a rider damage, and Anraí's experience with these had made him a spritely mover. He would have staked his winter's hay that this beast was neither homicidal nor hysterical, and so Anraí was without fear for himself. But embarrassed he was, for allowing a horse such liberties had a bad effect on

its training, and therefore Anraí cursed himself roundly for a
spavined, sickle-hocked, soft-pated, hammerheaded ass as
the grey horse flung itself down the road.

To the right of the road lay Lochán an Bhuilín, a lake of
some two dozen acres in size, circled by black winter gorse.
Its waters were mirror bright now that the wind had quieted
down. Straight ahead was Carraroe—An Cheathrú Rúa, The
Rough Quarter—which was called the poorest town in the
poorest parish in Ireland. The first plaster-finished stone
cottage rose up on the right of the road.

Anraí Ó Reachtaire coughed into his cupped hands. "I'm
sure you don't want to do this to me, my lad. Shooting me
down the main avenue of the town in this unconstrained
manner, like some equestrian exhibition in Galway." The
horse's fox-sharp ears folded back attentively, and it made a
sound of animal enthusiasm and nodded its white pony head.
It gave a smooth little hop and shuffle and entered Carraroe
dancing.

There was a small boy with no shoes but with a large rusty
barrel hoop, which he was driving with a stick before him.
He glanced appreciatively at the horse, which was large by
the area's standards. Then its state of undress became obvious to the boy, and his mouth opened and puckered, and
opened and puckered. The hoop got clean away from him and
rolled into the middle of the street, where the cobbles set it
into an awkward gyroscopic spin.

Anraí saw the hoop in front of them, and he set his legs
tight and grabbed mane, for he could imagine nothing more
frightening to a horse than a hoop spinning and singing in
the roadway. Indeed, the horse gave a little squeal as a signal
that something was about to happen, and it lifted up into the
air.

Anraí hadn't been sure they were jumping until they landed
on the stones beyond, and even that landing was marked by
only the slightest break in rhythm. The hoop was left behind
with the gawping boy, and here ahead was the shape of the
church to his left and the circles of bright red that meant
women walking together past the churchyard's cowgate.

"God to you, Anraí Ó Reachtaire!" called one of them. "I
have the weaving your own Áine spoke for!" Anraí stared
straight ahead of him with a face of forbidding majesty and

affected not to hear. One hand he carried clenched at the horse's withers, as though it held a rein of such fine and narrow leather it could not be seen from a distance, while with the other he fished in his waistcoat pocket and drew out his silver pocket watch, which he held in front of his face in a preoccupied, businesslike manner.

But this did not save him, for as he passed in front of the first hostelry on the left, a man who was resting diagonally in the doorway leaned out, pulled his cap to shade his eyes, and called out "Is it Anraí the son of Thurlaigh Ó Reachtaire riding bareback through the streets of An Cheathrú Rúa, like a petticoater on an old pony?"

Anraí would have ignored this hail as he had the other, except that the horse went into a splendid piaffe, with his hindquarters tucked under his belly and his muscular neck crested like a swan's. "God to you, Maurice," said Anraí, with great restraint.

Maurice Ó Ceallaigh stepped across the stabling yard, his cap in his hand, and his glance at Anraí was both respectful and wary. "A horse of Spanish blood, perhaps, for certainly you're teaching him the Spanish airs and dances, without so much as rope or halter on him, too."

Anraí cleared his throat and considered the possibility he might be able to slip down, now that the animal had ceased its forward progression. But although it is not particularly dangerous to sit a horse that is running away with you, getting off such a horse is quite hazardous, and Anraí disliked being hurt. "As all our horses in Connacht have a strong flavor of Spanish blood, Maurice, I cannot deny it in this son of the seasons. I have not gotten so far with him, however, as to be at teaching him the continental graces. In fact, if you were able to take an easy grip on his mane, there, and put a single hand gently over his nose, you'd have my share of gratitude."

Maurice Ó Ceallaigh was not a horseman by profession but a hosteler, but there was no human soul in Carraroe so ignorant of stock that he would not have been able to be of use in this situation. He reached a calm arm under the horse's jaw and grabbed a handful of mane, and he put his other beery-smelling hand over the smudged white nose. The horse snorted what he thought of the smell, and his

stationary trot exploded forward, dragging Maurice with him.
With every step he nodded, pulling the tavern keeper onto
his toes. "Ah, don't be that way," said Maurice in soothing
tones, while Anraí leaned back hard as a signal to stop.
But the horse quite calmly went on his way, as though he
could drag a town along with him as easily as not.

"Let go of him, Maurice," said Anraí, disheartened. "He's
determined to go, and he'll only pull you with him."

Maurice now looked up at the old man on the horse with
more understanding of the problem. "Why by the grace of
Jesus did you get up there, Anraí, with no halter nor bridle
on the animal?" He trotted along beside, for the horse was
not going at any speed. "Is it a sport or wager?"

"It is a penance for my sins," answered Anraí composedly,
as the horse sidestepped around a young woman in petticoat
and black shawl. The movement was as smooth as a cart
skidding on ice, and it ended with a gallant genuflection
toward the wearer of the shawl. Anraí felt a noticeable rising
of his stomach, as the horse so unexpectedly dipped. "This
animal is marvelously trained and not obedient at all," he
said to Maurice.

The hosteler was dropping behind, and he looked back
nervously at his untended bar. "I believe your only sin is
temper, old man, and if your rage ran away with you so
gently, it would be no sin at all. God bless you, I can't keep
up with a trotting horse."

"No reason why you should, Maurice. Keep you safe; I'll be
all right. Unless he drops me in the ocean," he added in more
private tones.

At these words the horse gave a squeal and slammed a
heavy foot onto the stones. Its ribs swelled and heaved
between the rider's legs.

"No need for you to take offense, you great bully," Anraí
told it. "This is the road to the water, after all."

But in three paces more the horse swerved right between
two walls of sand-stuccoed stone and took Anraí into the
backyard of Fenton the butcher, where white sheets of linen
hung on the rope, still damp from the morning's shower, and
equally white báinín work clothes lay stretched over the
hedge of stubby fuchsia. Anraí took a handful of mane and
prepared for trouble by relaxing. "It's no ghost or spirit, lad,

but only the washing," he whispered. "It won't do you a bit of harm."

The horse, standing surrounded by flapping banners of white, flicked its little ears forward and back. Suddenly it gave a warlike trumpeting and assaulted the length of twine from which the sheets depended, tearing stallion fashion with its teeth. There was a musical ping, and Anraí was struck in the forehead by a broken clothespin as his dirty white horse bounded into the mass of the fresh laundry and through it.

They came out onto the sidestreet between the ironmonger's and the old convent house, dragging a double tail of ruined linen. It was the length of the street before the horse got rid of it, and Anraí could barely hear the woman chasing behind them.

"You blackhearted, scoured, foul-tailed, cow-hocked, bog-spavined, unchristian . . ." Anraí could not think of an appropriate noun to end the string of calumny. He rubbed his forehead as the easy rolling canter carried him out of the town and between stony fields. "What worse could you do to an old man than shame him in his life's profession that way? Cruel! Why, you might as well be my son, and there is no insult worse than that."

Now the row houses, neat as hens along a roost, disappeared from the side of the way, their places taken by cottages of unplastered stone set at every convenient angle among the strips of stone-walled fields. The horse cantered nicely, with ears reversed for listening, and but for the fact that nothing he did had any influence on the beast, Anraí could have asked for little improvement in its manners. But the quality of the horse's movement did nothing to soften Anraí Ó Reachtaire; he was very angry.

He must have been very angry to have mentioned his son.

"And you can't cozen me into believing you felt a natural animal terror of those blowing sheets, for I know when a horse is afraid and when he has a nasty spirit in him. It was nothing but the desire to do me damage, as your own face itself betrayed to me. Well, I'm not a rich man, nor a young man, nor a healthy man, to endure being made sport of in this manner, and in the name of Christ I have had enough."

As Anraí chided, the horse's gait slowed and lost its elastic-

ity, until by the end of his jobation it was a shuffling trot.
Anraí saw his descent clear and heaved a great sigh.

"And now I'll have a miserable walk in front of me and a
great apology to make, all thanks to you, you great disgrace
to a fine race of beasts. And with my heart the way it is, who
knows the damage it may . . ."

He got no more out. Anraí had time only to slip an inch to
the left on the broad white back when the horse bugled again,
sank onto its haunches and leaped from a standstill off the
road and over the dry stone wall, where it took off galloping
over the dead sedge and glistening bog toward the north.

Its round black hooves splashed and sucked with every
step, filling the air with a noise almost like bells. Sometimes
one foot would slip in the standing puddles and sometimes
two or three feet at once would sink into a soft spot and
Anraí would prepare to be flung off. "Sweet Jesus, lad, haven't
you lived in this parish long enough to keep out of the
bogs?" Anraí's tenor voice cracked as he addressed the horse.

It was not personal fear that moved the old man, for
although the ground was scattered with stones just fit to
break a head, Anraí had fallen countless times and never
broken anything more than his collarbone. A man might get
stuck into the bog, certainly, but if he did he'd be more likely
to die of an ague than drowning, for here there was no bog
more than four feet deep.

But for a horse the story was different. The suckholes, the
pools, and the hidden boulders were all designed to snap a
leg like a green stick, and where was the winch and rope out
here to haul to safety a helpless beast weighing a half ton?

Here was the wall that divided O'Faoilin's garden patch
from the grazing. It was three feet high and held in place by
briar. The white horse came blowing up to it and skidded,
and from that skid it leaped the wall, its hindquarters advancing as it flew, so that it landed almost sideward and took
off in another direction, over the fallen ruins of a house.
Through all this, Anraí felt no jar or stumble.

That sparkle of blue at his left was Greatman's Bay, which
made the west shore of Carraroe. Ahead, once again, was
Lochán an Bhuilín, with the busy sky reflected in its flat
waters. This time Anraí came at the lake from the other, or
west, side, and the mad horse made a detour onto the stony

bottom, soaking its legs up to the knees and destroying the sky picture all around it.

Anraí considered flinging himself off at this juncture, for at least the water would be soft to land in. But though he was no sailor, still he could not swim, and he was not sure about the depth of the lake. Besides, until the horse came to grief, he would be fine where he was.

It took one small fence after another and bounded from stone hummock to dry grass to dead black heath. The bog sucked at it but did not hold it or strain the cables of its swinging legs. With his eyes closed, Anraí found, he could convince himself he was hacking quietly along the road. "If you were my horse," he said under his breath—and twin, perfectly matched impulses of fury and affection choked the horseman's breathing—"if you were my horse, I'd do a thing or two with you."

He opened his eyes again to find he *was* hacking quietly along the road. In fact, they were already as far north as Drumalegaun, where two men in báinín were hurrying a donkey cart filled with milk cans down the road in the direction of Glashnacally.

Anraí automatically took a deep breath and thought slow, quiet thoughts, for horses can be funny about donkeys. But this one wasn't, it seemed, for it cantered on, looking neither left nor right, its neck at such an arch that the rider might have been restraining it with hands of iron. Neither did Anraí look around, lest he recognize the men and be recognized in his turn.

But though the horse had no objection to donkeys, this donkey did not reciprocate. Anraí glanced around in time to see the cart and milk being propelled violently off the road in reverse, while the ass wore its ears laid backward, like a frightened rabbit's.

The horse did not tire, and Anraí's great concern wore itself off. By the time the sky clouded over and the drizzle took up, they had left behind the ruination of rocks that was the peninsula, and in front of him the earth was a soft, unbroken brown of bogland, with the perfect round cones of the hills to the right, and the tall Twelve Pins, the mountains of Connemara, winking in and out of the clouds ahead.

Anraí yawned. "Would it bother you too much to know

that you're taking me on my road home, lad? Would it ruin your pleasure in the day's sport if you found I wasn't lost at all?" The horse danced and shook its head, but made no sound. Perhaps it was finally getting tired.

The road went right and the horse with it. At the easy, rhythmic, but never mechanical pace they reached the Cashla River in a few minutes and crossed it. Evidently the animal had no fear of bridges. Anraí dropped his head forward so that the pervasive drizzle slid off his eyebrows, and he further closed his eyes to keep the rain out. Not for the first time in his life, he fell asleep on a moving horse.

He woke to a snort and a foot stamping to find the sky cracked with light once more and an afternoon wind blowing. The land before him dipped down in a dizzying smoothness of rock and dry grass, and he saw his own valley below, familiar to him as the face of his wife. He was sitting horseback on the dome of Knockduff Mountain, where he had often climbed in years past. The horse was still beneath him.

He gave a yawn and believed he would be sore soon. He scratched the wet wool and linen on his shoulders and felt a rough touch on his stomach, under the shirt.

It was the rope halter he had used on the yearling that morning. Half asleep, he took it out, pulled the rope through to adjust it for size, leaned forward, and clapped it over the grey horse's nose and behind its ears.

Anraí felt a jolt as though the horse had shied in place. Its sides went as stiff as wood. It hopped and trembled and before Anraí's eyes began to steam. Startled himself by this reaction, Anraí very warily tied the lead rope to both sides of the mouthpiece, making a sort of bridle out of the halter. "Don't tell me you're a stranger to the old rope halter, my lad," he whispered gently, close to the horse's ear. He saw a round eye ringed with white, and the long, unkempt yellow tail switched left and right. Anraí had a sinking feeling there would be a fight between himself and this horse on the stones of Knockduff Peak.

But he had to go home. At this season, there were no more than two more hours of light and likely no visible moon after that. He gave the horse an experimental squeeze of the legs. In perfect obedience it moved down the mountainside.

CHAPTER TWO

Knockduff, or Under the Black Hill

Áine said the pig's trotters were ruined. This was not true, of course, but it was the closest she could get to scolding Anraí for coming home wet and weary, when that had been no fault of his own. Anraí, wrapped in a blanket and with his feet in wool over a hot stone, sat by the kitchen fire and ate two trotters and a great heap of mash, both of which he covered with buttermilk and a crystalline layer of salt.

He told her about the horse, but not that he had mounted it without a bridle or halter. She told him how the chestnut filly had kicked Donncha, and what liniment she had used, but did not tell him about the letter from Seosamh, their only child. Áine and Anraí had been married for forty years.

Night fell and she saw her husband's face reflected by lamplight in the glass of the window, with his jaw working around the potatoes and the shadows licking in and out. It hurt her to see how old he was getting to be, and she scraped more mash onto his plate. The reflection glared at her in response, as though she had challenged his ability in some way.

One son she had given him and no daughters at all. And he had put her in a house of two storeys and seven rooms, with a girl to help her with the work, sometimes. Of course there was no knowing *she* was the one who lacked, as far as children went. If Anraí had sired a ragtag lot of babies before marriage, or even outside of it, then Áine would at least know. But that was not Anraí: nor did he drink or even wager more than one had to expect of a horseman. His only fault was in being at war with fully half the neighborhood at all times.

In the eight years since Áine had left off the possibility of another baby, she had begun to regret Anraí's fidelity that had once made her complacent. A love child was a great shame, but better than no child at all in this great echoing house. She would have taken it in as that of a cousin, if decency could have been preserved. That she might have had her own love child, and with greater secrecy, never occurred to her.

She took up Anraí's plate and fork and carried them to the sideboard. She heard him scratching his wiry hair with both hands as he got up.

"Are you going out again tonight, nursing a chill like that?" she asked, without turning.

"I am, of course, my dear. To the barn. I can't dump a strange horse in like a sack of bran and expect it to sit neat until morning. I won't catch cold in the fifty feet of drizzle."

Áine's plates each showed a little blue Chinese man and a little blue Chinese woman standing on a bridge like the one standing over the three-seasons stream in the close pasture. Over the bridge in the Chinese plate hung a sally wood: proof, as Tadhg Ó Murchú, the priest, said, that the Chinese were just like everyone else. The picture did not prove that, of course, for no Connemara man would let a willow grow uncut to such a height that its withies fell to the ground, however gracefully. Áine stared fixedly at the plate, thinking of that and thinking that she had to tell Anraí now.

"I got a letter from Seosamh today," she said. Her words rang loudly in the room and were followed by silence. Áine looked over her shoulder to find nothing but the table and the cupboard, with the spinet peeking through from the sitting room beyond. Anraí had gone out very quietly.

Donncha MacSiadhail had his right hand wrapped in linen, with blue fingertips protruding. The chestnut filly that had kicked him was stalled by the front door, for it seemed she needed to be worked with. Donncha gestured to the corner loose-box and winced from the pain of it. "He ate his dinner with the appetite of a sporting gentleman and has been paying calls ever since."

"Paying calls, Donncha?" In the light of the groom's oil lamp Anraí could see a pale shape, looking clean and ghostly against the darkness.

"Never doubt me. First he came out to visit the grain bins, and I found him standing there, peacefully, assessing our supplies. I put him back after that and made sure the latch had fallen. Next he was out calling on the little red girl, and she hiding behind the stall door in terrible timidity. (I wish I had that effect upon her.) This time I closed the top door on him as well."

"It isn't closed now," said Anraí, but not chidingly, for Donncha usually knew what he was about.

The groom glanced at the stall of the grey horse and then glanced at it again. "Indeed, it isn't."

Anraí walked the length of the damp, stone barn until he came to the loose-box, which was large and airy, made really for foaling. The horse stepped forward and waited for him.

It was the same glimmering as the priest's white lace frock at the mass, and the skin under the hair was black, casting a light of silver over the whole. Its dark eyes closed like the silent wingbeats of an owl. Anraí caught his breath.

"You've cleaned him up," was what he said to Donncha.

"Barely. A brush and a bucket. Clippers on the head of him: he makes no trouble in that way. He'll need more to be presentable."

All this was only Donncha's modesty. He was an artist with horses, though not Anraí's equal as a rider. He could take a shapeless rug of grey hair and force the attention and the admiration of all the horse-appreciating world. For this animal he had carved out the great eyes, and with four little snips, revealed the tiny, thoughtful ears, which by their minuteness multiplied the size and strength of the neck. Underneath, by shaving lightly under the chin, he had shown off that muzzle which was so oddly delicate compared with the strength of the horse's jaw and neck.

And behind the heavy round plates at the base of its jaw he had made a few tiny clips and revealed the throatlatch as clean and arched as a two-year-old blood colt's.

Anraí flipped the latch and slid in, shoving with his hip

lest the horse use that opportunity to escape again. He walked around the quietly attentive horse, and everything he saw was a fresh excuse for admiration. "Look at those forelegs, my friend. There's no more 'jewelry' upon them than upon an equestrian statue."

Donncha leaned over the top door, grinned, and scraped one hand over his own, unshaven chin. "Well, there're no splints, anyway. Probably means the old boy's had no work in his life."

"Never believe it, Donncha. He knows where to put his feet, is all." Anraí walked behind, grabbing the still-quite-yellow tail in his hand and stroking the beast's thigh and gaskin.

"I hear there's a letter from Seosamh come today," offered Donncha uncertainly, but Anraí was not hearing and the groom did not dare to repeat.

"I think you might use his hooves to cut biscuits." Anraí was now stroking the black sole of one of these perfect round feet with his hand. Its cleanness struck him, and he peered up around the yellow bracken that carpeted the loose-box. "Is he bound up, do you think?"

Donncha's grin exposed all his uneven teeth. "Not so. That was his other evening's errand—going out into the bushes like a Christian."

Anraí's face folded in little wrinkles away from his faded blue eyes. He edged out of the box door again. "A Christian! That he's not. Well, it's too bad, if he has such nice instincts, that we have to restrain him, but when I think of the devil that sits between those pointy white ears, I wish I had seven padlocks on him, and each of them blessed at the church font!" As he spoke, Anraí shoved the iron latch into its socket and then swung the top half of the door shut and did the same for it.

Donncha scratched at the hair that was in his ears with his good hand. "Anraí, you're in deadly danger of the sin of idol worship with that horse, and I don't know why."

"You don't know why?" Anraí's normally quiet voice doubled in volume. "You brushed, washed, and shaved the contours of that beast's frame and you don't know why?"

"I don't." Donncha sat himself on a hay bale, took a slow breath into his belly, and prepared for argument. "There's no direct fault in him, but still, what good? I would have to say I prefer the type of that filly there, though I haven't any reason to love her today. She's a Thoroughbred, while this is a chance meeting of someone's pony mare and a whistling stranger."

There was no change in Anraí Ó Reachtaire's face, except that it had gone turkey-cock red. "Donncha son of Eibhlín, you have a few tricks but there's no soundness to you. That filly has yellow hooves the thickness of my thumbnail and no more brain than any of Áine's laying hens. And cow hocks. And I'm not too certain of her vision on the right side, which you should thank God for, as otherwise she might have broken your head instead of your hand. You can commend your soul to heaven if that grey horse ever decides to strike a blow at you, for he has brain where she has only ... only nerves."

Unshaken, Donncha smiled more broadly than ever. "Yet her cow hocks and her nerves may win me fifty pounds, racing, which the brain of that bog splasher in there will not. What do I care for a horse's thinking, when what I want is for it to echo my own?"

Anraí knew that this was a made-up argument and that Donncha no more preferred the weedy chestnut filly to the grey than he had fifty pounds to wager. Every night that Anraí came out to the barns, which was almost every night, Donncha could be relied upon to produce some outrageous statement that would keep him there as long as possible. Anraí knew this, but as he was going back to a house with a fire and a spinet and a wife who heated bricks for him, and as Donncha was going to bed down in the empty stall between Squire Blondell's big hunter and the aforementioned filly, it seemed ungenerous not to give the groom his argument.

"Fifty years with horses, Donncha—and I have done my own share of racing *and* of wagering—has taught me that it's the clever horses that win races, time after time. And as for this grey horse ..." Anraí leaped forward and snapped the top latch open. The half door fell open forcefully and banged into the stone wall, for the horse had been leaning its head against it. The beast blinked a bit foolishly.

"... this horse has it in him to win a thousand races."

Donncha snorted derisively. "Make sense, Anraí! This is a workhorse! He has ribs like a barrel."

"You have a *head* like a barrel, Donncha MacSiadhail. There are all sorts of races to be bet on: hurdles, steeplechasing, town-to-town—and for all but a short distance on a shaved track, I'd put my money on this Connemara lad. If I were riding him, I would."

The ragged, bristly face of the horse groom went from cunning to blank with surprise. "You can't mean that, Anraí."

In fact, Anraí had been so stung (knowingly stung, but stung nonetheless) by his groom's aspersions that he hardly had known what he was saying. But he put one veined old hand up against the horse's neck and he repeated, "If I were riding him, I would."

The grey horse lowered its head until its silver-black muzzle rested on the top point of Anraí's shoulder. Donncha pointed, for it seemed to him that in another moment his employer and longtime friend would be bitten, not noticing. But Anraí was well aware of the horse's muzzle on his shoulder, and when the black-lipped mouth with its square teeth opened over the flesh and bone, so near his neck, he did not move.

With elaborate calmness, almost courtesy, the horse rocked Anraí back and forth by the shoulder three times. Then it released him, turned its hindquarters, and walked away to the far wall of the stall. Anraí looked away, at the far stone wall of the barn, and then quietly he closed the upper door once more.

Donncha was not a restless sleeper, and he did not know whether he had been half awake or all dreaming when he saw the long white body and the black-kneed legs of the new horse passing by his nest of hay. He rose, scratched out his ears, and found the horse lying at full length in the still-impeccable bracken, snoring gently. The top door was open and the bottom unlatched.

At the same hour of the night, Anraí sat up in bed. "Was I dreaming or did someone tell me I got a letter from that viper son of mine?"

"It's I who got the letter and I who told you," said Áine

from under the pillow, where she kept her face in sleeping. "But I'm not going to trade my sleep for a brawl about it."

Anraí grabbed the counterpane in tight fists and yanked up on it. Áine heard the hiss of a seam giving way, and she sighed.

Anraí would not lie down again. "How much?"

"Not now."

"Just tell me the amount, woman. I won't stint my horses for that boy's debts one more time."

"You never did, old man. You stinted yourself instead, and your wife as well. He only wants ten pounds toward a uniform, so there's no cause for melodrama."

"Ten pounds!" The ripping sound was louder. "Do you know how hard my man Donncha works for ten pounds? Or myself, for that matter."

"I know how hard I work for nothing at all, and without sleep," answered Áine. She put both hands over the pillow, pressing it against her one ear, while she pressed her head into the soft feather mattress below, and she did not come out again that night.

Not the next day but the one after, Anraí rode down to Carraroe again to pick up the cob he had left lame. It was an errand, said Áine, that might as well or better be left to Donncha, what with Anraí's age and the soaking he had gotten two days before.

But Anraí Ó Reachtaire would as soon have given his wife to Donncha as trade the chance to ride his new Spanish horse, on a day that glistened like summer.

Anraí had not been to Spain, but he had many times been to London in the course of his occupation, and had a great respect for the grey horses he had watched at the amphitheater, so much like his own Connemara beasts, and for the trainers who taught more than jumping breakneck over fences. So as he progressed down the Cois Fhairrge Road under January sunlight, he explored various possibilities.

The horse he rode bore very little resemblance to the yellow-tailed creature with sticks in its mane that he had found so recently. Given all yesterday morning and a free hand, Donncha had turned it into a carving of white marble, close clipped, with a neat-pulled mane that showed off both the masculine ruggedness of its neck and the fineness of feature. Its sweeping tail was full and silver and its knees mottled with gun-metal blue.

There was nothing it wouldn't do for Anraí: passage, piaffe, the Spanish Walk . . . At an extended trot its forelegs rent the air like scissors. And it did not collect by pulling in its neck, like a horse trained quickly and by force. Instead it coupled its whole body closer, and all the long motions rounded until Anraí remembered the sensation he had treasured as a boy, when he rode the springy end of a pine bough in place of the horse he did not have.

It was a warm day: too warm to be quite clear, for the soaked pastures and bogs released their water into the air, softening and wrinkling it. At the bridge of the Cashla River Anraí noticed the bloom of an early white violet poking from among the stiff twigs of a meager holly bush, which still wore its winter red berries. He pointed this out to the horse as they went over the bridge, making a confident music of horse hooves.

Grouse rose thundering up from the road on the other side of the bridge, causing Anraí, but not the horse, to start. A reed bunting gave a small interrogative call from the riverside, answered by a frog somewhere. The water standing in the fields was a dazzle to Anraí's eyes.

"Isn't this day a gift from God, bless His Holy Name?" said Anraí aloud, scratching his hat back and forth over his skull, where it itched from the heat. The horse gave none of the small replies Anraí expected, of ear, eye, or nostril. Anraí chose to regard this as slighting.

"Lad, the thing of it is, is that a fellow gets no credit in life, no matter how clever he is or how brawny his back, if he has not a generous heart. And I wonder to myself about you. It's certain you can trot, and it's certain you can run, but if you have any soul in you more than my pocket watch, you haven't shown it to me today."

Anraí didn't really doubt that it was a great-souled horse under him, but he did suspect it was the sort of beast that holds grudges and might resent the bit in its mouth. And although it was easy, on this sunny morning, to sympathize, he believed in his own soul that horses were there to be ridden, just as men were there to ride them.

"Haven't I picked out the gravel in your feet, a bhúachaill, including a lump the size of a hearthstone in your near fore that had ground a hole into the frog around it? And haven't I kept your manger as full of oats and bran as is good for a fellow? And didn't I tell Donncha to take a sponge and brush to those shameful and embarrassing stains on your . . ."

A fox ran into the road in front of them and barked three times. The horse gave a low and ominous rumble and stopped in place. Anraí stared at the red dogfox, which glowed like a fire in the sunlight. It didn't move, and neither did the horse. Or Anraí.

Seacoast Connemara was not great foxhunting country, for there breakneck riding leads ineluctably to breaking one's neck. But the red fox was no more popular among the poor Gaels of that place than elsewhere, and the vermin do not stop in the road to pass the time of day with men on horseback.

"Please God that the creature isn't mad," said Anraí, either to himself or the horse, and at the sound of these words the fox darted off the road, running low to the ground, as though on little wheels.

Anraí, like most men who get their living from nature, was very superstitious. He knew what three ravens meant, flying eastward, and he was familiar with the portents of the hooded crow. He knew that if a nightjar called out to one, one must turn clockwise, while this was no help against an owl. But if he had ever heard explained the meaning of a fox's blocking one's path and barking three times, he had forgotten it. He doubted it could signify any good.

"What did he mean by that, my boy?" he asked the horse, which nodded its head and leaned against the bit. Anraí pushed the horse forward, saying "Good. Now I'm no wiser than before. I should ask my questions only of Christians."

As he trotted the beast down toward Carraroe, with the waters of the bay blue at his left hand, it seemed that all the populace of the Cois Fhairrge were on the road. There were women in black and white and in red and white, and men in báinín, either cream colored or dirty. There were donkey carts hauling milk, though it was late in the morning already, and pony carts hauling stones to fix the road. There was hardly a donkey that did not in some way object to Anraí's passage, and not a pony that he had not to nudge his horse past, to prevent conversation.

Anraí was in a sweat, partly from the balmy air and partly because he expected at any moment that a man would stride out in fury and claim his wonderful horse.

Not that he'd be easy to recognize, smartened up as he was.

And the old man was hailed, not fifty yards from the granite dome where he had found the horse. Anraí stifled a desire to flee, and pushed into a halt.

But it was a woman's voice, and coming up the small road from the pier was Seán Standún, or John Stanton, with his two daughters. Seán was a fair man, tall and thin of face, like a blood horse. The youngest of his daughters, Eibhlín, resembled her father, though not too much, for she was a beauty, with small bones, wide blue eyes, and a very fresh complexion.

The other, elder daughter was as tall as Standún, but dark faced and square. Her eyes were black. Many in the parish had commented how little Máire Standún resembled her father, but most had long since decided why that was. It was she who had called out to Anraí.

"God to you, my dark rose," he answered her, relieved that he was not to be suddenly unhorsed, and he edged over to the walking party. He touched his hat to her and to her sister, continuing, "and how is the fairy lass of An Cheathrú Rúa today, and Seán Standún of the ships?"

Eibhlín giggled at this gallant appellation, though she had heard it often before. Standún did his best to look down his long nose at the man sitting above him.

"God and Mary to you, Anraí Thurlaigh," answered Máire. "It seemed to me, when I saw you at a distance, that you were riding a good friend of mine, though now I'm not so certain."

Anraí forced a smile, though he felt heat on his face. "Do you know this fellow, Máire?"

Máire Standún put her broad hand quietly on the horse's shoulder and looked at its head. It snorted into her full dark hair and showed its upper teeth in a horsey gesture of appreciation.

"I'm almost sure of it. He was a bit rougher to look at and

he wore more hair, but this is the horse that's always about the pier here, having sport with everyone."

"Not everyone, Mary," said Eibhlín, in her piping little voice. "I've never seen him, nor has father."

"You make too much of things," said Seán Standún, glancing reluctantly up at Anraí. "She wants a man to believe she knows a great deal more than she has any way of knowing."

Anraí, though not subtle in conversation, was a decent observer, and he did not miss the manner in which Máire Standún froze in place, not looking at her father, and how pretty Eibhlín was pleased by it.

Anraí's conscience convicted him. "In fact, I'd say you have a piercing eye, lass, for I did find this beast by the road here, just two days ago, and although he's the perfect horse for me, I'll be no thief. What man owns him and let him go to seed so badly?"

"I don't know," said Máire. "It was my idea he was a wild pony from the hills. They can be very forward, if someone encourages them." Then she laughed, for the horse, his head under strong rein control, still lipped at her and made a coarse, vulgar sound.

"That isn't it, for no animal learns what *he* knows by eating grass on a mountaintop."

"Ó Reachtaire, I will have my men ask around. When we find the horse's owner we will tell him where his horse is to be found."

Anraí looked down the man's hound nose into blue eyes with slight haws at the lower lid. Dislike almost overflowed from the rider. "I have no doubt but you will, my friend," he said, trusting himself to say no more. He gave them "health" and went on his way. From behind he heard Standún calling his big daughter a fool. In English.

Anraí took possession of his cob, and after only a short disagreement with the owner for putting his new yearling out to winter grass, he started home. It was an uncomfortable passage, for the dun cob didn't want to be ponied and it hung back behind the grey, and Anraí would be damned if he would sit the old pony's trot when he had so much finer under him.

The wind was up, too, and MacMathúna had not offered him eat or drink after his long ride down, so neither Anraí

nor the horses were at their patient best. At Crompán the
dun rebelled, pulling back, twisting Anraí half out of his
saddle, and the grey stood like a stone statue expressing
disapproval, when out of a two-window cottage came a very
elderly man, who pointed at the scene and cried out very
high: "An giolla! An giolla!" Then he ran back into the
cottage.

Anraí's heart sank and the rope slipped through his fingers. The dun cob left the road at a canter, his hogged tail
raised defiantly, like a flag. Anraí cursed the event, the
ancient who had pointed, and all the effort and caring he had
put into the grey horse that was not his.

Out of the cottage came a much younger woman. "God to
you, and I'm sorry if my father unsettled your horses."

The dun had stopped beside the dwelling, seduced by the
grass fed by thrown-out dishwater. "Never mind that, woman."
He squeezed his horse off the road and toward her. "For we
unsettled him first. Tell me, does he know this beast I'm
riding?"

She sighed and edged casually toward the dun cob, which
avoided her, equally casually. Anraí's horse took a few steps
forward. "No, man: it is all the confusion of his years. The
giolla is a seanchaí's story, is all."

Anraí took his feet out of the stirrups and slid to the
ground. "Well, life doesn't get any easier as we get old. Nor
are we easier on our children. It's a lucky old man who has
children to soften his evening. For the others, it's as hard as a
board from the bog." Anraí spoke without thought in prov-
erbs, and immediately afterward his mouth twisted tight.

The dun saw him coming and was also aware of the young
woman of the house, standing as a barrier in front with her
arms folded into her shawl. Cagily it backed away, meaning
to avoid the humans with least possible effort, when it found
itself at the end of a taut rope. It flattened its ears in anger for
a moment and then adopted philosophy.

Anraí and the woman were equally surprised to find the
horse caught, and tracing the rope back, found that the grey
had stepped on the end of it.

Anraí mounted again, and this time put a knot in the lead
rope, so the dun could not pull it through his fingers. He put

the grey into as fast a trot as the slower beast could maintain, for he didn't want to be out late again.

The black and white crows wheeled calmly through the sky, either looking for food or warming their wings in the rare winter sun. Anraí heard the bark of a fox as he neared the bridge, but he did not slow down for it.

An giolla, he thought. The servant, or helper. It wasn't a bad name for this grey horse, though such a servant would need a master with one eye open. Anraí could use some help. "It's a lucky old man who has children to soften his evening."

Ten pounds for a uniform. Cow shit, said Anraí to himself. Ten pounds to hold off creditors till the cards turned around, was more like it. The boy was a shame to his parents and a grief to his mother, better off in the queen's army and best off at the end of a rope. The fire of Anraí's anger grew hotter as he grew more weary and the sun's shadows lengthened, till he reached home, with Donncha in the barn and the good supper Áine was holding for him.

He had sent off the ten pounds already. Yesterday.

CHAPTER THREE

Ruairí MacEibhir, or Rory, Son of Granite out of Wind

"Mr. Blondell is coming," said Áine, standing in the doorway of the barn with her shawl pulled over her head to shed the rain.

"Well, what of it?" Anraí was trimming the hooves of the chestnut filly, who didn't like to stand still, and so he was sharper than he ought to have been with his wife.

Áine did not flinch. "This time, you must invite him to dinner. Three times he has been here this year, and a long ride for him, and never has he set foot in the house. He must think we are not Irish hearted, or have not a bite to eat!"

Anraí rumbled in his throat, and the filly hopped in place. "We're poor enough, by Jesus. Ten pounds poorer than a week ago."

So accustomed was Áine to her husband that she took this last as a comment uttered from Anraí to Anraí. "I'm expecting him, man. I will put out the white china and an extra place. And I'll add ham to the eggs." Áine faded into the drizzle, but the sound of her feet was heard, splashing.

"Won't she be disappointed if the man rides right by here," said Anraí to the filly, who stepped on the side of Anraí's foot.

Since Anraí had brought the grey stallion to the barn, the filly had not given herself a moment's rest. Sometimes she would hug the wall of her stall with her ears flat against her head for hours, and at other times she would fling herself away from her handler and scamper over to the wall of his loose-box and deliver to it a resounding kick, squealing. Of course she was a three-year-old, at the age when young mares don't know at all what they want out of life, but still it made working in the close barn very difficult. It had set the filly's learning, already very erratic and slow, back to nothing.

Anraí stopped, led the filly back, tied a rope onto the straw halter that he had never quite dared remove from the grey, and took that horse outside, to stand in the drizzle. He put an oilcloth over its back and apologized and then went back to finish the filly.

Mr. Blondell was a large man with a round chin and long side-whiskers. He came in while Anraí was finishing the trimming, accompanied by a man leading a huge red horse. His son Tobias, a boy of some eleven years, came behind. He also had a round chin.

"Nice little grey you have tied out there," Blondell said to Anraí.

"He makes his share of work."

Blondell shrugged his tweedy shoulders. "Bet he could give a good day's hunt, if the ground weren't too fast. For a lady, or a man up in years, who doesn't want to climb . . ."

Anraí clenched his teeth and reminded himself that this man was something of a squire. Neither Martin nor Ross, of course, but he had influence. "He'd give a good day's hunt to any man. Or woman. At any speed. But he still makes his share of work."

Good-naturedly, Blondell shrugged again. "Go by the height of him. Only a glimpse."

Blondell spoke in Irish, which language he knew imperfectly but used by principle, whenever speaking to a Gael. Anraí Ó Reachtaire answered him in English, which he knew somewhat better than Blondell did Irish, but which made him feel awkward.

"Do you want that I should be at training of that great ruddy thing?" Anraí pointed to the chestnut horse, which was rolling his eyes at the chestnut filly.

"I do want that," answered Blondell, giving the horse a look half admiring, half doubtful. He wrinkled his forehead, opened his mouth, and relapsed into English. "He used to be decent to handle, but all autumn and winter he's been a regular rogue. Come spring, when we need him . . ."

"He's for stud, then?"

The squire grinned. "He's a stakes winner and the father of others. That lass there is by him."

Anraí spared a glance for the filly, which was standing in her stall with a white-ringed eye fixed on her daddy and one hind foot raised to kick. The stallion's eyes were also excited and his nostrils whuffling. He raised his proud red tail and deposited a load at his owner's feet.

Anraí wanted suddenly to walk out of the barn and away across the fields. To forget horses, or at least his labor with horses, and stand on a rock over the ocean until the rain turned his hair into elf knots. He gave a silent sigh, looking at the Thoroughbred's sharp withers, which rose above Anraí's head. "I haven't forgotten this one," he said noncommittally. "We had him here three years ago, when he was fresh from the track."

I was a mass of bruises the whole time, he did not add aloud. He smashed me against every stone wall I own.

"I'll give you fifteen pounds to make him over," said Blondell, staring at the horse manure. "Again."

Anraí took a deep breath, considering the money and remembering his responsibilities. All his responsibilities. "You must stay for dinner," he said.

Mr. Blondell ate enthusiastically. He adopted the manners of a field hand, in an obvious attempt to make his hosts comfortable. Anraí ate delicately, because he didn't care whether Blondell felt comfortable or not. Áine hardly ate at all, so busy did she keep herself supplying ham, eggs, and buttermilk gravy to men who could not possibly have eaten the quantity presented, though Blondell gave it a good trial. Young Tobias stared at his plate.

The rain came down with the evenness of fabric. Anraí and Donncha returned to the barn while Mr. Blondell and his small party splashed off, leaving the bad actor to Anraí's correction.

The lanky red stallion in the loose-box kicked rhythmically against the wall and occasionally slapped his nose sideways against the door.

"He'll have the skin off his nose before nightfall," said

Anraí. He released the top door of the box and slouched over to the hay that was Donncha's bed, where he sat himself down to watch the stallion aggrievedly.

It shrieked three times, setting four of the other five horses in the barn into nervous motion. Then it wagged its very elongated head up and down at the end of its very elongated neck.

"It is a pity we have to promote that creature. He hasn't enough sense to chew with."

The grey horse, tied at the other end of the aisle, rumbled deeply, either in agreement with Anraí or in response to the red. The big horse chose to take it as an insult. It put its ears back and squealed like a pig, showing teeth.

Donncha joined his employer. "Anraí! The horse is a stakes winner. You don't appreciate quality when it stands there before you." Then he broke out into a stream of high-pitched giggles, very equine in effect. "Sweet mother of Christ! We might as well break a stoat to saddle. He's going to kill us both!" The idea of his impending demise reduced Donncha MacSiadhail to uncontrollable laughter, but old Anraí merely groaned.

Once again the grey spoke, and Anraí, glancing over, felt that he himself was addressed. The huge dark eyes, ringed in smudged black and set into a white face, looked spectral in the dim light of the barn. Solid and square the grey horse stood, paying no attention to the chestnut's antics, and it slammed one black hoof against the floor stones for emphasis.

Anraí stood, not knowing quite why, and took a few steps toward his horse, when he heard a bang, a crash, and the splinter of wood behind him.

He turned to see the chestnut standing on the wreckage of the loose-box door, which had been two inches thick and of oak. Anraí had never seen a horse look so much like a snake. Donncha, who had been sitting only two feet from the spot now occupied by the front feet, was now somehow perched nine feet up in the air, on the winter's supply of hay and bedding. Even as Anraí watched, the chestnut rose up on its hind legs once more, demonstrating how it had smashed its way out.

"I'll close the back door," cried Donncha, sliding down in that direction. "You edge your way to the front."

Anraí answered him from a tight throat. "Don't do it. A runaway is the best we can hope for."

Indeed, the tall chestnut stallion had no thought of flight. It advanced toward Anraí and the grey horse stiff legged, swinging its neck from side to side. Its face was the bony mask of an adder.

Anraí slipped between the grey and the wall and yanked sharply on the end of the rope that tied to a ring in the wall. The quick-release knot fell apart. Anraí slapped the grey hard on the shoulder. "Go, Son of My Heart. This is no time for heroics."

The grey didn't budge, but instead watched the advancing menace with calm, almost scholarly interest. "You ass! You can't fight a beast that hasn't the sense to feel pain!" This time, Anraí hit his horse over the nose. Hard. When this had no more effect than words, he backed away, lest he be smashed against the wall when the chestnut attacked.

It danced sideways, its head below the level of its withers. Yellow teeth snapped together with a sound of breaking wood.

The grey stood motionless, until the chestnut was ten feet from it. Then it put back its ears.

The chestnut stallion started so that both men in the barn heard it: a sound like a heavy drum beaten. It shied sideways into the wall of the dun cob's stall. It raised its head high into the air, snorted, and turned tail. Donncha very bravely swung the barn door in its face, and it was left no retreat except for the loose-box it had left so tumultuously sixty seconds before. Donncha closed the upper door and dragged a heavy feed box across the bottom, over the shards of oak.

"For this, Mary should get a tall candle at the altar, Anraí, for as I flew over the straw I promised it to her, if she'd keep me in one piece. You owe her another, old man."

Anraí, who had seen the incident drawn in shapes of light and shadow from the doorway of the barn, advanced to the grey horse again. He embraced the animal's hindquarters. "I do, Donncha. More than you, I owe it."

Donncha gave his yellow smile and looked slyly over at his employer. "If I left now, I could have this red weasel back at Blondell's door before supper, couldn't I?"

Anraí's arms fell to his sides and he leaned wearily against the cob's stall. "Donncha, I can't. We can't afford it right now. Stoat he may be, but he's James Blondell's stoat, and that man is half my business and more." Looking at the sheet of rain that appeared bright next to the dark of the barn, he continued, "But you needn't see to him, Donncha. Or ride him. I don't pay you enough to expect that."

"I should let you do it, old man?" asked Donncha. The man's puffy, unkempt face wore a tight grin. He added, "Look clever, now. Your wonderful white plow horse has found the oat bin."

It was toward the end of the same afternoon (no change in the rain) when Anraí came to where he had left the grey horse tied, by the grass harrow. He was not there, of course, but neither was he in the oat bin. Instead his silky, silver tail was seen twitching through the door of the harness room, where he stood looking at a row of bits, either in wonder or speculation.

Anraí sighed. "It seems you haven't the habit of leather chewing, at least." Anraí's breath smelt oddly, the horse noticed; it turned its muscular neck and snorted.

"Worse than a wife. I guess I won't fool you often. It's poitín. I had a thimbleful, and that's not a thing I do often. Not because of morals, you understand, but expense." He reached below the horse's chin and found the short lead rope that was part of the rope halter he had never dared take off this unconfinable horse. "But at the moment, I needed it."

He squeezed past the animal and then pushed it backward out of the little room. "Come with me, Son of My Heart," he said.

Out of the close barn he led, and into the rain. His hat was pushed down to his eyes. He sighed, again and again, and the horse rested its chin on his shoulder. "It's a very dirty world, horse," said Anraí, stepping through mud in his heaviest boots. "A stallion is valued for being able to hit his head against the barn roof, and the more valued because he is willing to do it! They're happier to stuff three times the food into a beast that uses it up in fidgets . . . And you know, it's as easy to bet on a fly on the window as it is on a horse race. You might lose your establishment equally quickly, and see Terrence Fenton throw your furniture onto the street.

"Even so, they show more wisdom in judging horseflesh than human. Why it should be that I work my bones crooked and Mr. Blondell hands me the horse he's ruined! Twice, he does. And on top of the whole, he has a son that obeys him."

Anraí gave a loose and unhappy laugh as he pulled the door of the far barn open on its track. "Time enough, though. It's when the young fellow comes into his manhood he'll ruin and scandalize his father. God my witness."

This barn was presided over by Anraí's other resident stallion, a black Thoroughbred of smallish size, used on the local pony mares for the production of hunters and driving horses. It was an innocuous beast, though not educated to any excellence.

It was also the home of a half dozen horses in training, as well as a harness ox and Áine's red cow. In the center of the floor was a rectangular frame of very sturdy stanchions, like a cattle chute, beside which stood the huge, pedal-powered clipping machine with which Donncha worked his wonders.

Donncha himself was in the far corner, his back turned to Anraí. He had a bucket in front of him and was washing tools. "Come on," said Anraí to the horse. "This place is nothing new to you; your white hair is still stuck in every crack of the floor."

Without hesitation the grey horse walked into the chute, for there was a small manger at the end, filled with sweetened oats. Anraí slammed the gate down behind. Four of the oak posts had wide leather bands riveted to them, which could be buckled around the legs of rowdy or belligerent horses.

The grey had never been either rowdy or belligerent, and when the first shackle was wrapped around his hock he seemed to react with surprise. He objected. But with Donncha on one side and Anraí on the other, the job was soon accomplished.

"I couldn't be more sorry for you, lad," said Anraí, taking a swig from the bottle Donncha presented him. "If I had my way, every horse in my barn would wear your face. But then we'd all starve, the horses and Áine and Donncha here and myself together."

Donncha took a thin, blue-bladed knife from the bucket. "I hate this," he murmured. "Worst thing we ever have to do, except for shooting them. And him a grown stallion and full of his pride . . ."

The horse tried to rear.

"It's just as hard on my own pride, my friend," answered Anraí sharply, in a voice filled with phlegm. "Hand me the knife now."

The grey horse gave a convulsion that shook the oak posts, so deeply sunk into stone. The front straps broke, and it rose up screaming, not as the furious chestnut had screamed, but very like a man.

It stood, and seemed to dwindle, and then toppled over in confusion. It shouted, "By heaven, man! Look what you are about!" And then there was no horse there.

Donncha's jaw fell open. He stumbled back. Anraí lost his breath entirely.

There was no grey horse, but the chute was not empty. Tangled in leather and with rope twisted around his head and neck, lay a man in a báinín shirt and canvas trousers. He had a cap on his head. He was very clean. Donncha took two looks at him and ran out of the barn.

Anraí could not have said which was the stronger emotion. Shock, that his horse could turn into something other than a horse, or anger and grief that it should not *be* a horse any longer. The man tied in the chute twisted and looked up at him with the horse's wide brown eyes. He pointed with a manicured hand at the knife that Anraí still held, and he giggled uncertainly.

Anraí let the knife drop to the stones and put both hands against his chest, for he felt a horrible cold pain spreading. It was as though a horse had kicked him over the heart. It *was* his heart, he knew. He fell to his knees and lay upon the pedal of the clippers.

Six inches from his face was that of the man who was a horse. The dark eyes stared at Anraí's grey skin and at the rictus of pain that spread over his face. They blinked.

"The halter, man. Anraí! Anraí son of Thurlaigh, take the halter off or I cannot help. Reach one hand!"

The words were slow and overpronounced, more in the manner of Kerry than Connemara. Or pronounced in an antique manner. Anraí barely heard them and did not understand much of what he heard. But he did make out that the young man there did not want a halter around his neck, as indeed who did? He reached a numbing arm over and pawed at it, and the twisted rope fell apart into the straw it was.

In another moment the bound man was free and wiggling out of the clipping chute. Anraí was picked up easily and squeezed. He dimly saw the two human hands pressed over his heart, while the man spoke words he could not understand. Not speaking to Anraí.

Warmth returned, and the gripping pain receded. Anraí could move his hands, and he put them around the strong arms that circled him. "You were . . . my horse?"

The fellow pushed his cap back, letting silver hair slide down his forehead. He was not at all old: no older than Anraí's perfect, Spanish horse, but even his eyelashes were silver around the dark eyes that had no white in them. "I am Ruairí MacEibhir, and my mother's name was Gaoth. And it might be I still am your horse, Anraí Ó Reachtaire."

Anraí took a deep breath, which hurt. "Why would that be? I don't remember paying a penny out for you. Nor signing a bill of hire with you, nor . . ." He winced.

Ruairí MacEibhir had a pleasant smile, which grew wider. "None of these, but only an unexpected rope at the top of a mountain. But as it seems I've almost killed you here, in your own barn, it may be I owe you something." He put his ear to Anraí's chest, listening.

Anraí was angry, in a weak way. He shoved the fellow away, or tried to. "I don't need pity now, from an unchristian creature that lives to play tricks on people." He tried to rise and failed.

Ruairí picked Anraí up in his two arms. "Are we arguing already, Anraí? It's no wonder I remained a horse until now. You were much kinder to me that way." He went out into the rain, guarding Anraí's head against it with his own, and took the old man in to Áine.

CHAPTER FOUR

❖

Tadhg Ó Murchú, or The Priest of the Parish

Ruairí MacEibhir stood beside the white-quilted bed and watched Áine pull off her husband's boots. She had paid no more attention to him than to give him an initial, confused glance when he entered bearing Anraí, and to show him to the bedroom. He stood with his legs braced and his hands in commodious trouser pockets. His tam was pulled far forward over his face.

The room was as white as the counterpane on the bed, under the soot-darkened beams of the roof. Against one wall stood a bureau of black bog wood, bearing a sock darner and a statue of the Virgin, which Áine, as a young woman, had painted herself. The clothes press was also dark and had a door that slid along the wall, like the barn door.

Ruairí looked at all of this with mild eyes.

Áine pulled the clothes off the patient, hauled the covers down to his feet and over, and beat an already shapeless pillow into greater softness. As she worked she whispered constantly, a steady stream of endearments and comforts. She called Anraí her love and her cavalier, her jewel, and life's long trust, things that might comfort a man of any age and through any sickness. But Áine uttered these sweetnesses in a whisper that Ruairí doubted Anraí could hear at all. He wondered if he should tell her as much, and he scratched his ear with a large-boned hand.

"I'll have to send Donncha for the priest," she said at last, much more clearly.

Anraí, whom the weariness of pain had made passive, opened his eyes in alarm. "I'm not so far gone, woman!"

Giving his pillow one more vigorous, almost bellicose blow of the fist, she turned away from Anraí. "You can't deny your danger, Anraí Ó Reachtaire! What if you should find yourself squatting at the foot of God's holy throne this very night, with all your sins crawling over you like lice on the shorn sheep? Besides, there's people in this very parish who have had the sacrament three times and more, and they're as healthy as the next fellow."

Anraí opened his mouth in rebuttal, but closed it again. He found himself looking at Ruairí MacEibhir's face.

Squarish, but not heavy to look at. Strong jaw, but with a delicate sort of chin. Not so long a nose as some men's. Wide, surprised-seeming eyes, all black inside, so you couldn't tell what he was looking at. Clean shaven and trimmed like a man for his own wedding, with only the neat black and silver ends of the hair slipping out from under the tam. It was a pleasant enough face, and save for the eyes, as ordinary as soda cake.

"I can go for the priest," said Ruairí. "Most likely faster than Donncha, even if we could find him. But you must tell me where the priest lives."

Áine blinked. "Forgive me, but are you such a stranger to the parish that you don't know where Tadhg Ó Murchú lives? Surely you're no foreigner."

Ruairí nodded, using his neck as well as his head. "That's true enough. But I've . . . been a while away."

"That man is my horse!" said Anraí from the bed, in a shaky, accusatory voice. He tried to point.

Áine shared a speaking glance with the young man and sent him for both the priest and the doctor.

Ten minutes later, while Áine was filling a hot-water bottle from the kettle on the turf stove, Donncha walked into the kitchen. "Áine NíAnluain, I think I'm a sick man." He lowered himself onto a rush-seated chair and hid his swart face in both hands. "Perhaps only mad. I don't know."

Áine did not raise her head from her pouring. "Unless you are very sick or very mad, Donncha, I haven't the time for it, with Anraí in the room behind us, after having a heart attack."

Donncha's eyes were red rimmed, like a hound's, and he showed the red all around them in his astonishment. "A heart attack?" He sat in this knowledge, breathing in and out of his open mouth. "Then perhaps I'm not mad after all, but merely a coward."

He reflected further, in silence.

"A terrible coward."

Tadhg Ó Murchú, the priest, was a small man and very dark. The roundness of his face owed nothing to fat, and he had two catlike cheekbones and a prominent cleft in his chin, which gave him a knobbly appearance, like that of raw Connemara fields.

When he heard a wagon being driven at speed into his yard, he was in the study speaking with a visitor, and although it was not a confessional visit, still he closed the study door behind himself before going to greet the newcomer.

"Anraí Ó Reachtaire desires the priest and the doctor," announced the driver, not rising from his seat. "For the sake of his heart."

Ó Murchú stepped out onto the muddy gravel. He saw the man black, against the striped, setting sun. He did not recognize either the shape or the face. He laughed at the phrase. "For the sake of his heart? You mean because his heart has gone out on him, I imagine. Two minutes."

They drove into increasing darkness, until the tail of the horse before them could not be made out. Ó Murchú kept his great hollow crucifix firmly on his lap, gripped with the one hand he did not need for holding on to the gig.

"We're going fast," he remarked.

"Indeed we are," replied the driver, and at that minute a stone flung the right wheel up off the road. The priest came down an instant after the wheel and the candles of beeswax stored in the stem of the crucifix rattled loudly.

"If we were to turn over . . ." Ó Murchú began again. "If we were to break our suffering necks—God between us and disaster—why then we wouldn't make it to old Anraí's bedside at all, would we?"

"Right enough, Priest of the Parish," replied the driver, and continued down the road in the same style. At last, with the priest's angry eye on him, he added, "We'll come to no grief. Not while I am driving and a horse is pulling. This red imp has a turn of speed, and as he's no worse fast than slow, we might as well use him at his best."

Ó Murchú sighed, unconvinced. It was now pitch black in the road and he wondered how even the horse could see.

"You're a Kerryman?" Ó Murchú hazarded.

Ruairí looked at him long before answering. "How could you tell?"

"Because of your speech, man. It is old-fashioned. You hold on to your words a long time, and pronounce them finely. Though I'd have thought only a Connemara man would have such poor manners with a priest. You haven't even told me the name of the man who holds my life in his hands."

The driver laughed heartily and reached out his solid left arm. For a moment the priest thought that he was either going to be hugged or throttled, but it was only that they were approaching a sharp turn.

"My name is Ruairí MacEibhir."

Now it was Ó Murchú's turn to laugh, but he smothered the desire. "Rory son of Granite? That is the perfect name for a Connemara crofter. It's too bad you're from Kerry, where the stone is rich lime."

"My name is Ruairí MacEibhir," the driver repeated. "And my mother's name was Gaoth." ("Gwee", or "wind" in Irish.) "I am Anraí's new horseman."

"Then God help him," murmured the priest, as the stallion bucked in the traces.

The doctor was not to be found in his home at Ros an Mhíl, for he was tending a man who had lost a hand to rot from the wound of a fish spine, so Father Ó Murchú left word for him to follow when he returned.

"The horse knows his way well," said the priest, as the gig swayed from darkness into darkness.

"I don't know why he should," replied Ruairí. "It's not his home we're going to, and until today, he has never pulled a chariot of any sort. This is James Blondell's crazy red stallion we have here."

Ó Murchú held tighter to his equipage. "I believe you are not a man of the truth," he said shortly. "I have an unhappy gift in that respect. I always know."

The unseen man on the seat next to him snorted, and at that moment the stallion decided to leap up into the air and come down sideways. Ruairí held Father Ó Murchú to the seat. "Indeed, for a man dedicated to God you have a hard attitude on you. It is the squire's red stallion, as a glimpse of his narrow hinder and thin tail should tell you. Donncha will identify the beast for you."

Ó Murchú waited for the trouble with the horse to be sorted out before he replied. "I didn't mean necessarily about the horse. I mean you have the flavor of a lying man about you."

"Is it that you doubt that Anraí is sick or that my name is Ruairí and my father's name was Eibhir? For I've said nothing more to you than these things, and I swear upon my mother's name that they are both true."

Ó Murchú could not choke back a laugh. "Then you swear upon the wind!" But his words broke off sharply, for they had come around the bulk of Knockduff much sooner than he had believed possible, and there were the lantern outside the door of Ó Reachtaire's house and a votive candle in each of the two lower windows.

"The mad brute *does* have a turn of speed," Father Ó Murchú murmured.

Ruairí MacEibhir sat himself down in the kitchen next to Donncha and regarded the man across the light of a white candle. Donncha showed his ridge of broken teeth and gripped the deal top of the table. "God's blessing, it *is* you."

Ruairí grinned back at him, black-eyed. He stamped one heavy-shod foot on the floor. "How I scared you, MacSiadhail!"

Donncha's own, droop-lidded eyes shot sparks. "No more than I frightened you, Fairy Man, with that great knife in my hand."

Ruairí smiled more broadly, exposing two rows of perfect, boxy, ivory teeth. "Grant you that! I had no idea the old man was so dissatisfied with me. He seemed to like my looks well enough."

Donncha chuckled, more at ease now, but he kept the body of the table between the stranger and himself. "Surely he does, Fairy Man, but he knows where the money comes from and what sort of horse brings it in. That sweet red songbird in the barn, now . . ."

Ruairí nodded. He picked the white length of the candle out of its candle holder and held it wrapped in his hands, so that they glowed. Big hands and square, but not fleshy. Donncha stared, thinking that he had manicured those hands. "You'll have no trouble with him these next few days. To-night he ran over twenty miles with Áine's gig behind him, and he's soft from confinement. Indeed, half his madness is confinement, though he'll never be sane."

Silently Donncha repeated Ruairí's words, a phrase behind. Then he cried, "The red stallion? Blondell's stakes-winning Thoroughbred? You harnessed that ugly devil up to the gig and flung off into the night with him? Fairy Man . . ."

The violence of Ruairí's mirth drove the candle flame licking over his face, where the two eyes were blind pools. "Not fairy, Donncha. Kerryman. The good Father Ó Murchú knows me to be from Kerry."

Donncha did not understand the joke. "He does?"

"He does! Even as he knows me for a lying man. Though I am not, Donncha, unless it is a lie not to say all you know."

"It's the path of wisdom, and our own employer should study it more closely," said the man, continuing, "so tell me why you have come to trouble his failing years. And my own prime."

Ruairí shot a canny glance over the candle flame and bobbed the white end of the candle in front of his nose. "If you must know, colleague, I am here by the seaside paying court to the queen of heaven."

"The queen . . . Mary the Virgin?"

"Forfend!" The candle slipped and the smell of burning hair spread around the table. Ruairí MacEibhir cursed, patted his damaged forelock, and returned the candle to its holder. "Don't be silly, Donncha. I mean the daughter of Seán Standún, of course."

*   *   *

When the priest left him, Anraí had Ruairí brought to his room. In actuality, he could not convince Áine to call him in, as she wanted her husband to sleep, so he was reduced to shouting down the stairs for him, but Ruairí MacEibhir entered the pale room as decorously as though ushered by deacons. He carried his tam and ran the brim in circles between his hands.

Anraí looked dwarfed by the bed, but his eyes glistened. "She's giving you poitín out there?"

The question was uttered sharply, but it brought a smile to Ruairí's lips. "It's government whiskey, I think."

"Worse and worse. That's because of the priest, although it's as strange a measure as any I've heard, with Tadhg Ó Murchú being as green a man as . . ." His voice trailed away. "Damn, I'm tired."

"I know it," said Ruairí. "And you have no need to talk to me tonight. In the morning . . ."

"To hell with that!" Anraí's face sharpened to boniness. "Before I sleep tonight, in this bed or in purgatory, I must know who you are."

"Ruairí MacEibhir . . ."

"Right. So you said. And are you a Christian man?"

"Not at all," said Ruairí, still smiling kindly.

Anraí lifted his head. "Human man at all, then?"

"I am not." He tossed his cap on the bed, and it landed on Anraí's stomach. "But I'm a pretty good horse, aren't I? The son of your heart, or so you said."

Anraí looked not at the brown eyes but at the cap. His head sank down. "If you knew me better, my lad, you would not try to endear yourself to me with a likeness to my son." He closed his eyes. "Why do you come bothering me, almost to death like this, creature?"

Ruairí stepped very quietly close enough to pick up his cap again. He left his hand resting on the covers. "Anraí son of Thurlaigh Ó Reachtaire, the damage I did you was inadvertent, and occurred only after your attempted violence upon myself."

Anraí found the impossible eyes six inches from his own. "You talk like a lawyer," he whispered, and then, remembering, he tried to laugh. "Oh dear God, what rubbish!"

In another moment he was serious again. "What do you want here?"

"Here, Anraí? Do you mean in your house, or on the earth itself? I come to this land and I go from it to the Other Place, according to whim." His mouth spread for a laugh, and then tightened again. "I'm not certain the whim is my own. Say I am like the rain: unreliable, except that you know it will show up again.

"But if you are asking why I am right here, in your house, then I must remind you that I didn't come here by choice." Ruairí raised his face to the black window and then looked over the room again. "But I think I could not have chosen better. I want to be in your service for a while, Anraí. And I am valuable; there is no better horseman remaining on the whole island than I."

Anraí blinked thoughtfully. "I believe that, if you're half so good riding as being ridden. But I can scarcely afford Donncha."

"You needn't pay me."

Anraí blinked again, this time squeezing his eyes shut. "I can scarcely *feed* Donncha. That's how bad things are for me."

The brown eyes remained mild. "Well, you needn't feed me either, as long as you've got grazing, and how could I say fairer than that? Anraí, I can make that red vandal behave himself for James Blondell."

"The priest told me," said Anraí dryly. He sighed. "And what in return, my lad? Are you a devil, that you have a fancy for my soul? Or is it my lovely wife you covet."

Ruairí laughed in his nose and put a foolish hand through his hair. "I could scarcely do better than Áine, it's true, but I doubt I have force of arms to tear her away from her old man. She'd hit me on the head first chance she had.

"And I have no more interest in your soul, Anraí, than . . . than Donncha has. Less by far than Tadhg Ó Murchú, who is in the kitchen drinking your whiskey now. What I need of you is the protection of your name and of your establishment."

The small man pulled himself up onto the pile of pillows. "The . . . the protection of my what?"

"I must convince Seán Standún of the ships that I am a respectable man, so that he will give me his daughter. She is the woman for whose birth I have waited, with beauty and strength on her like that of my own mother. And she is distant kin to me. You have no others like her in Ireland today."

Anraí blinked, drawn out of his own pain by curiosity. "Eibhlín? She is a beauty, certainly, but strength . . ."

Ruairí snorted. "She is a day-old chick. It's black Máire I mean, who is great-minded and courageous and sound from head to foot. How can a man who knows value in horses not know that of women?"

Anraí stared at the square face before him, and then through it, and into space. He sank back into the bed. "Go away, lad," he said quietly. "You make me tired."

Donncha drove the priest home, leaving Ruairí standing at the door of the house. He waved his cap to them.

The moon had risen by the time they began their sedate journey behind the dun cob, and it lit the rubbly road until the brightness made the eyes water. The stones that lay about in heaps were a lunar silver, but the dry winter heath drank all the light and gave nothing back.

Donncha wanted very much to tell Father Ó Murchú that Ruairí was a púca: a horse fairy. His eyes were round and glassy with the moon and with this desire to impart information, and his lips were constantly parted to speak, but he said nothing at all.

For horsemen are like gypsies: they may war among themselves lifelong, but they know the difference between one of their own and a man who is not a horseman by trade. He had shared whiskey with the creature. He had offered it the worst violence man can do to man (albeit ignorantly), and the fairy had laughed it off. There was a sort of debt there.

Most certainly the priest could not approve of fairies. St. Patrick himself had been their enemy. Besides, Father Ó Murchú had been severely educated in Rome, and it was quite possible he did not see fairies or believe in them.

Meanwhile, Tadhg Ó Murchú, who had smelled Ruairí out as a man of lies, sat next to the silent Donncha and merely supposed him to be dozing. He had no fears for his own safety, this ride, not even with a sleeping driver, for the cob's deliberate trot could not get them into danger very quickly.

He prayed: for Anraí's soul and for his body, for Áine, and

for the boy in the army. He also begged help against his own
abiding fault of distrust and wondered why he had accused
that foolish, good-natured MacEibhir of lying to him.

Donncha did doze off, and so did the priest. The cob
continued on at his own speed toward Carraroe, and up from
the shores of Cashla Bay moon-shining ponies came up to
inquire of them, still trailing strands of sweetish seaweed
from their mouths. These were mostly mares, swollen sided
with spring's babies, with weanlings like stick-legged bears
beside them. In unison they nodded at the gig, their ample
manes almost hiding their ears and eyes, and the neatly
trimmed cob snorted his dismissal of those who neither sow
nor reap.

Tadhg Ó Murchú heard the ponies through his dreams:
their hoof falls like rain and their thick nickering. He peered
through slitted eyes at them, looking Chinese and inscrutable,
and they blinked their big, brown mare eyes back at him. He
began to drift off again, hugging his shawl and his crucifix
against the late-night wind.

Now he was dreaming, for an arrangement of lights and
shadows at the side of the road became the face of Ruairí
MacEibhir, and the fellow looked at him and nod-nod-nodded
his head, like the little mares. The priest shivered, and the
dream figure laughed with moon-white teeth and impossible
eyes. Ó Murchú sat bolt upright, and it was not a man at all
but a white horse, neat and burly, standing head and shoulders above the pony mares. Its flanks glistened with sweat. It
was nodding.

They were at An Sruthán already. There, down the little
pier, *An Dreoilín,* one of Standún's Galway hookers, rested
creaking against its moorings. There were voices calling and
answering. Father Ó Murchú listened carefully, and one of
them was a woman's voice: the voice he had been expecting.
It was Máire, Standún's eldest daughter, bringing tea to the
men, as she did often before the day's fishing. It was gossiped
that she did so hoping to win some cold sailor's heart, and
that she came before dawn so that her sister's looks would
not cast her in total shade. But that was not true, Ó Murchú
knew, for he knew Máire well. Besides, Eibhlín never came
down to the boats, if she could help it.

The priest yawned, feeling the tears turn cold as they

leaked from his eyes down over his outsized cheekbones. When he wiped them away the horse and all the ponies were gone.

James Blondell walked into his wife's sitting room and tossed the newspaper onto the table next to her. She glanced up in irritation. "That print gets all over my canvas, James."

He picked it up again and looked at his grey-smudged hand. He turned a circuit of the little room, examining all the furniture, and at last, sighing, sat himself down and dropped the folded paper onto his own lap.

Hermione Blondell had a gold-rimmed lorgnette that she used to help her focus on her embroidery. James had often thought a simple pince nez would be more useful, freeing her left hand to steady the frame as she drove the needle. She had the proper nose for a pince nez, with a little shelf extending almost horizontally out between her eyes. Indeed, it was servants' gossip (which Blondell never admitted over-hearing) that it was this nose that impaired Hermione Blondell's near sight.

It was the true Delagardie nose, identical to her father's. James Blondell knew how to value that nose, as he did the extravagances of his chestnut stallion, and he never suggested the pince nez. He was a little sorry that Tobias, their only child, did not seem likely to develop the nose.

She was still working on the sunflowers: four of them, almost life-sized, in various shades of gold and green. Her stitches were astonishingly tiny and regular, and Blondell was surprised how realistic an effect they were producing. The tiny skeins of silk on the table did not look natural in color at all.

Not for the first time he noticed how close the pattern of Hermie's stitchery was to the wallpaper, which was also sunflowers. The wing chair on which she sat was mustard in tone, and Blondell's heavier armchair, a brassy green. The immortelles and the pampas plumes had been tinted daffodil color. The aspect of the room was south and, on bright days, tended to give off a glare oppressive to the senses.

In County Galway, however, that was no great drawback.

"I hear old Raftery the trainer has had a bit of a stroke. Or a heart attack or something."

Hermione glanced at her husband without moving her head. "Did you find that in the *Galway Intelligencer*, dear?"

He lifted the paper in his lap and dropped it again. "No, of course not. Beebs told me."

Her very delicate mouth curled tolerantly.

The paper rose and fell again as Blondell stared out the window onto clouds. "I wonder if I should in conscience take Imperator home again."

"Why 'in conscience,' James? Is there . . ." Hermione drove her needle into the canvas, which made a popping sound almost like rain. She turned her glasses to him. "I did not know that Raftery *had* the horse. Why on earth, when we have our own staff . . ."

The clouds were moving very fast. Blondell felt a sick impatience with this winter. "Kelly is kept busy enough."

"Oh, James, talk good English, with me at least."

Between one moment and the next, Blondell's palms went sweaty. He looked in from the window to his hands, which were now dangerously grimy from newsprint. " 'Busy enough' is good English," he said reasonably. "If I had said 'busy galore,' that would be different. And three grooms and a coachman can't be expected to keep a stallion like that in line as well as a stable full of carriage horses, my hacks, the farm horses in winter, your mare, and Toby's pony."

Her eye, through the lens, was first huge and then missing as she waved the lorgnette. "Toby never uses that pony. Why didn't you keep the stallion in Wicklow with your hunters?"

Blondell took a measured breath. "Because he's to stand here, that's why. It's in Galway we need a shot of quality in the young stock. Wicklow has no problems that way. Besides, I can hire Raftery cheaper than board a horse without training back east."

The golden thread made a ripping sound as it pulled taut in the canvas. "Yes, certainly. And you also have an excuse to sit down in his kitchen in your shirt-sleeves, drink poitín, and talk like a native."

"Hermie!" Blondell's mouth hung open in outrage for two seconds. "What *am* I, if not a native? I was born in this county. In this house!" He stamped his foot on the Aubusson floral carpet.

Hermione Blondell winced and leaned back into her chair.

She was not a large woman, and her hands appeared frail. "You know what I mean, James. Playing the Irish. You love to do it. Tobias told me about your social afternoon with Henry Raftery and his wife. Ham and potatoes, wasn't it? Do you want him to grow up talking Gaelic in the barns, too?"

"I'd be very happy—" Blondell almost shouted "—as long as he can also talk English in the drawing rooms, and there's no fear he'll fail at that! Toby is Irish, as I am Irish. You didn't seem to mind it when you married me!" Aggrievedly he added "You said the accent was pleasant to your ear."

She shrank further away from him, but there was no timidity in her reply. "In reasonable doses, it is, James. It's just that out here in the mud, with no society closer than Galway from autumn to spring . . ." She drove home the needle.

Blondell stood and bunched the paper in his sweaty hands. "I'm sorry, Hermie. I know. I'm sorry." He walked out of the room, still saying it.

CHAPTER FIVE

Máire Standún, or The Queen of Heaven Rides

Spring crawled out of the cracks between the rocks, too small for a man to notice. It was no taller than the narcissi in Áine NíAnluain's poor, horse-abused border garden, no wider than a spear of grass. It consisted of hard buds on the fruit trees and furry buds on the willow. It destroyed the heavy coats of the horses, leaving them harsh and staring. Diseaselike holes appeared in the raiment of the stable's one cow as she rubbed against the trees of the pasture, and birds fought over the pads of red hair that she left behind.

The season was as yet an uneasiness, marked by tiny flowers. It was not yet comfortable. It had not yet touched the sky.

Tobias Blondell, who was eleven, wandered the muddy edges of the roads near his house, soiling his black American-leather boots. Tobias was sorely beleaguered by tutors—three of them—and by the expectations of his father.

Mr. Blondell had very much wanted a sporting sort of son, with his own square physique, preferably with the Delagardie nose. He had gotten Tobias, with Hermione's neuresthenic build and a round, resentful face with hardly a nose at all. Tobias had no enthusiasm for sport, and indeed few enthusiasms at all. He was afraid of horses.

Today, a Tuesday of fast-moving cumulus clouds, Toby had gotten away. It was because of Mr. Chubb's septic throat, which Mrs. Blondell suspected to be contagious. Toby was still dressed for indoor work, for he had been afraid that in the time it took him to change, his father might have shown up and thought of some useful and strenuous activity to replace the lesson hour. His shirt was now damp with his effort to avoid this, and the wind stuck it against his narrow back. As he scrambled, his eyes on the gross imperfections of the road, he conjugated Latin verbs backward, from plural to singular and from third person to first, in an effort to further hex his sick tutor.

It was three miles into Carraroe, and his mother would not be happy if she found out he had been there, alone and on lesson time. She would think he was taking after his father. Given that circumstance, Toby had no choice but to drift toward the town.

Along the side of the road were scattered the two-window cottages lived in by the natives. The small stone buildings were set seemingly at random in their walled fields, pointing at various degrees of the compass and paying no attention to the road. Most of the roofs were of slate, and even these showed injuries where the wind had torn through. Sea pink bloomed under the stones and the air rang with the play of children in the yards of beaten earth.

The irregular houses seemed perfectly natural to Toby. The ten-minute-long gusts of rain, immediately followed by sun, were only to be expected. It was also natural and to be expected that Tobias Blondell should be walking alone, while eight boys in filthy homespun played hurley by the side of the road, sparing him only sidelong, sullen glances. They were not of his kind. Neither were the boys in Dorset, his cousins, of his kind. Indeed, Toby was not sure there were any of his kind on the face of the earth.

Footsteps advanced on him from behind. He slouched further off the road and examined his stick with great attention, but he was greeted anyway.

"Good morning to you, Master Blondell," said John Stanton in English. The boat owner was a fair man, thin faced and dressed in tweeds, as though (thought Toby) he were a gentleman. Toby had doubts.

He had his two daughters with him: the one that looked like him and the one that did not. Eibhlín, the pretty blonde

girl, gave him a smile, a giggle, and a slantwise look that
Toby was five years too young to appreciate. "Good morning,
Mr. Stanton," he answered very politely, his shoulders hunched
up to his ears. "Good morning, ladies."

"Answer the lad," said Standún to his daughters. "Don't
stand there like barefoot cailíns without English."

"Good morning, Master Blondell," said Eibhlín.

The dark girl who did not look like her father gave Toby a
slow, measuring stare. "You're going to catch it for ruining
those fine boots, Toby." There was nothing chiding in her
tone, and her black eyes held only a dry amusement. "Is the
game you're playing worth it, I wonder?"

Toby was rather surprised to find himself not offended.
"I'm only taking a walk into town, Miss Máire. My Latin
tutor's got an infected throat."

"And it's none of your business anyway, Mary," added
Stanton, who was clearly displeased. "He would afford his
father no satisfaction if he walked around dressed like a
spailpín."

Although Toby Blondell was exquisitely aware of his position in the community, he could not bear to hear it stated
this way. He winced, and Máire Standún saw it. They shared a
single black, resentful glance, and then Máire walked on ahead.

The air was balmy and seemed to bear her up. Her nose
was filled with the sweetness of wild hyacinth. Her skirt of
red wool was too warm.

"You make a very bad impression in front of the gentry,"
said her father, when his long legs had caught up with her.

"The gentry?" She answered slowly, as was her habit, and
in Irish. "You mean that little boy?"

"Mr. Blondell's boy. Who will be squire himself one day."

"Good for him." Máire yawned in the heat. "What's it to
me? If I'm nice to him, will he marry me when he grows up?"

Her father snorted. "Marriage is a thing you ought to think
about, for a change. I don't want to be supporting you when
you turn thirty!"

Her glance at her father's face was black and blank. "Do
you suggest I rob the Blondell's cradle? Go on with you,
Father! Toby Blondell is not going to look for an overage,
oversized Gael woman to wife. Besides which"—and she

tossed her hair back—"Eibhlín thinks of marriage enough for both of us."

"That's enough!" said her father.

The blonde girl recoiled. "And if I do, it's because there's some prospect of marriage before me! Perhaps I may pick and choose, while some . . ."

"Enough out of you also, my dear."

Máire turned slowly to her sister, with the force of a mountain moving. "You don't pick as much as collect, Eibhlín. And what you call choosing I call advertising, and people do not advertise unless they have something to sell."

Standún stopped dead and stared at his oldest daughter in shock.

Eibhlín crossed her arms in her black shawl and took a step backward, away from her sister's anger. "Ask her what she does with the priest at evenings, Father. There's only so many children's evenings or surplices to mend, and the woman who tends the rectory is known to be both deaf and blind. As God's my witness, she's not interested in marriage because she cannot marry the man she has caught!"

In another instant Eibhlín was cupping her hand around her split lip, while the air still rang with the sound of Máire's backhand blow. The dark girl still held in her left hand a handkerchief holding six hen's eggs, and she gazed blankly down at it, as though disbelieving they were unbroken.

Standún's first impulse was to glance around them, making certain no one had witnessed the violence. Toby Blondell was no longer in sight, and two men on a hill to the north, who were dipping sheep, did not seem to be paying attention. He regarded Máire distastefully. "You're a rude beast, lass," he said.

Máire opened her heavy eyes the slightest bit. "If she insults me so again, I'll hit her so again."

"You as much as called me a whore first!" Eibhlín winced and licked the bright red line on her lower lip.

"Did I?" There was no expression on the dark girl's face, but her sister took another step backward.

Standún stepped between. "A plague is no misfortune, compared to a pair of daughters. You have no shame, to be fighting like cats in a bag on the public road. If the men who sail my boats behaved so badly, they'd find no work in

Galway County! I'd have them keelhauled from the Claddagh
to An Cheathrú Rúa." He paused, looking from one girl to
the other.

"Eibhlín, keep your tongue to yourself, and you, Máire . . ."

Máire Standún gave her father the same look she had be-
stowed upon her sister. He paid no attention to it.

"You spend too much time with Ó Murchú. It raises talk."

"Talk raises up by itself, Father. All I do is help him in his
classes."

"That's bad enough, for there's no good odor to some of
the priest's classes."

"Would you have us ignorant of our history and language?" Máire's voice rose both in pitch and volume, and her
cheeks darkened as she spoke.

"I would have you at home, like a respectable girl."

"Respectable or no, you'll have her at home forever, Da,
because no one will take her off your hands."

Seán Standún shot a glare at Eibhlín, who skittered out of
her sister's range. Máire turned on her heel.

"Where are you going, Máire?" called Standún, seeing his
daughter climb the curb, her skirts lifted in both hands, and
her head held very high.

"Not to church!"

The sun shone down on Máire's very black hair. Her stance
was soldierly and her stride long. Standún watched her go
with a sort of relief.

"She'll end up in trouble for certain," offered Eibhlín,
eyeing her father's face carefully.

His blue eyes met hers without warmth. "See that you
don't yourself," he said, and then the two fair heads, looking
much alike, continued toward the pier.

Máire had no idea where she was going, when she set out
across the fields. Her anger, which was large, and her pride,
which was much larger, had only made it impossible that she
continue to the pier with her father and sister.

To be suspected of misbehavior with the priest! What
could be more wicked and less likely? And yet, she reminded
herself, as she stepped over a neat-blooming spring pink, she

had known from the beginning they would be open to gossip. Perhaps that was what made it worse.

And poor little Tadhg Ó Murchú, shorter than Máire herself and as dark as a Welshman. He might as well be a Welshman, with his tidy, clever, secretive ways. What woman would ruin her reputation for Ó Murchú?

Máire Standún would, she reminded herself, with a dry, involuntary smile. But not for the reasons people would imagine.

Where had she come? She stopped to look around, squinting in the bright sunlight of May. Here was the old house lived in once by Terrence Fenton's grandparents, now half roofed and, by the sounds coming from it, keeping calves. There were tiny bean-leaf plants growing out of the cracks between the stones, and these shone translucent. The quartz in the granite sparkled.

Máire's hopeless anger leaked away, leaving her no motivation to keep walking. She settled down by the old doorstep of the cottage, feeling the warm stone wall at her back. Her red petticoat spread out around her like a poppy on the new grass.

If Máire were a man, she considered, it would not matter that she were not her father's daughter. (Or son.) She was glad, in ways, not to be blood relation to a pale and mingy fellow like him. If she were a man, she would say to hell with Mister John Stanton and she'd go off to Dublin. If she were a man, she would enter politics. Or perhaps carry a gun. Certainly she would not become a priest, like poor Ó Murchú, pulled to the point of tearing by his bishop and his nationalism. She would have remained a free power.

But she was not a man and could not be rid of her father, who in turn could not be rid of her. Her income, apart from what Standún thought to give her, was the produce of ten speckled chickens and a single hive of bees which swarmed too often. If the chief constable discovered what she was teaching under the priest's supervision, she would probably go to prison.

Languidly, Máire was wondering whether prison would be more or less bearable than her present life, when a shadow fell across her face. She lifted her eyes.

"Och, it's you," she said to the horse.

It nickered very gently and tossed its neat mane left and right.

"Well, don't you look a gentleman, now that Anraí's taking care of you." The horse made no reply. Neither did it lower its pretty head to the grass, but gazed darkly and deeply at Máire, while its silver tail switched slowly.

"Does he know you're out, my man? It's a few miles between Knockduff and An Cheathrú Rúa, and Anraí Ó Reachtaire isn't one to let his good horses wander the roads."

The horse stepped closer, and with meditative care it placed its perfect small nose against Máire's face.

She was flattered, as any woman might be by this attention. It did not occur to her that the beast might bite. "Well!" she said, drawing back only slightly. "You're a horse, and that's to your advantage. But you're still a male, so my trust of you is limited. Of course my sister is female, so I can't say I prefer my own sex . . ."

It nuzzled her again and then danced away into sunlight. With a peculiar, complex gesture involving the head and both forefeet, it genuflected before Máire. White lashes fluttered over its black-brown eyes.

She rose to her feet in surprise. "That's quite a trick. But I don't have anything to give you for it except eggs, and I doubt you'd fancy them."

The horse made a disgusted noise, but remained on one knee, bobbing its head forcefully. Máire began to feel awkward about it. "I'm sorry, white horse. No sugar, honey, dulse, sweet cake. Nothing at all. My regrets." She lifted her red skirts and backed away.

The horse sprang up, bouncing straight into the air. It came down in front of her and knelt again. Máire's handkerchief of eggs slipped and nearly hit the ground. "Curse you, animal. Are you threatening me? You can't get sweets out of a stone!"

She started to edge sideways, between the kneeling horse and the wall. Inside the calves bawled.

The horse scooted with her, still kneeling. Máire hovered between perplexity and fury at being so cornered by the beast. At last, without warning, she broke into loud laughter. "You're getting your knees dirty, horse! Anraí's Donncha will be in a rage at you!"

It occurred to the girl, as she stared down at the smooth coat of hair and the wiry white mane, that she could sit right down on this horse's back. The idea came from nowhere, ridiculous and compelling. Máire had very limited experience with horses, having ridden docile ponies when available to her but never having been on anything that might frighten her. She could just lower herself sideways onto the horse here, so white and clean and friendly, and if it got up, she'd slip off easily. Better than sitting on a stone, and perhaps that would convince the beast to allow her past.

She found she was sitting on the horse, and (like Anraí, some months before) wondering why she had done something so foolish. For the horse had risen and she hadn't slipped off, and there she was sitting higher than ever she'd been, and holding a very short mane with the grip of fear. She gasped.

But the horse made no move. He stood like a statue, and the warmth of his skin could be felt even through her woolen petticoats. He smelled like earth and flowers.

"Mind your manners, now, my dear," said Máire nervously. "I'm no challenge to you at all, and if I fall off I'll lie in the road in two pieces, I'm sure." The horse glanced over his shoulder and nickered. He took a smooth step and Máire settled herself with one knee up over the withers.

"Well there!" she said, heartened. "I know I'm a fool, but I haven't suffered for it yet. I suspected a horse was more the natural gentleman than any man. I leave it to you, my brawny one."

And with this permission, if permission it was, the horse moved out from the cattle shed and over the field.

This was nothing like Anraí's wild ride, or the girl would have been on the grass in five seconds. The horse moved from a gliding walk to a pace as easy as a boat on calm waters. When he came to a fence, he stepped over, each foot in turn.

The bay was behind them, and the Cois Fhairrge Road. Ahead were fields of pinks and lupine and violets, with the first green of the heath cutting through winter's brown background. Máire felt herself impossibly high in the air. She let her left leg slip over until she was riding astride. With the bright skirt on the white coat the pair resembled a confection in peppermint. Bees rose up around them and filled her ears with sound.

They passed a man in high gaiters, walking with a black sheepdog. She waved graciously to him from her height. He stared and the little dog barked shrilly. Máire didn't care.

The horse was a galleon under sail. It was a white bird. Máire herself was a bird, exalted, exhilarated. She laughed again, and the horse broke into a round canter.

This was daunting at first, but she held on with the length of her legs. The hairy back was warm, warm. All the huts and cottages were behind them, and they splashed through empty bogland, scaring the sheep.

It did not occur to Máire that the horse might be caught in a bog. He knew his business. When they came to the first inclines of the highlands she felt the enormous strength of the hindquarters pushing her up and forward, and her dazed eyes opened wide. Then she began to be afraid of the gentle white horse.

They were in the hills already—the Twelve Pins—and the horse went at a mad roaring gallop. Máire clamped her legs tight and held on. "Dear God!" she exclaimed, but she enjoyed it. Her breath was fast, like the horse's, which boomed in time with his hooves. The skin on her arms was flushed. Hills of granite and of grass, streams and valleys, spun by, too quick to identify and shot with splashes of sky.

Máire Standún felt herself immortal, invulnerable, ready for great deeds and battle. "We are a nation of warriors!" she cried to the horse, as she had to the small, unadvertised classes in the inner rooms of the rectory. "A nation of poets and warriors." The horse made an odd gurgling noise in reply.

But the warrior in the red petticoat was getting tired even as she spoke, for both exaltation and equitation are hard work. Panting, she leaned over the horse's withers, holding the mane tightly in both hands.

The gallop slowed, turned to canter and then amble. In a sweet grassy thicket between two featureless hills, where there were not even sheep to break the privacy, the grey horse stopped. It stopped and then rose up on its hind legs.

Máire gave a small shriek as she began to slip backward.

She grabbed tight with hands and with legs, as the shape she held to did astonishing things.

Her left leg slipped and her heel hit a stone. The coarse hair in her hands changed to báinín and she was holding the back of the collar of a man's shirt. A man she was embracing in the most scandalous manner. She gave a great gasp and he kissed her.

It was spring. The air was fresh and warm, the grass new on the sides of the hills. Somewhere an ouzel sang its sweet few notes, and the man before her was not bad looking at all.

Máire hauled off and hit him such a blow he fell backward into the fresh cold waters of the rivulet. "Did you think I was such a babe and a weakling ..." Her anger outran her language, and her heel hurt like a bee sting where it had hit the stone.

Ruairí MacEibhir lay where he had been flung, and the little waters made trails over his woolen shirt. His black eyes blinked foolishly. "A weakling you certainly aren't! By my black mother, you have a fist to be proud of."

Máire Standún snorted at praise from such an unlikely source. She stepped backward up the side of the stony hill and looked around her at perfect loneliness. She became aware of her disadvantage and so did Ruairí. He sat up, sprinkling the turf around him. "It's a long walk home, isn't it, a Mháire mo Róisín?"

His open face, slightly reddened on one cheek, showed no resentment. Neither did he approach the girl closer.

"How do you know my name?" Not waiting for an answer she continued, "It's a long way, but I'd walk from here to Sligo before I'd take a ride at *your* price."

Ruairí sprang up and shook himself, left foot and then right. "Lovely lady, I haven't named a price at all. In weather like this, with the ground so firm it invites the hoof ... uh, the foot ..."

Guessing that the way they had entered the little dell was toward the Sound, Máire turned that way. She found the going slippery in the heavy shoes her father insisted she wear. Over her shoulder she said, "You were quick as a jarvey to collect your fare upon arriving here in the wilderness, fellow. I don't pay in that coin."

"Payment?" The voice was right behind her, and she hadn't

heard him come up. "There have been enough pretty lasses who didn't feel it as a payment to be kissed by Ruairí MacEibhir."

So that was his name. Máire did not turn.

"So kiss them. As for myself, you can let me be."

She heard splashing, and Ruairí was in the water, just beneath and to the left of her. "It's you I want to kiss, Máire my black rose. My big queen of women."

She flinched and laughed at herself. " 'Big' is not a word of flattery, for a girl."

With a leap, unexpected by Máire, he stood in front of her. "Should I call you a little, inconsequential thing, then? A toy? Like your sister Eibhlín?"

Eibhlín. That anger was still fresh, and she found she could not look at him. "Call me what you like, cowboy, but leave me be." She stepped around, or tried to. The hillside was steep and slippery with quartz and his arm was around her, supporting her. But he offered no further intimacy.

"I want you for my wife, Máire," he said, and then he stepped away.

Máire's face grew as hot and lonely as the place was; she felt surrounded by eyes. "Nonsense," she said. "I'm not so easily fooled as that."

Ruairí watched her discomfort—her shame—with incomprehension. He put his dirty-nailed hand into his grey hair and scratched. "Fooled? Máire, how could I be fooling you? I said it plain and under the sky. You are the choice of my heart, and I would marry you."

"Don't!"

She floundered off, handicapped by heavy shoes and a wealth of skirt. When she felt some control over her voice again, she called out, "I know something about fairies, Ruairí MacEibhir. And something about men, too!"

He scrambled behind, and soon the narrow valley opened up, revealing brown blankets of bog touched with green, and the grey rock and blue of the seacoast beyond. Sheep scattered in dim, sheepish alarm at their passage. "And if you do know something about fairies, so much the better for you, for you are a good part fairy yourself, mo Róisín. That pale man like a stalk of bleached celery is no kin to you."

Máire put both hands over her ears and skidded down the

side of a ditch. "Oh, leave that old story. It's done enough harm to my life."

"It should bring joy to your life, girl," said he, his face coming close to hers in the shadow. She sprang up the far side. ". . . for your father is not one to cause you shame."

Máire fixed her eyes on his. They were almost of equal darkness, but hers were human eyes. "Are *you* my father, Ruairí MacEibhir?"

His pleasant face went foolish and he let himself slip back into the drainage ditch. "Och! May stones bury my foolish tongue! I didn't mean to suggest *that*, Máire Standún. My interest in you is not fatherly. Or rather, it is, in that I would rejoice to be the father of your children."

"No more of that!" she shouted. "I'm hot and weary and I think I'll be very sore soon. And I doubt I'll find my six eggs, that I left home with this morning. More of your foolishness and I swear by Jesus I'll . . . I'll . . ." She could not, at the moment, think of any fate terrible enough to call down on the fairy man's head.

This vague threat, however, seemed to do. Ruairí MacEibhir pulled his head away from her, and his black eyes opened very wide. "I'll see you home," he said, and he turned into a white horse before her eyes.

Máire was still angry, but she was tired of being angry and plain tired, besides. She got on the horse, finding that she was sore already, and they went back to Carraroe very quietly.

The sunflowers in Hermione Blondell's sewing room gleamed an oppressive brass in the sunshine of the windows. James Blondell found himself squinting, as if with headache. "Well, what possible harm could come to him? Boys invariably dart off on sunny days."

He saw, by the angle of his wife's nose, that he was making no impression on her. "Dammit, Hermie. It isn't as though we were in London, surrounded by dangers . . ."

The nose sprang up. "If we *were* in London, the poor child would not be driven by boredom into risking himself this way. If we *were* in London, I wouldn't have to worry about his being plucked up by seditionists!"

Blondell's mouth sagged slowly, like a flower wilting in the sun. "Seditionists?" he repeated, but his moustache filtered all sound from the word. "Seditionists in Carraroe? What the bloody hell are you talking about, Hermione?"

Mrs. Blondell turned her stone face away, leaving her husband to grasp at straws for her meaning. He noticed (for the first time) that she was not sewing on her wallpaper print, but reading a magazine. He reached over her shoulder and took it up. For five seconds he read silently.

"Hermie, this is *Punch*," he said at last. "This article about seditionists is in *Punch*."

"I can read."

"But . . ." He waved the magazine in the air as he spoke. "*Punch* is humorous. Ironical. You are not supposed to take things seriously when you read them in *Punch*."

Hermione glanced at her husband's round, unsubtle countenance. She found the sight painful. "You don't take anything seriously, James."

"Certainly not *Punch*." He hit the rolled-up paper against his hand three times, and each time he did so, Hermione winced. At last he noticed this and stopped.

"You don't really suspect Toby has been abducted by nationalists, do you?"

She shrugged and moved to the window. Hermione Blondell had still a trim, womanly figure, and silhouetted by the window, she appeared breathtaking to her husband. Breathtaking and untouchable. "How can I know?" she said without emotion, and she raised her hands to her head, letting down a tumble of bright yellow hair. "He may be playing on the rocks in the bay, or have taken a ride in a canoe with some fellow."

Blondell's blue eyes softened at that very thought. "It'd be a grand day for that."

"Don't talk Irish, James," she answered, again without emotion. She was staring, unfocused, at the lily pond on the south lawn, which as yet was a mirror bare of green growth. After a silence of three minutes she said, "He must be sent to school, James. Don't you agree?"

There was no reply, and she turned around to find her husband gone. A flicker of movement caught her eye, and out the window she saw James Blondell striding toward the plantation, wearing heavy gaiters and no coat.

CHAPTER SIX

Tobias, or a Very Stiff Back

The morning was cold and windy, tearing the petals that yesterday had coaxed the first roses to open. Because it was Saturday, Máire Standún went to the rectory carrying a string bag filled with cheap paper primers. The ones that showed through the webbing were first texts in English and in elementary accounts.

The new orange brick of the building clashed with her scarlet and it tore at her black shawl with its roughness. Máire didn't notice.

The old woman who served the priest had eyes the color of sand-buried glass, but it was false to suppose she could not see with them. She admitted Máire with a lack of enthusiasm that was nothing new. Máire immediately sat down in the outside parlor, in the light of the bay window, so she could be seen from the street.

She began to sort lessons which were already sorted, and she was doing that when Tadhg Ó Murchú came in. He too stood in the light of the window and fixed his eyes on the papers.

"Your father came to me," he said without preamble.

"O dear God," replied Máire, brushing her hair from her face. She did not look up.

"But he did." She glanced sideways at Ó Murchú's face, and it was as bad as she had dreaded.

"If he doesn't want you to come here, there's nothing I can do about it."

Máire glanced much more directly around the parlor and along the dark hall where the old woman had disappeared. "I'm twenty-three years old, Father Murphy," she said, speaking English out of scorn for the subject. In Irish she added very quietly, "Two men will be coming in on the *Dreoilín* when she docks at An Sruthán tomorrow in the morning."

"French?" asked the priest quickly.

"American these twenty years," she replied. She handed him a very dog-eared, paperbound notebook, blotched with purple ink and scrawled over in a child's broad hand. He put it under his arm and did not look at it.

"Twenty-three or fifty-three, a Mháire NíStandún, you are living in your father's house."

"Where else can I live?" Now she looked directly at Ó Murchú's dark, foreign-looking face. "Wouldn't I create a stir if I were to take up residence by myself? I tell you, Father, I've thought of it lately."

He shrugged, turning his gaze out the window. "That's no solution, a Mháirín. All the town will think you're insane. Or a witch. Till you find yourself a husband, you must be careful."

"Careful?" Máire's voice cracked. "Sweet Jesus, Father, we could both of us be shot or more likely . . ."

"Hush!" he snapped, though her voice had been more of a hiss than a shout. The priest took a deep breath and leafed absently through the old primer, to the center, where the pages were white and the handwriting very different.

"I mean careful of your reputation. It's a vase you cannot mend, if you should . . ."

"Hush yourself, Ó Murchú. The only reputation I have is that my mother was unfaithful to my father, who is not my father at all. And that I have the sharpest tongue in the parish."

Ó Murchú might have glanced up. "That's not true, a Mháirín. There's old Anraí Ó Reachtaire, who has fought with nine-tenths of the parish, over his horses." At a sound from the street, he turned his attention outward again. The white sheets slipped to the carpet, and Máire picked them up again.

"I've never come to words with Anraí."

"That simply proves my point," said Ó Murchú, with a sly, small smile.

"Which was?"

"That you can't be too careful, a Mháire." Her smile died. "Don't come back here alone. Not for a while."

Máire whitened. She gestured at the pile of books. "And what about the men coming in . . . ? Am I to let Eibhlín in on the secret, so she can chaperone me? That would be ruination, believe me."

Tadhg Ó Murchú picked up the primers, one by one, at random. The white papers he folded and slipped through the false pocket in his cassock to his trouser pocket. "No. One of the other fishermen can take it over, as they used to. Or Morrie can handle it alone."

She picked up her string bag and wrapped it around her left hand. Her fingers poked through the holes. "Then because of the ill humors of a man who I'm glad is no relation to me, my career as a nationalist is over? Like that?"

Ó Murchú frowned. "You're feeling terribly sorry for yourself."

"I'm feeling damn angry, is what I'm feeling." Máire moved toward the hallway door, and as the priest did not get out of her way, she barged past him, nearly knocking him over. She stopped at the front door.

"I might as well marry Ruairí MacEibhir," she called back.

Ó Murchú himself was angry and feeling very bad. He had taken three strides away down the central hall, holding all the papers, the incriminatory and the plain. These words stopped him.

"Ruairí MacEibhir? That one? What do you know about him?"

She laughed. "He says he wants to marry me. A fine fellow, too, isn't he? Ó Reachtaire sets great store by him."

Ó Murchú remained sober. "I want you to be careful around that man, a Mháire. There is something about him . . ."

"There certainly is! At least one something." With a last, barking laugh, the girl was gone. Ó Murchú went back to looking out the window.

Donncha cursed the barn door, which would not stay closed against the wind. He put his hip to the square wooden bin for linseed meal, and he pushed that against the door. As it closed, the wind was compressed into the crack, and in revenge it tore the deck of cards out of his trouser pocket and scattered them into the piled hay. Ruairí MacEibhir, who had watched the process without offering help, picked a number of the cards from the air as they passed. These he handed back to the winded groom, and he yawned as he did so. His eyes were sleepy.

"Thanks and no thanks to you," said Donncha, and then he noticed the card that lay on top. "The Knave of Hearts. Doesn't that fit someone I know."

In no great hurry, Ruairí strolled about the barn, picking up the scattered pasteboards. His grin was benign. "At the moment, colleague, I feel more like the Fool. She'll have nothing to do with me from Saturday to Saturday."

Sunday to Sunday was how Donncha had always heard the expression. He watched Ruairí bend five times and paw blindly at the top of a hay pile once, each time coming out with a single card. "I'd think a fairy would be faster at this sort of job," he said. "Or is it only sand and ears of wheat you can sort in a rush?"

"Here's your deck." Ruairí extended the cards to Donncha and then lowered himself once more into the pile of straw where he'd been cleaning harness.

It was the complete deck, or so close to it Donncha could not tell the difference. He blinked from his companion's somnolent face to the evidence and back again. "I was watching you clearly, fellow, and you picked up only five cards. This is a trick."

Ruairí yawned so wide Donncha could see the grinding surfaces of his teeth, and he slipped onto his hand the glove stained with black daubing. "Of course it's a trick. So is sand and grain a trick. It's also your deck of cards, Donncha, so you have no complaint."

But Donncha put the deck on the lid of the meal bin and backed away from it, offended. "I'd never dare use them again. They couldn't run fair, after you've played with them."

"Don't play with them, then. Why should I care? You'd keep more of your pay if you played with no cards at all."

In the aisle of the barn stood the chestnut stallion, whom Ruairí had named Noble Brainless. He was perfectly free and unconfined within the shell of the barn, but he stood still and nodded his long neck up and down, as though through a stall door. He had been doing that in his spare time for so many years now, that he could not stop, whether indoors or out, come rain or shine.

After six weeks of work he was perfectly tame to handle, and the men had to feel sorry for him, but his piston-habit caused him sometimes to block the light in the barn.

Donncha let his bad mood extend to the horse. As he glared at it he swept the cards off the meal bin and slipped them into his pocket, without thought. He leaned against the bin and watched Ruairí work, as Ruairí had watched him.

"There are other lasses and some much nicer in behavior," he said.

"But none with a punch like the kick of a horse," answered Ruairí, not looking up.

Donncha rubbed his hands together, for he was still chilly. "And you think that's an attribute of beauty, do you?"

Now the black eyes did look up. "If it's swung in your own behalf, it is."

The red horse nodded and nodded. Under the door the wind wiggled, singing. Donncha put his hands up his shirt-sleeves.

"I'm told Eibhlín Standún is a sweet girl, and God knows she's prettier than her sister."

Now Ruairí MacEibhir stood at his full height, and he threw the black field harness, chain traces and all, at Donncha's head. "Speak such a lie again, Splay-tooth, and I'll put the pieces of you under a dozen rose bushes, and that'll make of you the first beauty you've known."

Donncha ducked with energy, but still caught the belly-band over his ear. It stung. "Jesus, man! I have a right to my opinion. And I beg you to remember who it was who cleaned you up to be presentable to a lass."

The barn filled with light, confusing both antagonists. Donncha saw moving shadows over Ruairí's shoulder and moved sideways to make out Mr. James Blondell standing in the doorway with his son behind him.

Blondell strode in, absently patting the red horse that nodded in the aisle. With equal lack of thought, he patted

Ruairí MacEibhir's shoulder. "Where might I Anraí Ó Reachtaire be found?" he said.

The fairy, who had not objected to being patted, took a step backward at this. Donncha, however, was used to Blondell's damaged Gaelic. "He's in the house, sir. These days he takes a nap after dinner."

Blondell nodded sapiently. "Well, perhaps Áine will let us cool our heels in the kitchen." His humility, while well meant, made Donncha feel very awkward. "I'm certain he'd be awake again by now, sir," he replied.

Blondell looked around him for Toby, to find that the boy had remained in the doorway, where he made a very small shadow against the light. "You're letting the wind in, son," he called, and his heavy boots rang against the flagstones of the aisle as he walked back the way he had come. He passed Ruairí, neither touching nor glancing, but at the red stallion he stopped.

"Is this fellow some get of my chestnut?" He lapsed into English. He looked to Ruairí for an answer.

The fairy stared intently.

"He hasn't a word of English," said Donncha for him, in that language. "But that fellow is your chestnut, Squire. The same horse that was dragged in here squealing only a few weeks since."

Blondell gazed at the unfettered horse, and it, which had been entertained by the activity, once more began its bobbing. "Now I know it's him. But is he well, to stand so docile, with other horses all about him?"

Blondell was chagrined to find he didn't understand the quick exchange between Raftery's grooms. But Donncha followed in English. "He is healthy. It is only Anraí's training that makes him so easy."

Blondell wiped his tweed sleeve across his smiling ruddy face. "Well then Anraí's sold his soul to the devil in exchange. There's no natural way that roughneck would start behaving like a lady's hack."

Blondell strained against the wind at the heavy barn door. Donncha went to help him too late. Ruairí never moved.

"Doesn't the man have a word of Gaelic?" he asked, when all was quiet again.

"A word," replied Donncha, pulling a grin. "It's just that it's difficult for a man to recognize what word it is." Then his smile grew broader as he added, "But the squire has more Gaelic than you have English, my lad. A man who speaks only his cradle tongue can't cast aspersions at others."

The fairy's grin was of the same sort as Donncha's. He sat himself on the hay directly in front of him. "Don't be mistaking Gaelic for *my* first language, Donncha. Nor me for a lad. I was born the day Pádraig the Bishop landed for the second time in Éirinn. A tragic day, my father, Eibhear, called it."

"Why so? Were you such a disappointment of a son?" Donncha MacSiadhail wiggled himself deeper into the pale green hay, as though to brace himself against Ruairí's drawling wit. He was quite proud of this last volley, but ready to duck if it set the púca off again.

But Ruairí stared, caught his breath, and erupted with a series of coarse, loud wheezes as much like the bray of a donkey as the laugh of a man. "Perhaps so, but he was too much the gentleman to say so to my face. Unlike you, Donncha, my bright joy! He meant because the end result of that Welshman's coming was to set your people against my own. He had strong feelings in the matter."

"And what of your mother? Was she a fairy, too?"

Ruairí MacEibhir lost his cunning smile. He met the groom in a dark, blank stare and said, "My mother was black. Her name was 'Wind' with reason, for no woman and no horse was faster than she. She was killed by Gaelic people, and burnt over a fire."

Donncha felt his hands like lead in his lap. He heard the barn door rattle as the wind hit it. "I'm sorry for you," he said. "I hope you yourself do not hold this against us." He paused, seeing no reflection in those eyes. "There is enough against us already, Fairy Man, and I don't think you'd gain much by ransacking all the Gaels of An Cheathrú Rúa together."

Ruairí pulled his head up and back. He snorted and the expression of his heavy face softened. "I was never much for grudges. They require too much work."

"And I know how you feel about work," said Donncha, rolling out of reach just in case.

Anraí came into the barn, pushing Toby Blondell very gently before him. Donncha and Ruairí were quartering a

horse between them, and Ruairí had the straw wisp in his
hand.

"We're to teach the young man to ride," said Anraí. As he
spoke English for Toby's sake, Ruairí leaned over the dun's
back for an explanation.

Toby stiffened. "I can ride already," he said quietly but
with undisguisable hostility.

This time the fairy did not ask for translation. He looked
down at the boy with strong interest.

Two or three expressions passed over Anraí's worn face and
were gone. "I said it badly then, Master Toby. We are to help
you perfect your riding."

Black eyes gazed at Anraí with the same strong and neutral
interest. But Donncha winced to hear his fiery employer so
meek.

Toby's hands were balled in his jacket pockets, but his
spine was militarily straight. He glanced from Donncha to the
rear end of the dun horse to Ruairí MacEibhir, and there he
stopped, wrinkling his small forehead. The barn light was
very low and he wasn't sure what he saw.

Anraí cleared his throat. "It happens that the pretty chestnut filly we have is destined for Master Toby, here."

"Dear God!" said Donncha, before he could think.

The boy pulled his attention from the silent groom. "My
father says there's no need to ruin oneself on a plug."

One could ruin oneself in a number of ways, was Donncha's
answer to this, but as Anraí's eye was upon him, he kept it
back.

Anraí took the boy outside, where there was a small,
round ring. The fence was wooden, though stone posts would
have been easier and cheaper. But wood was better to fall
upon, or to strike, or to have one's knee crushed against, and
this was a pen for breaking young horses.

Donncha went to tackle up the filly, while Anraí gave Toby
a short quiz on the subject of horse care. "Which way do you
stroke the horse's foot with the pick to clean them?"

Toby had been staring at Ruairí again, but he turned to the
old man and answered in a voice of ice, "The groom cleans
the horse's feet. I ride the horse."

Anraí went through the color changes of a turkey-cock and
then said evenly, "Your father cleans his horse's feet quite

often. He doesn't ask his groom to dismount and tie his own horse."

Toby stood very straight and raised his chin above the horizontal. "My father wants to be universally liked." Anraí had no way of knowing how much Toby's intonation and stance at that moment resembled that of his mother, for he had never spoken with Hermione Blondell.

There was a pause. "That's not a bad sort of ambition. But taking it from another direction, Master Toby: sometimes in the course of a hunt, where there is no groom beside you (I'm assuming you ride like your father), you feel your horse's gait going uneven, and you suspect there's a stone in the cleft or wedged in the shoe. You can't go on that way, or you'll lame your good beast for the season, and you must take care of the problem quickly, for the hounds . . ."

"Back to front," said Toby in an embarrassed rush. "Making sure you don't dig too hard into the central cleft, nor sore the heel."

Anraí's set face relaxed a trifle. "That's good. And to what use would you put the steel curry comb?"

Toby had to think about this one, for he knew there was a trick. His posture of battle eased and he rubbed the back of his sleeve over his mouth as his father had done, fifteen minutes before.

"It's to get out the mud from the coat of a work horse. On a high-blood horse I wouldn't use it at all."

"Except to clean the other brushes," added Anraí, but he was slightly better satisfied with the boy.

Ruairí MacEibhir watched all this, and when the flighty filly was led out, rolling her eyes and pulling up on the rein in Donncha's hand, he watched Toby's expression closely. Ruairí smiled.

Five minutes of instruction in mounting was ill tolerated, both by the boy and by the filly, and thirty seconds after his heels set the filly into motion, Toby lay flat on his back on the churned earth of the ring, and the horse was dancing from one end of the confinement to the other, panic and willfulness fighting for supremacy in her round, rolling eyes.

Donncha helped Toby up, and his mirth was not at the boy's expense. "She's a challenge, that little girl," he whispered. Toby's face was grey, but he allowed himself to be put back in place in the saddle and suffered a lecture about sitting deep in the saddle.

This time he was off within ten seconds.

He saw the grin on Donncha's wide mouth, showing all the wreckage of teeth. He did not stop to reflect that Donncha might be smiling in sympathy or, indeed, that he had never yet seen Donncha without a smile. Toby was not thinking at all, and as soon as he could speak, he shouted, "I will not be made a figure of fun in front of a group of . . . a group of . . ."

He stalked off, bending under the rail of the fence. Once outside, he paused to dust very ineffectually his jodhpur pants and his hacking jacket. Then he stalked off in the direction of Knockduff.

"It's a long way home, if he's walking," Donncha said to Anraí, who watched his pupil's departure without moving from the center of the ring. "And I wonder what it was that we were a group of?"

Toby cursed his father for telling him he had to ride that damned mad horse. He cursed his mother for not standing up to Father, though she thought this idea of his idiotic. He cursed himself, for showing emotion in front of the natives. He wished the damned, mad horse had broken his neck and solved all his problems at once. Now he had to go home and tell Father why he could never show his face back at Raftery's stable again.

And he would not. No matter what.

It was going to be a long walk home.

He was outgrowing these boots.

Knockduff rose up to the right and the main road was straight ahead. Perhaps he could get a ride with some farmer. Perhaps he would meet his father coming back for him. It would be too bad if Father missed him and went on to Raftery's and heard about all this first from the old man. As mother said about him, he'd always rather believe a native.

There was a sound of hooves from the meadow at the right, but Toby didn't look over, for these acres were Raftery's and full of foraging horse and pony mares and their off-spring. But five seconds later a figure stepped out onto the road. It was the man with the strange eyes: the peasant who didn't speak English.

He stood with one foot on a stone and the other on the plain dirt of the road and said to Toby, "I'd like to show you something."

Very odd. Toby's understanding had been wrong, for the fellow spoke without even a trace of Gaelic accent. He stood in bright light and the boy could see how perfectly dark and brown were his eyes, with only a dot of white at each corner.

Perhaps the color of his eye had broken in an accident, like the yolk of an egg, and run into the surrounding area. Toby's knowledge of human morphology did not deny the possibility of such a thing. He wondered if perhaps he shouldn't be staring. But the man seemed to see perfectly well, and if he didn't, then he wouldn't notice being stared at. Toby found he was following over the blooming fields.

The first foals had been born already, and followed their indolent mothers on broomstick legs. Three of the mares, two with babies and one perfectly enormous, tagged along after Raftery's groom, and one bear-furry infant blundered into Toby himself and sucked at the boy's fingers. No teeth at all.

Toby giggled. Such a thing had never happened to him before. He glanced to see whether the native had noticed his lapse, but Ruairí MacEibhir looked half asleep, and he was pulling great handfuls of dead hair from the croup of a bay mare who stood in glazed ecstasy to let him do it. They made a slow progress, and Toby had no idea where they were going until he looked up and found the small ring in front of him, with the nasty chestnut filly still in it, though her tackle had all been removed. No one else was about.

"Watch me," said Ruairí, and he squeezed between the rails.

The filly put her neck up into the air, until she looked like a picture of a camel. Her back hollowed and her tail came up. She bobbed her head like the daughter of her father that she was and stared at the approaching figure.

Ruairí MacEibhir walked over to her, his feet scuffing in the dust. He looked over her back and he yawned. Two yards from her hindquarters he stopped. "She'll go around the circle for me, now," he said, and Toby at the rail could scarcely hear him. Ruairí gave the filly a sudden glance.

She did. She went around the ring at a smart pace, and he did nothing but turn in a little circle within hers. Sometimes he looked at her and sometimes, in a bored fashion, he looked at Toby. His hands were in his pockets.

It wasn't just for one revolution the filly obeyed him; she kept in motion for five minutes, and soon she wasn't moving like a camel anymore. Her tight back was loosened and her quarters began to drive. She began to trot out like his father's hunter, who was a grand animal and a half-bred son of the same sire. She began to look pretty, in fact, and Toby felt a slight pang, knowing that he was not able to ride her.

As though he read the boy's mind, Ruairí said to him, "She looks lovely at the gallop, too." There was no great difference in the attitude Ruairí struck, standing in the middle of the round ring: a tension in the shoulders, a lowering of the head, a certain glower. But the filly sprang forward as though whip struck, and she did have a breathtaking gallop. Toby grinned through the dust, and the man in the center of the ring grinned with him.

Another ten minutes of speed and he brought the glistening horse to a walk, seemingly by no more than relaxing his shoulders. At last she stopped dead, in place, and her head hung to her knees. Ruairí MacEibhir squeezed between the rails, and he was dry faced and yawning again.

"Now, lad, you do it," he said, and he took Toby by the hand. Toby giggled in the manner he had always hated in himself, but at the moment he didn't notice. "I don't know the trick," he admitted. "I watched you, but I didn't catch it."

The strange fellow laughed, and the silver and black hair fell into his brown eyes. "There's no trick at all but the certainty of your own power. You're a human being and you're eleven years old. She's a filly horse and she's only three. You are much larger than she, if you'd but know it, and many times more dangerous. Know that and walk toward her hindquarters.

"Not directly behind, of course," he added in a droll manner. Toby took two steps. He did not feel in the slightest bit more dangerous than the tall filly, but he was used to acting a part he did not feel. With the same stiffness of spine he had shown in front of Anraí, he approached the filly, who rolled her eyes and shied. She did not move.

Damn you, you *will* move, he said to himself, and he thrust his head aggressively forward, as the man had done. The filly shot forward in an explosion that carried her all around the ring. As he was still in the same frame of mind when she came around again, and he glared at her face on, she skidded to a stop ten feet away from him and stood sweating.

"You've done it, my lad," said Ruairí. Quietly he stepped toward the filly, and he petted her, and was suddenly on her back, while Toby retreated to the rail, waiting for the fireworks.

A crow hop, no more. The filly stood with no tackle on her and the man's feet behind her elbow. His hands were on his thighs. "Go," he said quietly, for Toby's benefit, and he squeezed and leaned forward, and the filly did go. "Stop," he said again, and his weight went to the back, causing her steps to dwindle and fail. Again he set her trotting, and it seemed his very attention sent her right and left. At last he let her stop beside the boy.

"Now you," he whispered, and Toby's heart swelled with desire to the point of pain. Perhaps Ruairí took his expression for fear, for he said, "What could she do to you she hasn't already done, and left you whole?"

"I can't get up that far by myself," was all of Toby's reply, and when Ruairí offered a boost, he wasn't slow in taking it.

The red filly was very handsome, shining with sweat and with all the nonsense run out of her. It was fortunate for the boy that this had been done, but it was Toby's own intelligence and courage that moved her forward.

He put his hands on his thighs, as the man had done, though he wanted desperately to grab mane. He leaned and squeezed her forward. Glory of glories, the horse went into a good trot, and Toby sat that trot for half an hour, under the windy sky of April. She went left for him and right for him, and at the end of the lesson, she stopped for him. All without bridle or saddle.

Like a hero out of a story.

Toby slid off; his trousers and the skin on the inside of his thighs were wet with horse sweat. He loved it.

"I can ride her," he said, as though Ruairí MacEibhir needed to be told.

The man nodded his head, almost as the horse had done. He had such a nice face, thought Toby. He liked the broad cheekbones, the short nose, and the black, smiling eyes, even if they were like scrambled eggs. At the moment Toby liked everybody.

"You surely can. But she's too stupid for you, I think."

Toby blinked and looked back at the expensive filly.

"Oh, she may learn cleverness, but three-year-old horses are like babes in nappies. With the best will in the world, they can't be trusted to take care of their feet. I can find you a good pony who is so clever even I can't outthink him, and on him, you won't have to stay in a pen, like a monkey riding a dog."

"But . . ." Toby was doubtful. "My father meant this horse for me."

MacEibhir raised his head and gazed out over the hills. Over Knockduff. "If you show your father how you've mastered this girl, then perhaps he'll have no objection if we let her off to . . . to grow into you."

Toby giggled once more, thinking of the tall filly having to "grow into" him.

"However," continued Ruairí, and he leaned against the rail of the pen, as though too lazy to stand upright. "If I teach you, you must treat me with respect, and old Anraí too, for he is the best man on a horse in Connemara."

"I wouldn't dream of doing otherwise!" Toby really believed his own words; he had no memory of having had other feelings. "But . . . is he really better on a horse than you are?"

"Of course not," said Ruairí, and then James Blondell came trotting up the road on his covert hack, and Toby exploded away to tell him all about his lesson.

Blondell was pleased, and more pleased when Toby climbed onto the weary filly to take her naked around the ring once more. He acceded to Ruairí's request that the filly be given a "rest" while Toby was schooled on a horse of the trainer's choosing.

He went in the house, full of satisfaction, to speak with Anraí.

Anraí was very surprised, for he hadn't known there had been a lesson, and the last he had seen of the boy had been his dusty rear view as he had limped angrily away down the road. When the squire praised the English of his new hired man, his cup of confusion overflowed. He said little to Blondell, but only nodded and smiled.

Anraí walked out into the fresh air and wind to find the fairy helping Donncha pull a mane. "Are you teaching Blondell's son, then? And have you really excellent English?"

Donncha stared. Ruairí answered, "I'll teach the boy, if it's the same with you, Anraí. He's bold enough, though his tongue is awkward. But as for English . . ."

He left off what he was doing, and ran his hands through his heavy hair in thought. "In the center of four walls, my friend, and on a floor, I have no English, for I have never learned it. But on my own earth . . . there I can speak to anyone."

His eyes, intent on Anraí, were themselves holes into the brown earth.

CHAPTER SEVEN

Grand Shoulders

The spring night was very warm; moths of various colors dashed themselves against the chimney of the lamp.

"He's out there, all right," said Eibhlín Standún, who stood in willowy languor by the window, looking out sideways from beneath her lashes.

"What would I do without you to keep me abreast of things?" murmured her sister, who sat by the lamp, doing her poultry accounts. Máire Standún was very close about her egg money.

The girls' sitting room, which was also their bedroom, had glass in the window and curtains of lace woven by nuns. Their father owned five big boats: sleek Galway hookers that trolled out in Cashla Bay or further. It was simply furnished, however, and whitewashed instead of papered, because the Stantons, despite the name, were more or less Gaels. They did not hobnob with Hermione Blondell.

Máire's hair, falling in torrents to the tabletop, was the color of the ink she was using: more blue than brown. Eibhlín's hair was gold, and it caught the light no matter where she stood.

"He is a fine-looking man," she said. "He has grand shoulders."

"He does that." Máire's reply was vague.

"A uniform would become him, I think," added Eibhlín, which was one of her highest compliments.

Máire Standún tried to imagine Ruairí MacEibhir in the military uniform, and in the effort she made a blot in the shillings column.

Eibhlín's eyes were huge, and as bland as a baby's. She rarely looked straight at the thing she wanted to see. "He has been so faithful, Mary. Every clear night for weeks. Perhaps he has stood there in the rain, too, and we cannot see him. If he wanted to see me so badly, I'm sure I'd share a word with him."

"I'm sure you would," said Máire, even more vaguely.

". . . even if it were only to remind him his suit was hopeless."

Máire mumbled, "I'm sure it wouldn't be." Eibhlín glanced at her sharply, straight on, but only for a moment.

Fragrant breezes, not too warm, and moonlight. Máire Standún closed the door behind her gently. She had not sneaked out, exactly, but she had not made a great deal of noise.

Her sister's garden, with its roses and herbaceous border, had the south wall of the house. She passed through it and passed by the sally hedge, which was tall in this spring season, like stiff hair on a head. Beyond this was her chicken yard, its fence woven out of the willow shoots. Her hens were in the stone shed, their sleep noises barely audible. Beyond this stood her beehives: a wooden box in the modern system and three empty skeps, waiting for swarms to fill them.

This was Máire's garden. It had a few flowers, too, and pea plants on a trellis of willow. She stood by the hives, uncertain. Seeing no one about, she lowered her head and put an ear to the wall of the wooden hive.

"You're brave enough!" said Ruairí MacEibhir, stepping out from the shade of the hedge.

Máire straightened and made sure her shirt was tucked. "Bees don't want to sting you."

He laughed, raising his chin up. "Me, they do. The smell of me offends them terribly." He took a step into moonlight and his head shone white. "Not that I'm a dirty fellow, mind you. It's only the smell of horses."

Máire watched him advance. "They come out at night sometimes," she told him. "When the moon is this bright."

"Are you warning me off?" He chuckled, but he stopped in place. "Do you use your bees in the place of guard dogs?"

There was a faint buzzing in the air, or perhaps it was his imagination. Máire's teeth were bright as flowers in the illumination of the full moon. "I don't need guards, Ruairí. I am sufficient to myself."

The silver headed bobbed. "I believe you, woman! I would not . . . Ow!" With a flapping of hands, he retreated to the hedge again. "You may not need protection, but you certainly have it. I'm stung on the nose, by heaven!"

Máire herself backed away from the hive, though with a bit more dignity. She came to him in the shadow of the hedge and pulled him by the arm into moonlight. "Here. Don't pluck at it; you'll force the venom into your skin. Let me."

With a fingernail she scraped the pulsing venom sack from Ruairí's nose. The stinger, she made sure, came with it.

"It won't swell much, I don't think," she murmured. "It hadn't time to . . ."

Her hand was between his suddenly, and he had kissed it. She yanked back futilely, but he would not let go. "You'll hit me, lass. I know it, and now I don't dare release you." Her anger growing, she pulled with all her strength and almost pulled the man off his feet and on top of her.

"You see my problem," he whispered hurriedly. "I should have thought of it before I dared kiss you, but I'm not clever. I never was." Twice more she yanked against his hold, and the man followed in the most ludicrous manner, his feet always in his own way, apologizing that necessity had made him such a bother.

Máire sat down and tried to pry his hands off with her left hand. He caught that also. "You see, lass? If it weren't for the terror I have for you, I'd be able to let you go."

She gathered her shreds of control and glanced behind, at the darkened house. "Quiet. Now no more fooling. Let me go. I promise I won't hit you."

"Then you'll kick me," he answered, and held tight.

Máire took a deep breath which ended in a giggle. "I'll neither hit nor kick you nor do you harm in any fashion."

His eyes were black in the darkness. "How can I believe you?"

Now Máire laughed outright, but bitterly. "As I'm neither a

man nor a fairy, you *can* believe me, MacEibhir. I'll do you no harm."

Her hand was free, just like that. Ruairí stared at her intently with his invisible eyes. "And because I am both, Máire. Both a man and a fairy, you can believe me. I mean you no harm, but great good."

She stood up again, chagrined to find that the ground had been damp. "I've heard about fairies' promises."

He had remained sitting. "They are kept. It is only that they are sometimes carefully worded. But I say it plainly, with the night as my witness: I will do well by you, a Mháire daughter of beautiful Nóra NíGhallchóir by a child of Danu. In waking and in sleeping and in all seasons I will keep and guard you."

His serious expression dissolved. He stood up. "—at least as well as a bee can."

Máire tried to turn away from him and could not. "How would you do that? Keep me, I mean, when you're Anraí Ó Reachtaire's second groom and haven't even a cottage or an acre of your own?"

When his answer was not immediate, she added, "I knew it. You're after play, just like the man who ruined my mother." She headed back for the house, stumbling.

"Stop!" To her own surprise, Máire did.

"Don't you think I could find sport enough without spending the sweet season sitting under a hedge, like a dog waiting for his master?" The fairy man stepped over to her, soundlessly. "If I waited in my answer, a Mháirín, it was because there were so many answers among which to choose.

"I am now old Ó Reachtaire's horseboy, yes, but I needn't remain so. I could come to you dripping in gold and jewels, like a king, and riding a stallion shod with silver. I could put money into your lap."

For a moment she was breathless. "And in the morning it would all disappear?"

Ruairí had to smile. He scratched his grey head. "Some of it might, certainly. But fairies know about more than fairy gold, believe me. I know what the earth knows.

"With me, you could live better than with this corn-haired man who is not your father and who has so little love for you." He sighed softly. "For I do love you, a Mháire."

Máire frowned. She stared from the moon to her own white hands in confusion. Then she met his glance, and her full lips were tight. "You're not a Christian, Ruairí."

So unexpected was the statement that he left his mouth hanging in the breeze for a good while. "Not at all. How would you expect me to be?"

She nodded, and there was relief in her face. "I didn't expect it. But I am a Christian, you must know, and I cannot marry one who isn't without putting my immortal soul into risk."

"Is that so?" he said, and his smile was sly.

"It is, and I'll hear no fairy nonsense against my revealed religion, thank you!" As he said nothing to this she continued more softly, "So you see, I cannot marry you. You must find another like yourself. More like yourself.

"But . . ." a sudden idea brightened her moon-white face. "If indeed you know where treasure lies, there are hundreds of poor Gaels in this parish alone whose lives would be lightened . . ."

"Poor Gaels are nothing to me," said Ruairí shortly.

Máire's temper rose again. "Well, then, there is nothing more to say!" She stalked by the chickens and toward the back door.

He was trotting beside her. "Is that the only objection? That I'm not a Christian? It seems small enough. I will declare myself so."

"What?" So loud was her exclamation that Máire covered her own mouth with her hand and glanced guiltily at all the windows of the house. "You can't, Ruairí. Fairies are the enemies of the church. A touch of holy water to you would be acid on the skin!"

"Who says?" He snorted. "I'll bet I could endure it. Besides, it hasn't hurt you any, lass."

"I'm nothing like a fairy," Máire whispered, more composedly.

"You know nothing about it," he replied in an even quieter whisper. He kissed her on the lips before she could stop him, and then he ran off, making no noise on the short spring grass.

There were the white walls and the white sheets and the white spring coverlet that their mother had sewn before she died five years ago, but there was no Eibhlín against them.

Máire stood still in the doorway. She began to sweat and then to shiver. She looked out the window which gave onto the garden. At last she undressed and went back into her own bed.

What could the chippie say against her, even had she heard? (And what she heard she *would* tell, for she was Eibhlín.) She could accuse—no, convict her—of a clandestine meeting with a man in the garden. Of a kiss. That could ruin her, of course, if there was anything in big Máire Standún left to ruin. It would confirm her father's conviction that she was a whore born.

Like her mother.

But it was not as bad as if Eibhlín had gone through the dirty papers in Máire's "teaching" pile. Not as if she had discovered any one of Tadhg Ó Murchú's unobtrusive visitors. Eibhlín, with her mind irremovably fixed on young men, would not think to suspect her sister of misdeeds so unrewarding.

She was still hot with anger, however, and stiff under the covers, when pale Eibhlín drifted in. She shot a covert glance at Máire's bed and went back to her own, placing her black woven shawl ever so neatly on the peg by the bed.

"Where did you go?" asked Máire, and to her disgust her own voice betrayed her upset.

Eibhlín gave a well-rehearsed chuckle. "Where do you think, at this hour, and with the tea we were drinking all evening? But unless you were squatting in the garden to water the plants, a Mháire, I don't know where you were, for I didn't see you at the little house. Perhaps I shouldn't bother about it."

"Perhaps you shouldn't," said Máire. "Perhaps you shouldn't bother with a lot of the business you bother about." She turned over with great energy and lay as though asleep.

Eibhlín lay down without messing the covers and folded her hands over her stomach. She slept neatly, but snored.

A light spatter of rain made both the saddles and the horses smell. Anraí Ó Reachtaire, on the black Thoroughbred, peered with weather-worn eyes down at the rippling summer grass and sedges in the valley below. Ruairí, sitting the crazy chestnut indolently, looked further, at the wild hell of fuchsia and gorse on the far slope.

"We don't know where he is, but I make no doubt that he knows where *we* are," murmured the old horseman.

"Oh, but I know where he's hiding," said Ruairí. His complacency roused Anraí.

"Damn you if you do. We've been searching all morning, MacEibhir, and I think you don't like to waste your time any more than the rest of us."

Ruairí still sat at ease, and his peaceable face went even sleepier. "But it's no waste, Anraí, son of Thurlaigh. To ride a fast horse on a fair morning . . . ?"

"Fair!"

"Well I've endured many worse. I'll follow you like the good hand I am, Anraí, but if you'd have me bring you this horse, you must tell me what you'll do with him. Shoot him, as Diarmuid Ó Cadhain wants you to?"

Anraí had a long rifle slung behind his saddle. He did not look at it. "If he's as vicious as they tell me, I'll have to, Ruairí. I'm told he'd be no loss to the race of ponies."

MacEibhir colored, in one of his rare moments of temper. "The little king? Indeed he is not vicious, or not as vicious as you are, horsekeeper. And as for being a loss to the race, well, I think the race might have some say in that. I know he is very good to his mares."

Anraí's eyes widened, but he was not one to back away from an argument. "Except that his mares are actually Diarmuid's mares. And James Blondell's mares as well, which he has stolen. And the babes they could be breeding for good gain for their owners are rough pony babes, and uncatchable."

Ruairí smiled, as though Anraí had actually agreed with him, but the red stallion took a sudden opportunity to snap at his black colleague, who shied away.

"Sorry, my oversight," said Ruairí, turning his mount's head.

"I'm sure it was!" Now it was Anraí's turn to get hot. "You make that kind of mistake all the time, you unholy creature. Let me tell you I've never been happy to kill a horse my life long. Much rather would I kill a human man, but sometimes it comes to that." He pointed a gnarled finger at the fairy.

"I've spent my little share of strength covering this mountain, and I won't be made fool of. If you can catch me this wild hammerheaded pony, then do so, and I'll see he gets no bullet. But if I have to sweat much more, I'll shoot him as I see him, to spare my own life!"

Anraí had no intention of shooting the wild horse unless it attacked him, and Ruairí did not believe for a moment that he had. He replied, "If I catch him, can I do my own will with him?"

The old man stared. "If that doesn't include turning him loose again or breeding him to my mares, then you can."

The red horse dropped its head and pawed, as though it and not its rider were considering. "It doesn't include either of those, though by preference I'd let him remain king of his little country, for he has qualities, and I have known him since his birth." He turned his horse's limber neck.

"I'll catch you this horse, Anraí. Sit here at your leisure and I'll bring him to you."

Anraí watched him start down the hill, sparing the Thoroughbred's delicate legs. The horseman felt somehow badly used. It was Ruairí's eternal command that bothered him. Damn all, Anraí was boss.

He thought of something hurtful to say. "You know, Ruairí, that a decent man does not go courting at night without a father's permission."

In surprise the other reined his mount. "Doesn't he? But when am I to court, if you keep me working all day?"

The black horse stirred at the grip of Anraí's legs. "A decent man doesn't go courting at all, but leaves that to wise friends, who take a good bottle to the man of the house and discuss the matter."

The fairy produced an incredulous expression, which made Anraí angrier. "That's what a Christian does, you heathen. But you wouldn't understand!"

Now Ruairí settled back in the saddle. "It's true that I don't, Anraí. But I must learn to, for a Christian is exactly what I intend to become."

And as the old man stared, he rode down the hill after the hammerheaded pony.

Anraí sat in the mist, while the black horse shifted left and right. After a while he could no longer see the chestnut spot against the grass that meant Ruairí.

He began to consider his finances, as he always did when

he had time. He wondered whether the summer would be impossibly tight or only a decent pinch. With pounds on one side and bales weighed against them, it seemed possible that they would manage.

Because of the fairy, of course. He was more use than any two assistants, and as yet Anraí had not paid out a shilling to him. Even Donncha could not be jealous of that.

Wet wind blew under Anraí's hat. His horse snorted. There was nothing to see but the green, barren valley below and the thorn across the way.

Of course Ruairí MacEibhir had not asked for money, but only an opportunity to make himself known to the parish. To Standún's black daughter, specifically.

Anraí sighed, and so did his horse under him. His agreement with Ruairí MacEibhir might be more costly than the pennies he saved, if the fellow got Máire in trouble. Carraroe would not like that and would ask Anraí why he'd taken such a villain into his household and where he had gotten him in the first place. Was he to answer that he met him in the form of a great pony on the hills? The priest thought he was a Kerryman, by his slow, old-fashioned speech. Old-fashioned, indeed! And little Toby, the young squire, who walked about telling folks that Ruairí had come off a horse and broken his eyeballs like egg yolks! Dear Lord, what a tale! Who in his right mind could believe that man would come off a horse?

If Ruairí MacEibhir came to grief, be sure he'd drag Anraí down with him. Or in his place. But Máire . . .

His head nodded under the spatter of rain.

Máire Standún might take care of herself very well.

When Ruairí MacEibhir came back, Anraí was asleep on an uncomfortable, wet black horse. The scrape of hooves over rock did not disturb him, but the snorts and groans of fright from the horse Ruairí led behind him woke the old man in an instant. Before he opened his eyes, his hand was stroking the neck of his mount, and he was crooning to it.

There was the grey-haired fellow with the black eyes and the young face, looking as sleepy as ever—though the red horse he rode was clearly unhappy. And behind them, frozen in shock and dread, was a small, stocky, dust-black stallion, with a rope of grass draped around its thick neck. Its nose was pinched, its lips pulled, and the expression in its round eyes made Anraí catch his breath. His unkempt coat was wet through by sweat more than by rainwater, and steam rose.

"By sweet Jesus, man! What did you do to him to put him in that state? He is a horse terrified to the edge of death!" Anraí Ó Reachtaire was flooded with outrage.

Ruairí cleared his throat, which was thick. "I told him his reign was over," he said, and there was none of the accustomed cheerfulness in his voice. "That his reign was over and his family broken. What would you expect him to look like, after hearing that?"

Anraí looked at the stocky pony, not fourteen hands high, and tried to see a king within.

To call the beast hammerheaded was unfair, though its jaw was heavy enough and its throatlatch almost drafty. Its ribs were broad, but not quite barrel shaped. Its shaggy short legs were foursquare. "And yet he came with you? On a little grass rope, not even tied?"

Ruairí put both hands on the pommel of his saddle and let his head hang forward. Anraí thought he said, "What choice had he?" but realized then that he had heard wrongly. "What choice had we?" was what the fellow had said.

The black pony stood very still, all his legs braced, as though he were falling asleep. Anraí knew better. "It might have been kinder to shoot him," he said, and he raised his eyes away from the sight.

But behind the black pony and Ruairí on the red horse there was another horse, coming slowly up the hill. It was long limbed and very elegant, and it came freely. The red stallion nickered and pawed, and the black turned his head an inch.

It was Diarmuid Ó Cadhain's Thoroughbred mare, half sister to Anraí's own black stallion. A dark, burnished bay, fully eight inches taller than the little pony, she walked a large circle around the red stallion to approach from the pony's side, and she lay her very expensive head across his slanting croup.

"There's loyalty for you," said Anraí.

There was a shrill call from the opposite slope, and Anraí

could barely make out other horses, or ponies, most likely, half hidden amid the gorse. They did not approach.

"Don't be hard on them, old man. They're not tame to man, like the big girl," said Ruairí.

At the far whinny, the pony turned his head all the way behind, raised his ears, and took one step to the side. Ruairí gave the slightest of pulls upon the grass rope, and from his human throat came a deep, equine grunting.

The prick ears slid back again and the black eyes glazed over. Anraí circled his horse to come up on the pony's other side. They started toward Mám Cross, where Ó Cadhain had his barn, and the black pony and the bay Thoroughbred came with them.

"He'll scarcely let you keep her, too," said Anraí, roughly.

Ruairí was unmoved. "I never led the horse to believe he could."

There was silence broken only by hoof falls and the black pony's frequent stumble. They passed sheep and a man in black gaiters, who was accompanied by a black, barking dog. The sun came out. It was over ten miles to the crossing.

"So how do I do it?"

It was the fairy's question, and Anraí, who was nodding again, squinted at him in confusion. "Are you asking me to guess how you convinced that poor pony to give up all . . ."

Chuckling, Ruairí shook the rain from his hair. "That wouldn't be fair, Anraí. I'm asking you how it is I become a Christian."

Old Anraí snorted very much like a horse, and the bay mare he was leading lifted her nose to him. "Why, you become a Christian by being baptized, of course. That is, after you believe what the holy church has to teach you."

Ruairí was examining the pony's eyes, but he caught at least part of it. "Baptized! Of course. That's what the man Pádraig came to do, isn't it. With a lance through the foot?"

Anraí blinked. "I'm sorry?"

"I asked you whether you still baptize with a lance through the foot, as the old bishop did in my early years?"

"He never!" Anraí's forehead wrinkled so that he let the drops from his wet hair run into his eyes.

And Ruairí giggled. "Ah, but he did! Who should know

better than I, who was there, although a small foal at the time."

Looking at Anraí's scandalized face, he giggled again. "Ara! Anraí, I never lie to you. Not outright, that is."

They were on the wooden bridge of Mám Cross, with the high hills rising behind. "Well, Tadhg Ó Murchú does not baptize with a lance through the foot," Anraí stated.

"I'm glad of it," answered Ruairí.

They turned left and went a half mile.

"Anraí," said Ruairí. "If you take my advice, you'll exchange the payment Diarmuid has offered you for the foal that bay mare carries. He'll be glad to dispose of it, feeling as he does, and it . . ."

"Do you think I'm an idiot?" Anraí tried to frown, but a sly grin broke through instead. "Why, Son of My Heart, I no sooner saw the two of these, but I'd decided on that. It will be a grand baby!"

They were both laughing as they came to Ó Cadhain's barn, leading the lovely Thoroughbred mare and the little broken king.

CHAPTER EIGHT

Grand Shoulders, Continued

Tadhg Ó Murchú tore his newspaper into tiny bits as he gazed at the sky through his parlor window. He was angry at the news, but he shredded the paper more because he had the habit of shredding papers, once read, than for any immediate reason.

Outside it was a lovely day, and the people on the street outside were dawdling. There was a cluster of women outside the tobacconist and grocer's shop, and they hadn't moved for twenty minutes. He wondered what they were discussing.

So Gladstone had finally lost his temper (or his reason) and stuffed Parnell into Kilmainham Gaol. The priest himself had predicted it, but that didn't make it any easier to live with, now that it was fact. It would be very hard to preach restraint in the pulpit as well as to certain of his back-parlor friends.

More immediately upsetting, however, was the plan to boycott Ó Cadhain, who was taking up the lease on ten acres from which Seán Garvaí had been evicted. This would be the first boycott on James Blondell's land, and Ó Murchú had rather had hopes for Blondell. It would make more sense if they did the boycott on the bailiff, Fenton, if they were going to do it at all. Fenton was every landowner's bailiff, at his price. This very day he would descend on the Séamas Ó Conaola family, not a quarter mile down the street, and pitch them into the road. Perhaps he would have to tear the roof down, for Bríd NíAnluain, Séamas's wife, would not leave easily.

Ó Murchú would have liked to have someone to talk to about all this, but the only person he could trust, and who might understand both the issues and his reservations, he dared not approach. He would have to keep his mouth shut.

He was used to it.

The newspaper was confetti over the embroidered pillow on the window seat. His housekeeper would shake her head. He tried to gather it up in his hands.

There was movement out the window. Not the women at the shop—that knot was stable, even larger. Two men ascended the rectory drive, dressed not in báinín but in rough hacking jackets. One wore high boots and one heavy gaiters, and for a moment Ó Murchú had no idea who they might be. His stomach twisted, for he could not imagine anything good out of the day.

As they neared the door and passed behind the forsythia, which was in thick leaf, he could see stripes of them.

It was Anraí Ó Reachtaire, of all people, with his new horseboy. Ó Murchú let out a very relieved sigh and rose to get the door before the housekeeper could be bothered.

"God to you, Father. Good evening," said Anraí, though it was near noon. He had his hat in his hands, and his face and hands had been scrubbed to the point of irritation.

Ó Murchú wondered if he himself were half that clean. He felt a pang of guilt, that the man should go to such trouble for a call. Of course it was the office, not the man. He gave Anraí a "God and Mary" in return and held the door for both men.

Ó Reachtaire wore boots and the assistant rude leather gaiters, as was only fitting. But somehow, on him, they looked less demeaning and more like . . . the priest couldn't put a name to it.

As he looked politely into the man's face, Ó Murchú suffered a small shock. He had never seen MacEibhir in the light of day.

The eyes were enough. Unlike most of the residents of Carraroe, Father Ó Murchú had traveled. He knew that eyes of such peculiar size and color did not exist. Not anywhere.

Not out of disease, or accident, or strange, foreign blood.
Nowhere.

But the eyes were not all. As Tadhg Ó Murchú stared at
the brawny, neat form, his own sharp eyes played him a
trick. He blinked, twice, sure that the whiteness was tears or
sun glare. Or perhaps he was going faint.

Ruairí MacEibhir caught the priest as his knees buckled,
and with one hand he held him upright. When Ó Murchú
could focus again, he found that the fellow was grinning at
him, as though they shared a secret.

"You must remember Ruairí," Anraí was saying. "When I
had that spell, this winter before, he's the one who . . ."

"I do remember," answered Ó Murchú. "Very well." He
swayed on his feet.

"Are you all right, Father?"

He took a hard breath. Ruairí MacEibhir was still there in
front of him, and aside from the eyes, he was just a fine-
looking young man with prematurely grey hair. Very well
groomed. Smiled a lot.

Ó Murchú felt the hair on the back of his neck rising
against his collar.

"It's because of Ruairí that we've come, Tadhg." Anraí
began to relax. He sailed his hat onto the chair by the door
and followed Ó Murchú into the parlor, where he stared at
the large pile of shredded paper on the pillow, wondering
what it could mean.

The priest's quick eyes glanced from one man to the other.
"Couldn't Ruairí come to me by himself? I'm the priest for
all the parish."

Ruairí lifted one foot, absent-mindedly, and stamped it on
the floor. "That's the problem, Uí Mhurchú. You are priest to
all the parish, but not to me."

Anraí cleared his throat. "He means, Father . . ."

"He can explain what he means."

Ruairí stamped again, his thumbs in his belt. "I mean I am
not of your tribe. I am not a Christian. I have not been
baptized."

Ó Murchú's face expressed incredulity. "You mean you
don't remember being baptized."

"Of course that's what I mean. But I doubt it was done
while I wasn't noticing!"

Ó Murchú lowered himself into a hard, spindly armchair which sat beneath a lithograph of St. Peter's in Rome. Anraí quickly deposited himself in the chair opposite, and Ruairí MacEibhir sat on the pile of shreddings. Seeing immediately what he had done, he laughed and dusted himself, sending bits of paper all over. Some remained on the seat of his canvas trousers. "Very few people remember being baptized, Ruairí. It happens when we are infants. I presume your parents are dead, or they would have told you. If you ask any surviving members of your parents' generation, or perhaps if you could find the midwife who bore you, she would tell you that you had been baptized properly."

The grin spread from ear to ear. "The midwife who attended my mother was a stranger, a poor woman whom my father hired in the very night of my arrival and who was sent home never knowing clearly where she'd been. Such is the custom of my family. And I have reason to believe that she is dust on this earth. My own people were killed long ago and did not come back."

The priest glanced over to Anraí, and his eyes asked quite clearly whether he was supposed to understand that Ruairí MacEibhir was one of God's simple ones. Anraí looked agonized and his fingernails gripped his trouser knees. "You see, Tadhg, it's like this with Ruairí . . ."

Feeling he understood plainly, the priest shushed him with a gesture. "Be easy, Anraí. Remember you aren't strong yet.

"What about the priest of your parish in Kerry? He would have records."

Ruairí put his elbows onto his knees. "Though I have been to Kerry in my years. Ó Murchú, it is scarcely my home. I am out of Connemara." He said each word of the phrase again, with emphasis: "out—of—Connemara."

The priest turned his head half away, like a dubious bird. "Not so."

The grin came back. "No one more so. I am of Connemara and I am not baptized. If you doubt me, it is easy to prove it." He stood, and his pleasant face knew a moment's uncertainty. "How strong is your floor?"

"Ruairí, my son. Don't do it!" cried Anraí.

Ó Murchú rose along with Ruairí. "How strong is . . . Why, what on earth are you going to . . .

Father Ó Murchú was down on the beach, with the grey horse trotting beside him. The stones that cluttered the shore were rounded and gold, some of them the size of sheep and some the size of a man's head. Ó Murchú hopped them with the ease of a child; his black cassock was wet up to the knees.

The horse kept to higher, smoother ground.

"Why do you want me to baptize you?" asked the priest, looking straight in front of him.

"Máire NíStandún has made that a condition," replied Ruairí MacEibhir, who pounced onto the same rock that supported Ó Murchú and skidded over it neatly and down to the next.

"Clever with your feet." The priest said it as though it were no compliment.

"I should hope so."

"What do you mean, 'a condition'?" Ó Murchú shouted, because the wind was high and so was the blowing surf.

"A condition of our betrothal." As Ruairí raised his voice, it went into his nose more, as happens with the people of Connemara. And with horses.

Ó Murchú stopped dead. "Of your . . ." His quick eyes moved over the receding waves. "Was she serious?" His question was addressed to the water. Then he said, "She's too good for you."

The grey head nodded. "I should hope so." Then his grin stretched tight. "Do you want her, too?"

Ó Murchú growled, like a cat. "You can't be that ignorant of my calling, pagan though you are."

"I'm not ignorant at all," answered Ruairí, and he kicked a large stone with his foot.

Ó Murchú noticed the heavy shoe and the leather gaiter, which was getting wet. "Where do your clothes come from, when you turn from horse to man?"

"They are with me from the time I was given them, thirty-seven years ago."

Ó Murchú stared, turned off, and began to walk again. "You've worn them for thirty-seven years and they haven't fallen apart? Is that fairy magic?"

Ruairí scrambled in the surf to keep up with him. "Not at all! I haven't worn them for all those years, for it was thirty-seven years since I took this form in this place."

A cold wind hit the priest in the back. "What do you mean? You spent all those years as a pony on the hill? And did nobody ever see you?"

"I was not a horse, Ó Murchú, nor yet a man." He flopped his hands against his sides in a floundering attempt to explain. "I told you, Priest, I am out of Connemara."

Ó Murchú's hands were balled in his pockets. He stopped at the end of a spit of land, with the fairy behind him. "Out of . . . In the earth, as the stories put you? With the dead?"

The usual grin faded from Ruairí MacEibhir's face. He looked at Ó Murchú with a peculiar reserve. "Don't you know all about it, Tadhg Ó Murchú? Weren't you born knowing what you know?" He took one step closer. "This shirt of mine, now. I got it from off a dead man, the last time I came out here, among . . ."

The priest gave a sudden scream, for he had recoiled and was falling. He hung ten feet above the water, dangling from the fairy's hand. Without much trouble, Ruairí pulled him up and onto the rock again.

"Clever . . . with your hands, too." Ó Murchú's voice shook.

"Legs and hands. All but my head, as my father was fond of saying." The grin broke through again. "Ó Murchú, did you think I was about to slay you for your cassock? Believe me, dead men are not stingy of their old belongings." With exaggerated care, he stepped backward off the rock, letting the priest pass without touching him.

Ó Murchú began to laugh. "I believe I have pulled my seams. What a bother: I'll have to sew them at night, lest my housekeeper finds out." As he smoothed the garment flat, a thought struck. "Thirty-seven years ago was forty-five. That was the famine."

"It was a bad time enough," answered the fairy soberly.

Ó Murchú pulled the windblown hair from his eyes and he stared at the other as though he were a sheet of newsprint, while Ruairí shifted from foot to foot. "And you haven't been back since."

"Didn't want to."

The small black eyes at last relented. "What do you remember about that time?"

Ruairí hugged himself, perhaps from cold, and gazed out

to sea. "I remember that gold could not buy food for those who needed it."

"It could in Galway," said the priest. "It could in Dublin."

Ruairí sighed. "I don't go to Galway by choice. I don't go to Dublin."

"Was it you, then, who was trying to buy food? For yourself?"

At this Ruairí showed teeth to Ó Murchú, but not in a grin. "By all the black hounds, man, grant me some credit!"

"And where did you get the gold?"

"From the dead, of course. From the dead!" And then the angry grey horse stamped along beside Ó Murchú, toward the pier at Carraroe.

"It's not enough reason," said the priest to the horse. His ears were now red and chapped, and he stood at the place where the road ended in the water. "Wanting to marry is not enough. I'm not at all sure you were meant to be baptized. You are not a human."

"So my father said," replied Ruairí, who had recovered his temper. "That we were another race and a much better one than you."

Ó Murchú smiled tightly. "I don't say he's wrong. I don't know that you—whatever you are—came in need of a saviour."

The black-shod foot of the priest skidded on the gravel of the road. "And all the stories I have heard of meetings between my church and your people have ended badly for you. You might dissolve at the touch of holy water. Or turn into stone."

Ruairí stepped along beside the shorter man, and his feet on the road surface still sounded like hooves. "Naturally, Ó Murchú. The stories are told by you, and not us. But if your magic is so potent against my kind, why do you worry?"

Ó Murchú gave him a black, birdlike glance of disgust. "Do you think I want to do you harm?"

"Why not?" The fairy shook his head as a sort of shrug. "Wasn't it you who said I was a liar?"

"Ah! You have me wrong. I said you were a lie. And I was right, since you are pretending to be man when you are not. But for the love of God, I want to do no damage to an Irish spirit. Spirits may be the only thing these poor folk have left. And fairy spirits do less harm than the liquorous kind."

They were on the street now, with the chemist's shop at the right. The dray horses waiting in the yard sang out to Ruairí as they went by, and he acknowledged them. "It's odd, though, Ó Murchú, but liquor has no power over me. It can't make me one whit happier."

The priest saluted three worried-looking women, who did not reply. "If you were one whit happier, lad, there would be no enduring you. But what is the reason for that? Are all fairies immune to liquor?"

Ruairí stopped. He was staring straight ahead and up the street, with his legs braced and hands in pockets. "Not fairies, Ó Murchú. Horses." He gave a sigh that was almost a groan.

The intensity of his stare caused the priest to look, too. "What is it?" he said. "Are all those really people gathered there? Or is it someone doing the wash in the street?"

Ruairí raised his head and then lowered it, still staring. "They are women, mostly," he said. "And one man with his fists in the air. The women are wound together."

Wound together? In an instant it was clear to Father Ó Murchú. He remembered his anxiety over Gladstone, and Parnell, and the boycott, and . . .

"The eviction!" he said aloud. "It's Fenton, the bailiff, throwing Séamas Ó Conaola and his family onto the street. Perhaps it is the wash all over that I see.'"

Ruairí strode out now, to keep up with the priest's hurry. "My eyes know wash from women. And I would know the figure of my black Máire under a basket in a cave at midnight with no moon and it raining."

Now they were close enough that there was no doubt. They could hear Terrence Fenton shouting and the loose ring of barefoot children peeping like birds and frogs in time to him. Fenton stood in the middle of the street, wearing a bottle-green coat, with his two deputies in báinín, looking bewildered, behind him. And the páistí, the little children, hopped in place from sheer excitement, staying out of reach and calling him names.

Cáit NíChonaola was on her porch with her daughter-in-law behind her, and the tiniest Conaolach in the woman's arms. The babe, though only a year old, had his grandmother's long chin. There was no Séamas Ó Conaola to be seen, but between Fenton and the house were women like a fence of sweet peas in bloom.

Each wore her best red petticoat and had her arms twined and tangled into her neighbors' so there was no getting through, unless you were willing to break them. And the tallest of the peas, in the middle, between Fenton and the Ó Conaola door, was Máire Standún.

"Oh dear God," whispered the priest. "What does she mean by this?" Between Ruairí and the man who had squeezed up beside them, the priest seemed to fade and shrink, until he was the size of a child, or of a man of eighty.

Ruairí, on the other hand, swelled visibly, and like the little urchins of Carraroe, he danced from foot to foot. "She means to stop the fellow, I think! And by the grass of May, she'll have her way. Now I could stand beside her and win her cause and her favor in one charge, and . . ."

"Stop!" The priest's voice was not loud, nor was his hand on the big fairy's arm enough to hold him, but Ruairí stood still, blinking at Ó Murchú.

"Stand quiet, if you have any feeling for the girl. Who knows where the guns are, in this crowd, and the introduction of a big man against him will put anger onto the bailiff."

"Guns?" Ruairí repeated the word twice, as though he had never heard of such a weapon as a gun, and then Terrence Fenton's voice cut through their talk.

"Damn you, girl, I'm only doing my given job!"

There were over twenty pairs of locked arms in the row facing him, but Fenton spoke to Máire Standún.

She stood very straight and unafraid against him, and her eyes were dry and sparking, like mica in stone. "A man makes his own work, Terrence son of Nóirín-the-Harelip. You weren't born a crow, to drop eggs out of other birds' nests."

The bottle-green coat tightened, for the children behind made it clear they thought this a lovely hit. "Nor does a man have to let his rent go for nine months of the year," he answered, speaking to the crowd.

"In this parish and in this time, he does." The fence of sweet peas let out a small shout, much like that of the children. It was not a confident shout, but one of the women followed it with a cat's hiss.

"Dare you!" Fenton pointed his finger at this one as if it were a gun. She hissed louder.

Fenton's deputies were standing very close together, and between them was a tall, ancient, black–and–red-rusty shotgun of two barrels. Each of the men had one hand on it, and neither would look at it at all. A rock—a piece of gravel, really—hit the stock of the gun, and the deputies both let the thing fall. It did not go off.

"Up the Land League!" came a cry from the crowd, and Father Ó Murchú choked on his breath. Ruairí MacEibhir glanced curiously at him.

"Is that a cry to disgust you, Ó Murchú? Perhaps you're with the man with no shoulders in the shiny coat?"

The priest's laugh was short and very painful. "I have to get out of here," he said. "It'll go badly if I'm connected with this. Take care of her."

Ruairí grabbed him by the shoulder. "I'm not likely to leave. But what about my being a Christian?"

"I don't know. Come see me tomorrow or the next day. If we're all still alive."

"I will be," said the fairy, with a great, broad grin, and he let the priest go.

Fenton blustered but the women stood, and occasionally the matriarch on the stoop pronounced what she called the full curse of her age upon him. He was called a gaimbín man, which he was, and "the dog which tears the udder from the cow," which was more questionable. The collar of his bottle-green suit grew black with sweat.

At last the bailiff made a direct attack upon the fence of sweet peas, only to find himself dragging a line of women and half smothered in it. He found this distasteful and he backed out, looking around for his troops.

They were no longer there, but had left the gun behind upon the street, where two small lads and a lass in pigtails were investigating the mechanism. "Let that be!" Fenton ran at them, and the young birds flew, leaving him in possession of the rusty shotgun, which Fenton had never in his life used.

And now he was farther from the Ó Conaola door than ever, and the street was filled with people, some of whom were singing. Fenton was alone.

"Well done, Queen of My Heart!" whispered Ruairí, for the crush was close enough so that he could speak to her unobserved.

Máire was flushed, but not yet trusting of her victory. "Do you think so? But no. You're saying that because you want me to like you."

Now someone was shouting "Parnell," but very halfheartedly. Ruairí nudged Máire and whispered, "I hope you do that already, lover. I'm saying it because it's true. Only you should have taken that gelding's nose off for him."

She giggled, a strained little sound. "I thought I might, if he got any closer." Máire listened, but the singing had stopped, and the political fellow run out of his small store of passion. "Was . . . was that Father Ó Murchú with you, before?"

"It was. He said he had to go."

Máire's exaltation evaporated. "He would have to," she said in a little voice. "Being . . . what he is."

"Which is an odd one!" Ruairí danced clownishly in place, grinning, for he was standing very close now, and the girl made no objection.

There was a jog at Ruairí's elbow, which he ignored until it became a furious shove. Seán Standún's yellow head thrust between Ruairí and Máire. He put his mouth close to her ear, and what he called her made her draw back her hand, nails curved.

Ruairí stepped on the man's foot and stood there.

"Now there is no sense to calling a lass names with her sweetheart standing beside her, is there? You can only get in trouble."

Standún screamed, pulling at his trapped foot, but it might as well have had the weight of Knockduff on it. He put his other foot against Ruairí's ankle and gave it the force of his six feet of height, and when that didn't budge it, he flung himself on the street and writhed. Only after all this did the man have the sense to cry, "Off! Get off!" and then Ruairí calmly got off his foot.

"I'll have you in prison for this," cried Standún, and a crowd began to gather.

Ruairí glanced around and met a half dozen interested gazes. "For what, man? For stepping on your foot?"

"I saw it. He did no more than step on the man's foot," said a man to a woman.

"Fenton's gone. Just run away," said a woman to a child.

"Seán Standún is a delicate man," said another to the first man. "Just look at his coloring."

Ruairí bent down and put his arms solicitously around Standún's shoulders. As Standún had whispered into his daughter's ear, so did Ruairí to Standún.

"Since you tell the lass to her face that she's not your kin, then I don't know what father's rights you can claim. But I'll do you the courtesy of telling you that I intend to have her as mine, and I won't put up with the donkey's treatment you are giving her."

There came white spots in the center of Seán Standún's flushed cheeks and over the bridge of his nose. "I will certainly have the law on you, boyo."

"Ara, he only stepped on your foot," said Pádraig Ó Ceallaigh, the man who had reached to support Standún on the other side. Standún glared at him as well as at the horse trainer, but he staggered off on Ó Ceallaigh's arm. As he went he whispered more cautiously, and away from his supporter's ear: "Máire was raised under a good slate roof, fellow. Painted paper on the walls and glass in the windows. She has never had a dinner of potatoes without meat, save in Lent. A fine helpmeet she'll make for a ham-handed ploughboy." He laughed: a strained titter. "Oh, I wish you both great joy!"

All this while Máire Standún had been silent in confusion, hearing only scattered words of the dialogue between Ruairí and her father, broken by the singing of the crowd, which had gone from "The Brown-Backed Cow" all the way to "A Eibhlín, a Rún." Now she glanced about, uncertain, and at last she unlaced her arms from the community of sweet peas.

"Did you . . . did you hurt him? Father, I mean."

His face wore a winning simplicity as he answered her. "Oh, I did! I broke his foot, certainly. He'll not be chasing you around again soon."

As Máire stood staring at him, the singing became nonsense buzzing in her ears. "You . . . you broke my father's foot? By Mary and the saints, why?"

The pleased look began to fade as Ruairí answered, "Because he was giving you trouble, love. I won't permit that!"

The crowd that had gathered to pester the eviction remained now for whatever was coming along. It seemed to be an argument between black Máire and Ó Reachtaire's horseboy. At least judging by the girl's face, it was, so they pressed their circle around those two.

"Parnell," stated the political fellow, without emphasis.

"You broke my father's foot on *my* behalf?" Máire's soft and heavy voice was shaking. Her hands made fists.

"Oh, he only stepped on it, lass," came the reassuring voice from the circle. "Things like that happen, in a crush."

"Don't be so hard on the man. Look at his grand shoulders!" That came from another angle.

". . . not her father. Not her father!" It was a child's chant, quickly stifled and leading to a moment's unhappy silence all around.

Ruairí was very disappointed, and his "grand shoulders" sagged as much as they were able. "But he did say I could marry you, love. If I had a house with a slate roof and painted wallpaper. And if I fed you meat."

Ruairí MacEibhir took two steps away from the look on Máire's face. He blundered into the young Ó Conaola, with baby.

The deep growl in Máire's throat found words. "*He* may have said you could marry me, you coot, you loon, you great, fat *horse*! But *I* didn't say you could marry me! Get away from young Nóra and her baby before you do more damage. Take a gallop into the ocean! Go hide under a rock in the fields and be done with you!"

"Oh, that's harsh!" called a rather sentimental voice from the circle.

"Can you say that to his sweet eyes?"

"Where's Fenton?"

This last gave everyone pause, even Máire and Ruairí. The circle dissolved, became a shapeless crowd again, and at last it was discovered that Fenton was not anywhere on the street.

The eviction was declared averted, and general merriment ensued, at least for those who had not really been involved. The fence of sweet peas, now sundered, sat themselves down on assorted stoops to catch up on their breathing. The children mourned the loss of the black steel shotgun, which they remembered to have had a faded primrose painted on the end of the stock.

Ruairí reached out an imploring hand to Máire, to find instead the flat bosom of old Cáit NíChonaola. "Lad, do you want the curse of my age upon you?" she asked him.

He backed away with alacrity and shoved out of the crowd. Behind him he heard the singing resume. The political fellow called out, "Parnell is in Kilmainham Gaol."

This time he sounded really moved.

CHAPTER NINE

Some Dreams

Under the north shadow of Knockduff, Ruairí MacEibhir squatted barefoot on a shelf of stone. It was a warm rain coming down, and it didn't bother him. Out beyond the shade of the mountain it shook in silver sheets with the wind.

His fine big face was intent, but upon what was not apparent. He was not smiling, and his hands were interlocked around his knees. Occasionally he spoke, not in Gaelic.

He was speaking to the stone.

"It seems to me you might come back, Father. You were never so old, nor home so changed, that there was no bearing it. I can bear it easily, and I am more your image than Mother's."

There was no sound, but he must have felt the stone had contradicted him, for he replied, "But if that were the case, old White, then I'd be stronger than I am, for in the battle of wind and rock there is only one winner.

"Now, don't get cold with me for saying what is only a truth you yourself told me when I was a baby."

Ruairí's eyes were unhappy and his face was wet, but as he was a fairy, the wetness was likely only rain. "I'm never your equal, Father. I am not so hard as you, and I cannot maintain without forgetting, let alone forgiving. Who would I play with, if I kept the old anger, with none but enemies over the land? But I might as well be at odds with them; being not so clever, I am always offending these Milesians by accident.

And that's no fairy gift!" Except for his tragic eyes, his face
gave no clue to his misery, for it was not a face made to
express misery.

"And you know, I must live with them, or pass away in my
youth from my own land and leave it, which would be a
sorrow to it and my own shame."

Lightning licked the sky, though a good strip to the south
was blue. Thunder was a sound of ripping cloth, and the
púca lifted his head to it. "Our ways are far parted, Mother,
and I fear you're not happy with me. But I need more of a
mother's blessing than heaven's whips, right now. How I
wish to hear your hoofbeats on the hard road coming to me!"

And he did hear hoofbeats, and a black form, glossy with
rain, came speeding up the bare slope of the mountain.
Ruairí sprang up, and for a moment he wavered in mind and
body, being neither horse nor man, but a glimmer lost in the
rain.

It was not the wind, however. It was the little, stocky black
king, whom Ruairí had left at the foot of the incline. He
danced his front feet as he came, and shook his long head
like a pendulum left and right, expressing his distress in
birdlike noises.

Ruairí snorted. "What kind of stallion is it, terrified of a
bit of thunder? Did you hide behind your wives, fat in
increase, so that the lightning might hit them and spare
you?"

The pony stopped square, and his tiny ears made a flip-
ping back and forth that was equal to reasoned paragraphs of
essay. Finally he turned and presented Ruairí with his butt
end.

The fairy chuckled, and his face returned to its normal
placidity. "Never mind, my old child," he said, and he scuffed
over the flat stone to where he'd left his heavy shoes. They
were filled with water, which he spilled out. "Why should I
snub you because my own sire and dam have no time for
me?" He came to the square, black beast and rested his arm
over its back.

"It's a terrible life, little black, for *her* father hates me, *my*
father is not speaking, and the lass herself would sooner see
my tail." The black king grunted and shook, adding dirt and
stones to the water that coated Ruairí.

"But she's a lance upright, to me. A tree in silver bloom. A pool the color of the moon, is she, and with eyes like clear day. I'm a fish in the net for her. I'm tied and thrown."

The pony nodded, and he whipped his tail in perfect understanding, for he was fond of the ladies, too. They went down the mountain together, and by the hideous scowl on Ruairí's face, it was clear that he was thinking.

Mr. Blondell rode out from town under sunlight, on a strong, half-bred gelding that was by his chestnut Thoroughbred. He liked this horse; they got on well together. Toby rode beside him, his little grey in a determined trot which would have done damage to kidneys older than the boy's. Occasionally the pony had to break into a canter to keep up.

It was a shame about the red filly. Blondell had dwelt upon the notion of his son having a mount to match his own favorite. But he understood what Ó Reachtaire's horseman had told him, about the filly's bones being unfinished and her education in process. Such an intelligent fellow, MacEibhir. Good English. Not the sort you found under every hedge these days. Not the sort to make trouble.

And he was glad Toby had finally taken to horses. He glanced at the boy, who had taken the reins in his left hand and was pulling his shirt out of his trousers with the right. Hot afternoon.

It was in the blood, thought Blondell. A son of his was born to ride. And a Delagardie son, too. They were bruising hunters in the shires. Even Hermione had been a rider, in her younger days.

Blondell remembered the sight of his wife as a young lady, in a primrose habit seated upon her black hunter, the horse she had left in Lancashire when he brought her to his home. Again, that was a shame, for he would have been happy to have the beast shipped. Or replaced by another, because (good God) this was Ireland and full of horseflesh.

He thought of his wife in her sitting room, doing sunflowers on a canvas like wallpaper. "Toby," he said aloud.

Toby looked over, warily. He had hoped to get away with his shirttails out. Hot afternoon.

"There's no need," said Blondell, "to mention to your mother that we spoke to the priest while we were in town.'"

Toby's blue eyes measured his father's face without sentiment. "She wouldn't like it."

"I don't really know." Blondell smiled, but kept his attention between his horse's ears. "But it was our business, after all."

Toby meditated for a while, as sweet airs crawled up his shirt and dried him. He could smell the sweat of this old pony, and he wondered why he should like that smell better than his own sweat. "She doesn't like him because he's a Roman. After I talk to them, she wants me to go wash up."

Blondell started. "After you talk to whom? To priests?"

"To any Romans, though I expect a Roman priest would be worse."

The subsequent silence was broken by the heavy beats of the half-bred and the hoof spatter of the pony next to it. "Your mother . . ." began James Blondell.

Toby hated it when his father said "your mother" like that. Or when his mother said "your father." It was not fair to hold him responsible.

". . . Your mother was not born in this area, and she isn't used to the locals. It's true," and he laughed, making the gelding's ears prick, "they *do* take a deal of getting used to."

"She's a foreigner," interjected Toby. "She's not Irish."

Blondell's easy smile turned into a frown. "That's not strictly true, Tobias. She's British, and Irish is . . ."

"Rory says we're all foreigners, even Anraí and Áine."

"Don't interrupt when I'm speaking," said his father by reflex. But he wasn't actually unhappy about having his thoughts cut off. "All foreigners, eh? Well, that's a good philosophy, I think."

"Except him. Rory, that is." Toby nudged his pony, which had fallen behind. He had to nudge quite hard before the pony sighed and cantered up. Toby spoke with more animation in his voice than was usual, and as his face stretched, he began to show a hint of his mother's nose. "He says that he was here before the Milesians, who were called 'fir bogs,' I think, and that there were trees over . . ."

"Toby . . ."

". . . over all Ireland except Connemara, where the lime goes to granite, and . . ." Toby heard his father retroactively, and mumbled to a stop.

Blondell was looking down at his son with a face both irritated and smug. "You've lived among the Irish all your life, son, and you ought to know by now that they make stories. They are not lies, precisely, because they more than half believe them themselves. It's the basic childlike-ness of the race, and it's appealing in its way. But you are going to have responsibilities, and you have to know the difference."

Toby blushed angrily. "I thought we *were* Irish," he said, very quietly. His father set his horse into a canter and chose not to hear.

Both beasts glistened with sweat, and Toby had a pad of white hairs shed off from the pony's coat onto his trouser legs. But the canter made a lovely breeze, and when they passed the donkey cart and the man waved, looking slightly dazzled at their speed, he lost all his resentment.

Toby was not afraid to gallop nowadays. Nor to fall.

Blondell pulled in first. His round face was slick. "Spare your mount in the first heat of spring, and he'll do you fine in September."

Toby looked solemnly at his father, and gave no hint that he knew him to be winded. "What did the priest say, Father? About the rents?"

Blondell loomed close to his son. "What would you know about that, Toby? I left you outside."

The white pony sidestepped neatly away from his bulky neighbor, but Toby was unafraid. "You told me before we left. That we would stop at the Catholic rectory after the saddler's."

Blondell remembered. He loosened his own shirt from around his neck. "He really didn't know as much about things as I'd hoped."

Toby had an odd thought; he wondered if his own lies were as obvious to his father as his father's were to him. He made a note to himself to be careful. He looked ahead down the gravelly road. Perhaps he would overhear Father telling Mother. Or likely Mother would tell him straight out. She would if the news were bad.

"I can't believe that little grain sack can take a fence," said Blondell, and was surprised at the hostility in his own voice. He really had no feelings against the old pony.

"She can," answered the boy with more than childish

restraint. "But my jumping lessons are not with her. Anraí puts me on a grey hunter horse. I really like him."

"Henry? I thought you preferred the young fellow: MacEibhir."

"I mean I like the horse. It's Henry who gives me the lessons. I never see Rory while I'm jumping. Henry says he doesn't want to be there when I fall on my head." Toby laughed very pleasantly, but his father gave a small wince.

"And do you think you're going to fall on your head, Toby?"

"Oh, no. Jumping isn't much. It's the horse that does it, after all."

Tadhg Ó Murchú's thoughts were quite similar to those of Blondell. He was disturbed; he had believed the landowner to know more about the people around him than seemed to be the case.

He sat beneath the lithograph of St. Peter's, with a tea tray beside him. He had drunk his tea but taken the cake that went with it and shredded it into a pile. His jam he had dissolved into his tea and drank, so that Nóra would not be able to tell he hadn't eaten. His small Welshman's face was intent on nothing; he had a headache.

The letter from the bishop had been scathing, and yet the bishop had no idea what Ó Murchú's involvement was, but only suspected he had not condemned the Land League in language strong enough. Such a shame about the church. Usually Ó Murchú could keep Catholicism and nationalism in two separate bins in his mind, but now that was difficult. Perhaps he would get a visit from some monsignor or another.

The bell tinkled for a visitor, but Ó Murchú didn't move. He waited until Nóra shuffled forward and told the woman that Father Ó Murchú was at his tea. Then he caught up as many of the crumbs as he could, leaned toward the open window, and threw them into the bushes. For the birds, he said to himself, although birds would have a hard time getting in to them.

That Bondell should have taken such a hard attitude at the first hint of unsettlement among his tenants! And have expected the parish priest to act as his bailiff! Ó Murchú's hands, greased with crumby butter, grew hot at the thought. Englishman, aping the Gaels when it amused him.

Was a landlord on the land any better than a landlord in England? Of course he was, because he would care at least for the soil, if not for the human cattle that tilled it. But better infinitely was a hundred families on their own holds. There was really no lasting rapprochement between the people and men like Blondell, thought the priest, and each party knew it.

Ó Murchú heard Nóra outside the door of the parlor. He was suddenly aware of the state of his hands, which gave away his subterfuge. In an effort at concealment, he wound his fingers together and rested his nose upon them. Entering the room, Nóra found the priest at prayer. So she thought. And the old woman had endless respect for Ó Murchú in that role, though she had none in any other, so she stood silent until he was forced to look up at her.

"That girl was here," she said.

"What girl, out of all the girls in the parish?"

"Black Máire Standún. She wanted to see you, but you were at your bit of tea, here."

The priest felt disappointment sluice through him, as though he had taken cold water instead of tea. "Thank you, Nóra," he said.

Ó Murchú was a steady dreamer, though he didn't usually take account of his dreams, and that night he had a very clear one.

There was a noise outside his bedroom window, and he thought he heard Ruairí MacEibhir's breathy, inconsequential voice. He rose, feeling the cold, and stepped over to chide him for making noise on the town streets. But it was not Ruairí, but a strange man, slight boned, long nosed, with curling black hair and beard, and wearing a white shawl.

A tinker, thought Ó Murchú.

The tinker said nothing, but met Ó Murchú's gaze with the welcome of an old friend. With a bare, swarthy arm he gave through the window a wand with leaves on it.

The priest took it and yelped like a dog, for it was a living nettle. But instead of dropping the thing, he found he was grasping it harder. He glanced up in surprise, and then he recognized the dark tinker, and he knelt down on the boards of the floor.

"Dear Lord," he said.

There was a snort and a stamp, and the Tinker floated away from the window. In actuality he wasn't floating, but was sitting on the back of a horse, which shone in the night like clouds around the moon. This horse backed away from the window and nodded, nodded its unconfined head. It crossed the garden, high stepping, and bounced over the garden wall.

The Tinker had been wearing báinín, but no shoes. He had sat bareback as neatly as a boy. But, then, Tinkers were legendary in their way with horses.

Ó Murchú was left alone in the cold of the open window, with a stinging nettle in his hand. It reminded him somehow of Máire Standún, so he flung it away from himself and went back to bed.

A warm Sunday had brought Donncha MacSiadhail to the pier at An Sruthán, to watch other people work. Morrie Ó Nigh, fisherman on one of Standún's hookers, ought to have been cleaning and stowing after the night's haul, but he wasn't. Instead he squatted on the stone next to Donncha's stone, with a whistle stamped and rolled out of tin.

The sun washed over Donncha's rough countenance and touched the bald spot on the top of his head. He allowed it to do so: unlikely it would stay long enough to burn.

"How is it you work on the sabbath, anyway, Morrie? What does the priest say to that?"

The fisherman was tall. He wore a dark geansaí with chains knit into the sleeves, and a cap over his carroty hair. "Ask about the boss, not the priest, my friend. Seán Standún tells us that the sabbath begins at midnight, so the night's fishing actually belongs to Saturday."

"Whereas, we all know that the day begins at sunset the night before, so that's false."

Morrie grinned with his teeth around the whistle, which had suffered in its paint from such usage. "You tell what's true and what's false to the owner of the boats, Donncha. I'll listen from around the corner."

"And then, do you have off the night of Sunday, which is

really Monday? Or does he come round weekly to the church's way of thinking?"

"We leave after midnight, that's all."

Donncha's face was intent. "And what does the priest say for the good of your souls?"

A painfully shrill whine of the whistle prefaced Morrie's answer. "He's sorry for us, poor lads that we are. The man has a heart under his black robes."

Donncha touched the end of the whistle with his finger. "Let's hear the tune again."

Morrie put his hands to the holes of the tube, which rested in the far left corner of his mouth. It was a swinging hornpipe, with three parts. He repeated each of them twice.

Donncha listened, hiding his face in his hands for better memory. When it was done he said, "And that's called 'The Broken Foot'?"

"Either that or 'Fenton's Rout.' People have not settled yet."

"Two very different names."

Morrie put the whistle in his pocket and scooted his behind down the face of the rock, which then became his pillow. "You weren't on the street at the time, or you might think they fit better. Actually, I would have liked to call it 'Máire Standún,' only there's already a tune by that name."

Where Donncha was seated he could see both the waters of the bay, where the *Dreoilín* lay moored, and the road down to the pier from the land above. "Fancy gig coming," he said quietly to his companion.

Morrie sprang up skidding. He spanked his trousers furiously. "Is it Seán Standún?"

"Who else?" Donncha accompanied Morrie to the side of the boat, moving with less energy. He watched the owner's fair head bob with every rut of the road, and saw the blue eyes in the narrow face, measuring men and rigging as he drew near.

"I get my money from a Gael who is a Gael," said Donncha, neither loudly nor whispering. "There is no 'Mr. Ó Reachtaire' there, and no labor on the sabbath, except what the horses need to live. And Anraí is a better horseman than I am, I say freely. Is Mr. Standún a better sailor than you?"

Morrie gave Donncha an owl's look, and Donncha giggled.

As Standún's cart approached, the groom pushed himself off the cloth bumpers, still chuckling.

"Health to you, Morrie."

"Health to you and to Parnell," whispered the fisherman.

This evening there was the bright moonshine of four days past first quarter, and no clouds in the spring sky. Eibhlín's rose arbor was heavy with pink bud, so that the branches of the climbers drooped. Within the trellis of willow, hidden from moonlight by the sweet weight of flowers, sat the fair girl herself. She was alone and sitting very still, but her eyes looked left and right.

Eibhlín was very pretty. She had an oval face which was all pink flesh and no bones. Her lips were a pink rosebud and her yellow hair was pulled back, very smooth. She had been there a while, listening to her father shout orders to Máire and the nurse.

Now she heard another sound: hooves at a rolling, slow canter, soon muffled but drawing near the house. She stood up, sat down, and waited more quietly than ever.

Ruairí MacEibhir stepped in through the wicker garden gate, and his greying hair shone white. He passed the hen yard and made a large circle away from the beehive. When he reached the rose arbor he went directly to Eibhlín in the shadows and stood before her.

She fluttered slightly and turned her head away. "How did you know I was here?"

"I heard you breathing," he answered. "It was either someone in the roses or the bees out again."

The whites of her eyes were brighter than milk, and their blue centers colorless. She took in his face, his broad shoulders, and the way his shirt fitted him.

He, in turn, was not unaware of the lace of her shawl, which had been tied in a tight cross over the heart. "You're still breathing," he said, and took a step closer.

Eibhlín played with her fringe. "Where . . . where did you leave your horse? I heard it."

"Where he'll be no bother to you."

"It's a long way to be coming here from Knockduff every evening, Ruairí."

"Not every evening. Last night there was a foal coming."

With a sigh, Ruairí lowered himself down onto the same bench which held Eibhlín. Close. She gave a little gasp and inched away.

"Well, it is a pity that Máire will not see you."

"Oh, she will." He went to staring at his right hand finger-nails, where there was something that bothered him. Out of his pocket he drew a sharpened hoof-pick and began to work on it. "It's just that she knows she needn't hurry. If I were a clever sort, I would fix it so she weren't so sure of my heart. "But . . ." He sighed again, but not from muscle soreness. He lifted his legs off the ground and onto the bench, tailor fashion. "Then I'd be someone else entirely, and not my father's son, Ruairí."

Eibhlín reached out and touched his arm, with a moth-wing pressure. "I'm afraid it's more than that. She won't hear your name mentioned, day or night."

"She won't?" He perked up. His hair rubbed against the pink roses, where it stuck like cobwebs. "That's a better sign than I expected."

Eibhlín stared, with her forehead worked into what would someday become frown lines. "I am very sorry for your case," she said in English.

"What's that? Again?"

She repeated the sentence, and Ruairí just shook his head.

"But Mr. Blondell was telling Father about your good English."

His quick smile caught the light. "That man's Gaelic is a thousand times beyond my English. I have none."

Now the ripples in her forehead became creases. "How could he make such a mistake?"

"Ask him," answered Ruairí, and he smiled and sat, en-tirely at ease. Eibhlín looked at him only for moments, and then away. For a while both of them listened to Seán Standún's parting comments on the day, and then the amount of light in the arbor was lessened further as his bedroom lamp went out.

"I'm sorry I broke your father's foot. It seems that was the wrong thing to do," whispered Ruairí at last, and he shot the girl a glance half remorseful and half mischievous.

It was Eibhlín's turn to sigh. "It has made him into a fury, but still I have a sympathy with you in that matter."

"You do?" He edged closer, staring.

She did not move. "Indeed. Father is not a reasonable man, and he has made life difficult for both my sister and I."

His eyes were as uncommunicative as those of an animal. "You mean he doesn't approve of your chemist's assistant either?"

Eibhlín started, pressed her lips together, and edged away on the bench. "What have I to do with a chemist's assistant?"

"You can answer that better than I."

"Then the answer is that I have nothing to do with him. Nothing at all."

Now Ruairí's smile returned. "Poor man. I'm sorry for him." He absorbed the distance between them by the amount she had created. "So you don't care for your sire at all? You don't want to please him?"

She sniffed. "There is no pleasing him."

"Ah. And your sister will not speak to me." He raised his voice a little. Eibhlín glanced in fear up at her father's window and put her hand across Ruairí's mouth. He did not seem at all reluctant at the touch, nor was she too quick to draw away.

"No. I'm afraid she will not," she whispered, close to his ear.

"And she told you to tell me so."

"She did." Eibhlín's little voice was husky.

"Indeed!"

Máire did not speak loudly, but Eibhlín jumped as though a gun had been shot off by her ear. Ruairí, who blocked Eibhlín's view of her sister, continued to look at Eibhlín and grin and grin.

"I don't remember a word of that, Eibhlín. It's a shame. I didn't know my memory had become so bad. It must be old age overtaking me."

Eibhlín was on her feet. She backed into the roses, which was not comfortable, and she pointed up at the dark window, with the forefinger of her other hand to her lips. Then, with a nervous little giggle, she plunged into the flowerbed and was away.

Máire, in her plain skirt, black shawled, stood before Ruairí. He did not get up. After the rustling of Eibhlín's departure had died away he said very casually, "Grand moon tonight, isn't it?"

She gave a sigh that was half a hiss and leaned against the corner post of the arbor, facing away. "Is that all you've got to say?"

Before answering, he scraped the heel of his boot on the gravel. "Your father doesn't honor you, and your sister is faithless. But I'm not allowed to resent the one or notice the other, so what should I say but, 'Grand moon tonight'?"

Máire turned her head to meet his eyes, but she could not maintain it. "Do you like her?" she said at last. "Isn't she very pretty?"

She felt him take her hand, though she hadn't heard him rising. He led her over the shining gravel and past the bees and the hens onto the poor grass behind the garden hedge. There they could look back at the house, where one small yellow light came alive as they watched.

"I wonder if she's woken Father," said Máire, absently.

"She's not such a fool as that," answered Ruairí. "Though almost." He sat down on the grass. She spread her skirt not too close to him.

"I'm building a house, Light of Heaven," he told her.

Under moonlight, her eyes were as black as his. "My congratulations, Ruairí MacEibhir agus Mac Gaoithe. I hope it's not meant for me."

"It's yours if you'll have it."

"I won't."

His grin flashed. "Then I'll build another, more to your taste. And another. I'm in the world for nothing else, my dark lovely."

The compliment returned Máire's mind to Eibhlín. "I asked you if you didn't think my sister is lovely. Don't you remember?"

"She has no more bone than one of your hens, Máire. Less sense than a day-old foal."

She pulled her black shawl closer, for the night was reaching toward cold. "It's neither bone nor sense that a man looks for in a girl."

"Then he'll get the offspring he deserves!" Ruairí hugged himself laughing, for he thought he had said something very witty.

Máire did not agree. "Do you take *me* for a broodmare?"

The laughter froze, to be replaced by a look of puzzlement. "There is nothing under heaven better than a broodmare, love. She is the protector of infants, the teacher and molder of young hearts, and the mother of the race."

Máire snorted. "And she stands in a field all day, eating and growing fat. What a life!"

"It's the rare mare in Connemara that can get by standing still," said Ruairí. "More likely she will pull and haul up to the time she drops her foal and then work with the pesky child beside her. No, a Mháire Dhubh, there is nothing of more worth or honor than a good mare."

Now Máire raised her face to the moon. Her giggle was abrupt and explosive, like that of a little boy. "O lad, how you compliment me. No girl in Galway County has such a smooth suitor. Are you planning to turn me into a horse next?"

Ruairí had been pulling the blades off from a strand of cowgrass. Now he let the pieces fall in his lap. "Alas, my love, your father is not of the púca line."

She fell back on the grass, but her face was taut. "No, he was of the philandering variety."

Coolly Ruairí replied. "He broke no oaths that I know of, Queen of Heaven. That was your mother's business."

Máire came up with both hands balled into fists. "How dare . . . Well, he left her, didn't he, more shame to him."

"No, as a matter of fact. She left off meeting with him and would not return. She ran back to her yellow flag of a husband, my dear, and soon died of her mistake, leaving you to be raised by him.

"Would you like to meet your father, a Mháire?" The moon glinted on his hair.

"Would I . . ." Máire came to her feet. She was a black pillar against the stars, and her two white arms clutched at her shawl. "Oh, dear God have mercy on me!" She ran over the grass toward home.

And came smack against the warm white side of a horse. Against Ruairí MacEibhir. "Enough, love. I won't ask you again. Here, don't breathe so hard or you'll wake your 'father' "

Máire stepped back. Her right foot was sore, for she had

twisted the ankle. "I . . . don't want to know any more about my . . . father. Please."

"I am your servant. Your giolla. There! That's an idea. If you were to come for a ride, then I couldn't disturb you with my uneasy talk, could I?"

Máire shook her head. "I don't trust you."

"Oh, but you do. You know I'm on my parole with you. I won't kiss you again without permission—I take an oath to that—nor touch you in any way you don't want. I won't even trot without permission." His voice grew breathy, almost a whisper, and his face was close. She could see a glinting of silver beard.

Máire took a breath and looked around her. The single yellow light was out, and all was bright and colorless. The air was decidedly chill. "All right," she said to him. "But if I fall off, it will be your fault, for I don't really know how to ride."

"I know that well enough. But if you fall off, Queen of Heaven, it will be because you tried to." And those were his last words before the grey horse came down onto its four legs, shining under the moon.

Máire did not touch the earth, either in body or mind. There was no sound of hooves on the soft grass of spring-time, and when the horse walked hock deep into the ocean, the phosphorescence rivaled the moonlight.

The fairy, as he had promised, made no trouble, and when Máire came home and slid off his side, it felt very heavy to be walking again, and she tiptoed up to bed favoring her muscles.

I've been out all night, she said to herself, after making sure Eibhlín was asleep. With a man. As she slipped into bed she could smell horse all over her.

CHAPTER TEN

Ó Murchú's Sacrament

Áine was tying the peas to the fence when the priest came walking up the path. She was also cursing, very mildly but undeniably cursing, because Ruairí had let out the old grey pony and it had done some damage to the kitchen garden. When she saw Father Ó Murchú she took three steps backward and broke a vine off at the root, but this time she didn't curse.

"God to you, Father. How is it that I didn't hear you coming?" She beat her apron with her hands, as though it were dirty.

Ó Murchú stopped five feet from her. Though Áine was an older woman and not a likely target for gossip, neither the priest nor she would have been comfortable with closer proximity. "I don't stomp as I walk, Áine, and the day is so gentle it would have been a crime to make more noise."

Áine opened the garden gate and then trotted around behind Ó Murchú, where she attempted to push him through like a very respectful sheepdog. But Tadhg Ó Murchú did not want to be pushed, and so he lounged in the gate as though he hadn't noticed, fingering the broken pea vine and appearing perfectly at ease.

"You won't tell me that you walked all the way from the parish house."

Ó Murchú smiled until his small dark face appeared Chinese. "I won't. I took a kind ride from Tim Ó Súilleabháin in

the beer dray and only turned up your long drive here. Two
miles. It was a lovely day for a walk."

Áine glanced up, though she knew already that the sky
was unbroken blue. She realized that her hand wringing was
making a mess of her apron and she let it drop. She took a
breath. "Well enough, Father, but you don't need to stand
out under the heat now. Do go in and I'll run to find Anraí,
who is out playing he is still a young man, fool that he is."

The priest leaned more fixedly and smiled harder. "I'd like
to see him, certainly. But it was with the excuse of talking to
Ruairí MacEibhir that I've taken this holiday." He lowered
the bag he was carrying gently onto the grass.

"Ruairí? That scamp? Well, forgive me, I won't cast names,
but surely you might have only sent a lad out to tell him to
come to you."

Ó Murchú looked very like a scamp himself as he replied,
". . . and I'll do that, the next time it rains, Áine. But I wanted
not to be home to people this afternoon, and there is a matter
of a baptism."

Áine took in a shuddering breath and turned to go. But she
could not endure the uncertainty and so came back to ask,
"Has he really done so much harm as that? I hadn't thought
he'd been in the county long enough for such a . . ."

"Áine! It's his own baptism at issue here, and there's no
need for a woman who works so hard to run my errands. Just
tell me where he is and I'll find him."

Flustered and red in the face, Áine could hardly speak.
"He'll be on a horse, is all I can say. But better than running,
I'll ring the bell for him."

She went past the priest, who moved out of the gateway so
they would not touch by accident. On the small front porch
there was a bell hanging, of a copper-green color. She hit it
with a stick of willow, three times. The echoes, which were
alarming, died away after five seconds, and she did it again.

Ó Murchú gazed out over the fields toward the barns, and
soon a face with a cap peeked out from one and a face with
dark hair out of the other. "There's my old man and Donncha,"
said Áine, beside him. "Ruairí is likely doing something
wild."

Ó Murchú was in no hurry. His dream was still with him,

and much pleasanter in retrospect. The sun and his walk had
warmed him, and the hard-won prosperity of this farm under
Knockduff soothed his mind. The fields were not lawns, such
as Blondell or even Seán Standún might have; they were
weedy and unevenly cropped by horses. But the little fences
were regular, and there was no lack of whitewash. Anraí and
Áine had done well.

Only one child, of course.

There was a flicker of movement and at the same moment,
a noise of hooves. Out beyond the second barn a red shape
rose up and sank again. It was a horse and rider taking the
paddock fence. As the priest watched, another horse came
over: this one without a rider. It was black. Together they
came over the grass toward the house.

It was a chestnut under Ruairí MacEibhir, and she moved
with heartbreaking elegance as he brought her down to a trot
that sliced the grain of the grass from its root. The little black
tried to match her and failed. It went back to a canter.

Together they popped the near fence and slowed to a walk.

"You shouldn't be taking that filly over fences, Ruairí.
She'll come down in a heap someday!" Áine spoke firmly and
in a voice lower than was her wont. A voice like Anraí's.

Ruairí greeted the priest and slipped off the filly's back.
There was no saddle. The black, six inches shorter than the
filly and of equal weight, stood at parade attention on his
other side.

"Peace, Áine. I'll know long before she does, when she's
had enough. And bored as she is, I have to do something to
hold her attention." While addressing the woman, he kept
his eyes to Ó Murchú.

"Have you come to see me, Priest of the Parish?"

"That's no language to . . ."

Ó Murchú pretended he hadn't heard Áine, and he stepped
up to the chestnut filly and made a face to indicate he
understood horseflesh. "Lovely mare, Ruairí. Real quality in
her."

"She is hollow backed and has a neck like a goose," replied
the other, "but such things can be fixed. Her nerves are
another thing entirely. Now this gentleman"—he touched the
stocky pony respectfully on the throatlatch—"hasn't her reach,

but he'd take me home if I were one-handed and with a leg
cut off at the knee. What's more, he'd probably find the
villain who served me so and throw him over Knockduff."

The pony bobbed his head and made a sound of frantic
agreement through his nostrils. Or perhaps he was only
flirting with the filly, who squealed.

Ó Murchú's shoulders fell, just a trifle. "All right, my lad,
so I'm not a horse coper. I'm sure I'd rather ride the pony,
just because it would be less far to fall.

"But I've not come here to talk horses. I've come here to
baptize you, if you still want."

The fairy's face lit from within, slowly. "Ah. Well, then.
Are you sure that it *doesn't* have to do with horses, Ó
Murchú?"

Áine, who did not understand entirely, pinched Ruairí on
the elbow for his manners.

"Or with the men who ride them?"

Ó Murchú's smile was tight. "Was it a false dream that you
sent me two nights ago?"

For only a moment, Ruairí was solemn. "I don't deal in
dreams, Tadhg Ó Murchú. Horses are enough."

The moment was over, and Ruairí nudged the priest.
"Besides, when do dreams leave nettle welts on your hand?"
Ó Murchú opened and closed his right hand, where the
welts had long faded, and at that moment Donncha came up
to them, half supporting Anraí, who was puffing and blowing.

In the parlor it was much cooler. The light off the limed
walls was blue as skimmed milk. Anraí came and Áine with
him, for they were to be godparents to the fairy, which was
an absurdity to threaten any composure. Donncha came in
also, because he had an interest. As Father Ó Murchú set out
the vestments, the book, and the water on Áine's mother's
heavy wooden sideboard, all assembled stood so still that the
air began to smell dusty.

It was like a dentist's surgery: that long table with its
instruments. Anraí swallowed loudly. In a colorless voice the
priest asked, "Will a bit of water do harm to your carpet
here?"

Áine clucked. "It couldn't do more than a dozen puppies

have done in their . . ." She realized her own indelicacy and trailed off.

Alone of the company, Ruairí MacEibhir seemed at ease. He leaned over Ó Murchú's shoulder and peered at the stole and the book. He fluttered his small nostrils above the water bottle and eyed the crystal ewer sidelong. He paid great attention to the manner in which the priest put on his stole, which he had brought only because he knew Anraí and Áine would expect it.

Tadhg Ó Murchú gave a look of challenge out of his dark, Pictish eyes. "Ruairí MacEibhir, do you know that this is dangerous for you?"

"No matter to me if it is," he replied, offhand.

"Well, it is matter to me!" The priest seemed almost angry. "I am not sure whether I'm being *called* to do this or only fairy led, and it will be your own suffering you've made if you're the fairy that did it!"

Ruairí blinked his mild eyes and scratched his small nose. "By the blossoms of May, Ó Murchú—and better, by the Tinker Man (and he's not bad a rider for a man who never rode anything but a donkey)—I swear to you I'm not in the business of leading folks astray. Nor am I the sort of Caledonian rogue who flings them into the ocean, either. It was never my family's course."

"Ara, but you don't bring them straight home, exactly, do you?" asked Anraí, with surprising spleen. Both Ruairí and the priest ignored him.

"And you're only doing it to please Máire Standún?"

The broad brown eyes opened wider for an instant. "You know she's a woman well worth pleasing, Priest of the Parish. But ask her, and she'll tell you the idea is mine and not hers. I have a fancy for it."

Ó Murchú sighed bitterly. "A fancy! And here I am, submitting to it, God help me. And do you at least promise to follow the commandments and the rules of the church?"

Ruairí snorted. "The ten commandments Áine has described to me, all but one which she sent me to Anraí to learn, for her gentility's sake. They seem cumbersome enough; what are these other rules?"

Ó Murchú smiled slowly. "Never mind. They are implicit in the ten, if you are careful with them."

"Ten is a large number. If I forget one once?"

"Then you will suffer for it, like all the rest of us," said Ó Murchú simply. He shrugged the stole into place.

He poured water from the bottle into the ewer, and he was either praying or muttering to himself as he did so. Anraí, who had combed his hair, stood on one side of Ruairí. Áine, who had replaced her apron with one identical to it, stood on his other. "Kneel down," said Ó Murchú, in the tones one uses to a disobedient dog.

Ruairí went down on his knees with great deliberation, first the right and then the left. Áine wrapped her arms together, for she had never been at a baptism without the strong desire to hold an infant. Donncha stepped back against the window and made himself small.

Ó Murchú put his hand gently on the head of black hairs and white hairs. His eyes were worried as he picked up the ewer. He dribbled water delicately onto the hairs, where it hung like the dew of morning.

Ó Murchú spoke aloud. "Si non es baptizatus, ego te baptizo in nomine Patris, et Filii, et Spiritus Sancti." Anraí nodded his head in happy agreement, for he had once had decent Latin and was glad to understand.

The priest thought he was beginning to cry, despite himself. Then he thought he was going blind, for his world became misted in a whiteness that thickened and rose before him. It was coming out of Ruairí MacEibhir, who knelt and swayed before him, with brown eyes glazed and staring.

It was a curtain in the air, a veil, a ghostly fire that spread up toward the low ceiling. It took the shape of a horse's head, thrown back in panic. And all the while Áine smiled and Anraí stood there, smugly nodding.

Ó Murchú was filled with fury. "Fool!" he hissed through clenched teeth, meaning Ruairí. Or himself. Then he reached his short, swarthy arms up into the air and he caught the veil—the shape of the horse—by its filmy edge and he shook it like a bedsheet. "Back with you!" He shouted in a bull voice not usually his to command. He snapped the sheet in the air and smashed it down again over Ruairí's collapsing form. "And stay there!"

The fairy took a great breath and then another.

Anraí cleared his throat. "I was never at a grown-up baptism before, Tadhg. I had no idea it would be so different."

Suddenly, noisily, Ruairí struggled to his feet. He was still swaying. "Am I baptized now?" he asked.

Ó Murchú had sunk down as he raised up, and was squatting like a primitive against the front wall of the sideboard. "What? Are you . . . I don't know. Or rather . . ." He noticed that the ends of the silken stole were dragging the carpet and he climbed up again. "Or rather, of course you are. What happened does not invalidate it. You are baptized, Ruairí MacEibhir.

"Now. Let's see you turn into a horse."

"Here? In the parlor!" It was Áine's cry.

"Right here," answered Ó Murchú. "For there is such a heavy weariness come over me I don't know whether I'll live the hour out and I want to know."

Ruairí blinked. He shook his head as all moved away from him. Donncha scooted the small tea table against the wall. The shape of the fairy rose up as a cloud of snow and the grey horse settled his front feet delicately on the carpet.

"Glory be to God," whispered the priest in such a reverent manner that three in the room echoed him.

Ruairí came back, brown eyes to booted feet. "Well, I have to say it's better than the rites of old Pádraig. No lance in the foot."

Anraí harrumphed. "You have been laboring under a misunderstanding, lad. There was never . . ."

"Would someone drive me home?" asked the priest, as he gripped the handles of the cupboard doors for support. "I am very tired. Or I am becoming ill."

Ruairí caught him as he fell. "You are not used to this, Priest of the Parish? The powers wear you out?"

"Take me home!" Ó Murchú would have snapped more sharply if he could have, for the spirits and energy of the fairy offended him and indeed he did not feel well.

"I can drive him myself," said Anraí, making an ineffectual effort to press between Ruairí and Ó Murchú.

"Or I," added Áine, with no great hope of being heard.

"Let the new convert do the work," said Ó Murchú. "He has strength enough, it seems."

Donncha harnessed up the cob in only a few seconds, and

Father Ó Murchú was half lifted into Áine's springy gig.
Ruairí MacEibhir sprang up beside him and put the cob into
a trot.

"He isn't nearly as fast as the red horse you drove last time
you had the hauling of me," said Ó Murchú, after ten minutes' exhausted silence.

"No, but he'll go the distance." Ruairí turned his head on
his neck to look at his companion. Ó Murchú wondered if he
could even see out of the corners of his eyes, human fashion.
The sun was passing in and out of clouds, and the wind was
brisk.

"I worried the baptism might be the death of you, fellow.
It never occurred to me I was the one in danger."

The fairy smiled and the air went bright for a moment.
"You'll be fine, Ó Murchú. But I am no small thing, flitting
from flower to flower. To put me back together when I am
coming apart is heavy work, and not many could do it. I
chose well."

This last phrase stuck in Ó Murchú's ears, not pleasantly.
Anger bubbled through his weariness. "*You* chose? Do you
pick and choose, among human beings, to serve your will?"

Ruairí winced under this heat. "Peace, man! We all choose
among each other, to serve our desires a hundred ways.
Surely I would come more willingly to a man of the hidden
people than to . . ."

"What?" Now Ó Murchú's weariness was forgotten. He sat
straight up on the padded bench. "Are you trying to say to
me . . ." The cob's ears folded back, and he sighed as he
trotted.

"Are you telling me . . ." Again his angry words trailed off,
and the priest took a breath. "Exactly what *are* you telling
me?"

The fairy blinked his long-lashed eyes. "Only what you
know already, Priest. That you are out of an old and forgotten race on this island. That you touch the different worlds,
whereas most men do not or will not."

Now the sweat of Ó Murchú's anger turned into a sudden
chill. He felt his back prickle, as well as the hair on his arms.
"I know nothing of the kind," he said in a quelling voice.
Then he swallowed hard and wrapped his shawl around his
shoulders.

"Then you don't know that there is fairy blood in you?" asked Ruairí, almost diffidently.

"There is fairy blood in most Irishmen," answered the priest, though he had no idea where the words came from.

The sun went in and out, and the wind kept the drive from being ever comfortable. After half an hour, Ó Murchú said something else.

"Do you know what I really am, Rory son of Granite? What I am is a nationalist!" And he let out a great, growling groan.

Ruairí turned his brown eyes to him. "Oh. Is that what it is? I had wondered." He tickled the cob on the ear with the holly whip.

"But you must never tell anyone that I said that."

"Then I won't," answered Ruairí equably, and they drove on to the rectory.

It was in the evening and threatening rain. Ruairí MacEibhir was in the pocket of land that Anraí had given him: land blooming with large rocks and gorse-grown, which ran full up to the side of Knockduff itself. It was by an undercut of the mountain that Ruairí planned to build Máire's house.

It was to be of stone, and it was two feet high so far. Donncha, who had amazed himself by helping to gather the rocks, stood leaning against the brown side of the ox in its harness.

"I hesitate to speak what is not my business, Ruairí . . ."

Ruairí straightened with a hundredweight chip of granite in his arms. "But you don't hesitate, Donncha. Not for a moment. So tell me what is bothering you."

Donncha slouched forward, pointing. "Your foundation here is neither a square nor a rectangle, but a circle."

"So it is." Ruairí put the stone very neatly on another and between two on either side.

Donncha remained deadpan, though with difficulty. "Well, is it the garden wall you're building first? For it's large enough, but I warn you it'll be harder to get the rest of the stones past it once it's in place."

Ruairí followed the pointing finger and grinned. His face was shiny with sweat. "I know it! But you must understand, Donncha, that Máire Standún has lived all her life in a large house. Could I ask her to move in with me and trim her wings back like that?"

Donncha left the ox and walked the perimeter of the house. It was one hundred and twenty paces along the stones, plus some forty feet where it butted the flat mountainside. "You're going to put her in a fairy ráth, then?"

Ruairí heaved another stone, and another. "She wouldn't like that a bit. Most of them are filled with bones, not fairies." He went back to his work.

When night fell it did rain, but the light of the full moon penetrated the clouds. Ruairí MacEibhir did not return with Donncha to the barn where he slept (slept in theory, at least). The groom waited for lazy Ruairí to cast off this enchantment of work he was suffering and return to dry straw bed and steaming potatoes. He had saved up a number of good thrusts against Ruairí's folly, both in building a circular house and building it for a woman who would have none of him. But Donncha was a good sleeper, unless a horse groaned, and rarely knew when his colleague was out on the tiles. By midnight, with the moon high in the sky, he had given up waiting and let all the witticisms he was saving run out his ears. He was asleep.

The sky cleared gently, unnoticed by man. Wet earth sparkled under the cold, planetary light, and the ponies of the mountains came over the broad stone and bogland toward Knockduff. They ran as lightly as goats. Some were black and some were white and some you could see through like the pools of rain.

Some had riders.

There were laughter and bells sounding in the circle of wet stone that Ruairí built, and then was added a tinny, thin wailing whistle, like Morrie's whistle, but smaller and better played.

The singing and the crying out were not entirely peaceful. Not entirely happy. Ruairí's own black pony grunted in the yard, where the stone moving had scraped the earth bare. Shaking his mane, he walked deliberately away.

Ruairí, or perhaps one of his visitors, had lit a fire in the stone circle. It burned clean and golden, though there was no dry wood around Knockduff, and it cast splashes against the undercut mountainside. There was gesture in those golden splashes, and there was dance.

Someone cried out in gladness. Someone cried. At dawn one could not tell the mounds of granite stone from the backs of the sleeping ponies: the black ones and the white ones only. Ruairí MacEibhir came out of the door of his stone house and peered up the high walls in satisfaction. He yawned and shook the dew from his clothes.

Mr. James Blondell did not know that the wall had been raised by night, as he sat his red hunter with his gloved hands on the pommel of the saddle. He found it noteworthy for other reasons.

He called the builder over, across the grass. "Ruairí. Is Anraí building a fortress here? Is he expecting it to come to this?"

Ruairí MacEibhir felt a little the worse for wear this morning and he could not follow Blondell's meaning. He stared upward at the man. "It is not Anraí's, a Shéamais. By his grace it is mine, and it is Máire Standún who will come to it, I hope."

Blondell looked down on the other's pleasant countenance and thought that Ruairí MacEibhir was the image of all that the peasantry ought to be: solid but never sullen, well conformed and conforming. His shirt was dirty, but that was understandable. His hair and nails were respectably cut, and that meant he cared. Blondell grinned at Ruairí in the way he would have had Ruairí grin at him.

Ruairí, however, was too tired. "What can I do for you, a Shéamais?"

It made Bondell feel very good about himself to know he could hear this assistant horse trainer call him by his first name, Gaelic fashion, without becoming offended. It was a sign of just how reasonable and fair a man he was. "Have you heard they're talking of . . . of boycotting me, Rory?"

Ruairí's frown of concentration became deeper. "I didn't know that. All I've heard concerning yourself lately is about the fight with your wife."

"The what?" Blondell's question was sharp.

"I don't know more than that, because I was too busy to listen. I'm sorry." He managed a smile at last.

Blondell decided to let the apology cover the reference to Hermione, and put to the back of his mind his chagrin at having his domestic troubles put all over the country. Irish domestics, of course.

"What I've come for is to offer you a job."

Ruairí blinked.

"Head groom. Double your present salary. At least."

Ruairí blinked again and again. He seemed incapable of understanding, so Blondell slowed down and began again.

"My own head groom . . . left me in the lurch. I'd like you to replace him. Live on the estate. Either eat at our tables or set up your own, when you marry. Good money and the best horses in Connemara under your supervision."

Now Ruairí's full grin returned, not at the offer but at the mention of "the best horses in Connemara." He remembered the red stallion in the barn aisle, nodding and nodding.

"That is indeed a generous offer, a Shéamais Blondell. But I think your estates would be a little far from my house." He gestured behind him at the wall.

Blondell glanced over in better appreciation of what he saw. "That's to be your house, Rory? Twenty feet high and no roof? It looks more like a Norman fortification."

Ruairí accepted the humor of it, but he replied, "I've just begun, you see. The roof will be slate and the walls plastered, so that no rain or wind will touch Máire my blackbird."

Blondell was Irish enough that he knew very well the story of Ruairí and the strapping "blackbird" who would not have him. But he was English enough that he would not let on that he knew it to the fellow's face.

"At my estate you will live in a house of brick."

Very slowly Ruairí walked off, looking for a stone on which to sit. As he had pulled all the stones in the immediate area, he had to go fifty feet. Blondell followed on his horse.

"You see, a Shéamais, I am promised to the service of Anraí MacThurlaigh Ó Reachtaire. And with his heart being bad in him, he needs me here."

"He has Donncha MacSiadhail."

Now Ruairí had to find a blade of grass to tear, which took him a while. "One man was barely enough when Anraí's health was unbroken. I would not leave him now."

Blondell brushed this aside. "I think Toby needs you as

much, Rory. He talks about you constantly, as though you invented horses."

Ruairí looked up. "Say that they invented me, first."

"Before he began studying with you, Rory, the boy didn't like anything or anyone. Now he's ... he's a regular boy again. Do come."

Now Ruairí raised his brown eyes to Blondell and regarded him steadily. Blondell had not meant to use his son as a draw for the stableman, for in truth he wasn't certain he'd be able to keep Toby at home much longer. Hermie was so set on an English school, and she had a lot of sense on her side. Blondell found he was looking at his folded hands instead of the horseman.

He hadn't expected he'd have to talk him into it.

"Toby can come to Knockduff, as he has been," said Ruairí.

"Once a week isn't enough."

"Then he can sleep in the barn with Donncha and myself and ride for Anraí at sixpence a week."

Blondell had to laugh at the idea. Toby would probably love it. But not Hermione. No. And Toby had better things to learn than the grooms' rough manners. It was too bad. He shook his head and a thought came into it. "Ruairí, you're not boycotting me right now, are you?"

Ruairí lifted his eyebrows, which were much darker than his hair. "How, when I'm speaking to you at the moment?"

"You do know what it means—'boycott'?" Blondell leaned out, disturbing his horse.

"I won't pretend to more ignorance than I have. I know about the boycotts. But as you're not buying or selling much of anything, and aren't one of the Irish people, to be hurt by the lack of their society, I don't know what harm a boycott could do to you."

Blondell, stung by these words as though by whips, swung his hunter around and kicked it into a smart canter, leaving Ruairí standing weary and openmouthed by the wall of his house.

In the middle of the day, Eibhlín Standún was coming out of the chemist's shop with a basket of flowers under her arm. Under the flowers lay a bottle of laudanum for her father, but

Eibhlín did not think it ladylike to be carrying a parcel from
the chemist through Carraroe: hence the flowers.

The breeze whipped her skirt around her ankles, display-
ing the hem of lace to good advantage. It raised the tendrils
of her yellow hair.

The pony trap, with Ó Máille, their man of work, was
parked at the other end of the street, so that the Standún
household (or at least Eibhlín) might not be marked as
spending their mornings at the chemist. It also gave her the
chance to let the wind blow her lace around for a while.

Unfortunately, the same wind had kept many of the inhabitants indoors; the only other figure on the street was Maurice, the publican, who had nothing to do yet at this hour
and was leaning against his door in the sun. He gave her a
high "God to you" and pushed himself off into the road.

"Eibhlín, I hear the 'good fellow,' your sister's swain, is
building a house up at Knockduff. Looks as though the
announcement is any day, isn't it?"

"The 'good fellow'? You mean Ruairí MacEibhir, the horse
trainer? Why do you call him that?"

Maurice grinned. "It's a joke in the pub, lass. If you ever
watched us drink your health there, you'd know such things.
It's because of his great black eyes and his old way of talking,
and because no man has succeeded in getting him to show
the trace of drink, though they've sunk their week's pay in
the effort. It's as though he is : . . you know."

Eibhlín did not know, but did not want to admit it.
"Ruairí spends time in the pub?"

"Not as much as we could wish, for he's a funny, funny
man. But Knockduff is long miles away. Tell me now if I'm
right; Máire has accepted him."

Eibhlín held her basket to her waist and stood very straight.
Speaking to Maurice was almost as low as setting foot into
the local itself. "You're completely in error, Maurice. She will
not have him at any price."

"She won't?" Maurice gazed down at the girl with measuring eyes. "Why not?"

The publican's near presence was unsettling. Eibhlín wished
he would stand back, but she didn't wish it wholeheartedly.
He was not a bad-looking man. "He broke Father's foot," she
said.

Maurice's face lit eagerly. "What a story! She won't have him because of that? And what better way to make up to the man than to marry his oldest daughter? Come, sweet one, you'll have to do better than that!"

Maurice had a sly face, and something in Eibhlín responded to that. "I think that the truth is she doesn't trust the fellow. She thinks he's making sport with her."

Now Maurice did step back, thinking very hard. "Well. Well! He *does* play tricks, that one. But to build a house for the purpose of a joke seems excessive."

Eibhlín shrugged. "A man needs a house, with a wife or without. And it doesn't have her name on it."

The publican had a rubber face and eyes that glittered in the sun. "What do you think the reward would be to him, though? The feeling in the town would be against him if he dropped the girl, after wearing his heart pinned to his sleeve all springtime."

On impulse Eibhlín said, "I think it was a wager with some friend. That he could break a heart as hard as Máire's."

The rubber face opened and closed. "You'd say that about your own sister?"

Eibhlín knew, in a cold rush of feeling, that she had said too much. And she remembered that there was another reason to avoid Maurice; he was the center of all the gossip in Carraroe. "Of course not. I only thought that . . . that he might. I must go now. Ó Máille's waiting."

The publican let her go, for he had a bellyful of information. He leaned back against the door again, to settle it in the sun.

Eibhlín hurried on, scuffing her little shoe soles on the walk. She found the breeze unpleasantly cool and was bothered by the way it pulled (like fingers) at her skirt.

Ó Máille was waiting five doors down, just this side of the priest's house. It was better not to go by the rectory in that particular skirt, with the ankles visible through the lace. The door of the grocer's opened, blocking her view, and when it closed, there was a man in front of her. He was not tall, but very straight. His shirt was thin linen and his trousers were those of a soldier. He was dark. He was young. He had a scar. He looked straight at her.

"You don't remember me, do you, Eileen?" he asked in English.

She stared and blushed and did not.

"I'm Joe Raftery. Henry's son. Home from the army."

"Oh, my." She remembered a boy much smaller and with an angry face. She thought that might be him. "Yes, of course."

"I remember you," he said.

In the end, Ó Máille had to come and get her.

CHAPTER ELEVEN

Challenges

Ruairí had the help of Donncha in putting the roof atop and the wooden floor between the stories of his house. Diarmuid Ó Cadhain, who had brought Ruairí together with his black pony, came to lend a hand also. He had heard how odd a house it was.

Anraí Ó Reachtaire did not work, but spent long hours staring and calling advice, and so was as weary as any.

It was partly of bog wood, which was delivered by night and was found almost impossible to cut or plane, but with willow where it did not have to be so strong. In two weeks that part was done, and the chief fault it had, as a house, was that it did not hold out the rain.

Ruairí labored hard in thought, during evenings in the barn with the horses and Donncha, but he could not imagine how he was to come by slate enough for the task and to cleave it into neat shingles.

"By the Tinker, man, I wish she'd be content with yellow straw. There's no fault to it, and it gives a home to many little creatures besides the owners of the house."

Donncha was lying on his back and trying to roll a cigarette on his chest. As he had no paper but used discarded writing paper, it was not an easy task. "That's part of the problem, my friend. So few people spare an affection for the little things: fleas, ticks, earwigs, silverfish ... But rather wish that the girl would have you in any sort of house, for it's the father's wish you're following, and none of hers."

"I will build as I said I would build," said Ruairí, and he seeemed to lay his ears back.

Donncha put his construction in his mouth and reached for a match. A powder of tobacco tumbled out the end of the tube, all over his chest. He sighed and began again.

"There are great blocks of the stuff in the east, where the land is lime," continued Ruairí. "With four great horses and a heavy wagon I could haul a few of them out here and take a chisel and mallet to them. But it's not work I've done before. It's not in our line."

Donncha glanced over at the stolid, squatting figure, but he didn't ask for elaboration. "I wonder when Blondell will come for that stallion?"

"What does it matter?"

"Someone is in a very bad mood," said Donncha airily. This time the cigarette made it to the match and he sucked on it greedily. Coughed.

"There are some houses I have seen in the north by Moyard that were abandoned. Last time I was there they still had their shingles. I could . . ."

"When were you last there?"

Ruairí counted on his fingers. "Thirty-seven years."

"Don't bother. They won't still be there." Donncha was pleased with his cigarette. His companion put a large hay bale between them.

"Then I shall have to rip them out of a house where folk are living!"

Donncha peered around the bale, to find Ruairí squatting like a red Indian with a fierce frown covering his face. He sat back again and sighed smoke and burned paper into the air. "Too bad. If we were gentry, now, you'd just buy so many shingles. You'd say, 'and make sure they are even and uniform and *no cracks*!' Other men would labor, and money would see it done."

There was no reply. Donncha wondered if he had offended his strange barn mate, whom he still could not predict. Then Ruairí's head appeared around the straw bale. "Buy shingles?" he asked. "Slate shingles?"

"Certainly. How do you think most people get them?"

Ruairí crawled onto the bale and stared down at Donncha. He sneezed. "If I had known, I would not have pondered so deeply. There are men who sell shingles, like they were cabbages?"

"Dear Lord, of course there are!"

The irritation returned to the overhanging face. "And you never told me?"

Donncha took a last, heavy drag upon his cigarette, for it was coming apart. He pounded out the embers on his chest. "How could I know you'd be so ignorant? And besides, you don't have a penny, as I well know."

Ruairí stared, as though he would contradict Donncha, and then he lowered his gaze and merely stared. He stood slowly, pointed his finger at his companion for a moment, and then let it drop. Without another word he left the barn.

Donncha sat with smoke dribbling out of his mouth and from his shirt. "What new trouble . . .?" he asked the air.

Ruairí MacEibhir did not return that night or the next morning. But as it was the morning that Seosamh Ó Reachtaire walked up to the back door of the house and announced his return, he was not missed a great deal, except by the horses.

"Term of duty is over?" echoed Anraí. "What do you mean? I thought the army was your career, a Sheosaimh. That, at least, was what you gave me to understand when . . ."

"Too expensive a career, for too little reward," answered Seosamh. He sat across from his father with one arm over the back of the chair and his other hand wrapped around the little glass that Áine had set before him, looking completely at home.

His father, on the other hand, sat on the edge of his seat rigidly, with his hands balled on his thighs.

Seosamh took a breath before continuing, "There is no way a man in the ranks can establish himself, Da. You just grow older and less ambitious as the years . . ."

"Did you get your uniform money that your father sent you?" Áine broke in nervously, looking from father to son.

"Uniform . . . Oh, of course, Ma. I did."

Anraí's color had been deepening ever since he sat down, and now was like the inside of a sweet cherry. Still, he made an attempt at composure. "I'm told by Maurice at the local that the queen buys your uniforms for you."

Seosamh's eyebrows rose at his father's queer phrasing. In

this position he bore a strong resemblance to Anraí. "The queen? Wouldn't that be bloody good of her!" He slapped his hand hard against the back of the chair and downed the government whiskey in a single swallow. He ignored the small protest in Áine's throat concerning his language and spoke to his father. "They buy some uniforms for you."

"And how many do you need? You can only wear one at a time," replied Anraí, but his words were almost placatory in effect.

Seosamh allowed the fumes of the whiskey to escape through his nose. He leaned back in the chair, which squeaked. "I'll tell you, Da. The British army is no place for an Irishman."

"Was it four years ago, when you were so hot on it?" asked Anraí in the same small voice.

Donncha put his head in the door to tell them that Ruairí had not come home, but at that moment Seosamh slammed both his hands on the enamel-topped table, making the glasses rattle. "How the dirty hell should I have known what it would be, four years ago when I hadn't joined?"

Anraí came to his feet roaring, "Because I told you!"

Donncha met Áine's eyes, winced, and ducked out again.

That evening it was Donncha and Áine, sitting by the light of his lantern, amid the company of the horses.

"It'll be the death of my old man. There's nothing the boy can say that doesn't set him off. He's certain that Seosamh was drummed out of his corps, and all because he didn't bring him the little piece of paper to show."

Donncha, who was equally convinced that young Ó Reachtaire had been cashiered, shook his ungainly head. "So unfortunate, Áine. How was he to know it would be wanted?"

"Indeed! And Seosamh never has been reliable with things written. Or with finance."

Donncha nodded. He recalled, now that he sat and thought about it, that it had been partly a lack of financial reliability that had impelled Seosamh Ó Reachtaire to leave his father's establishment in the first place. (Accepting payments from clients which did not then find their way into the books of the stable. Among other things.)

"And the boy wants to set his father off, like gunpowder." Áine shook her head mournfully and wandered over to get whatever consolation her red cow's smooth back had to offer. "It's as though he does it on purpose. And yet this very morning I told him he had to be careful, for his father's health hangs on a thread, what with his bad heart."

Donncha was usually quick to make connections, and this one caused him to drop the chew straw from his mouth. "You told him? Has . . . has Anraí made a will?" Immediately Donncha regretted his question, but Áine turned to look blankly at him. So did the cow.

"I said, 'Indeed, they sometimes will.' " Donncha's grin was weak.

There was a grinding of the old door of the barn, and a sprinkling of rain came in, along with Anraí Ó Reachtaire. He glared at them both, until it occurred to him that he wasn't angry with either one of them. "I've left His Majesty the whole house to himself," he declared.

Áine sighed and sat down on an oat bin. Her husband came to join her and committed himself to putting his arm around his wife's shoulder, right in front of Donncha and the horses. "I'm sorry for you, my lass," he whispered.

She replied, "I'm sorry I only gave you the one, and him such a disappointment to you. Another woman . . ."

". . . Would have murdered me in my bed for my tempers and rough ways, Áine. Believe me, I know that Seosamh is a mirror of myself. It's for that reason I can't bear him. If he were more like his mother . . ."

Donncha wandered away, gazing vacantly at the roof of the barn. He came to the stall of the red stallion and gave the horse a few strokes along its elegant muzzle. The stallion, which did not have Donncha's inhibitions, craned its neck out to watch the courting couple.

Again the door groaned, and all tightened for the confrontation with Seosamh. It occurred to Anraí that he had left the boy with the entire bottle of whiskey.

What entered instead was a figure in grave dirt, dripping clods. Its features were the color of clay, streaked with white where the rain had hit it. It was dragging something heavy. Every beast in the barn cried out.

Áine shrieked, a sound that descended as she recognized the ghastly visitor. "Ruairí! By our Lord, what has happened to you?"

White teeth shone and disappeared. "I'm dirty, Áine. I've been digging."

Donncha stepped up. "You've been digging? All night and all day? While I did two men's work for you?"

"Three men's work, if you did mine too," replied Ruairí. He strode across the barn to the water butt and dipped himself a pail.

"Here's soap," said Áine, pointing.

But Ruairí lifted the heavy pail to his lips and drank half of it. The rest he spilled over his head, turning it silver again.

Anraí, meanwhile, had approached the rough object that Ruairí had dragged in with him. It appeared to be of wood. It was hollow, and hurt the knuckles when rapped.

"What is this: treasure?"

Ruairí bent over it with him, dripping water from his forelock over the shaped wooden boards of it. "You will have to tell me that, Anraí Thurlaigh."

It was about a foot in length and eighteen inches high. The top was rounded, and there was an iron lock, long broken. It smelled of dirt and turf and rain. Ruairí and Anraí lifted the lid.

Paper met their eyes, paper turned the color of yellow onion skin. It was the first page in a book which had been bound crudely with needle and linen cord. Carefully Anraí lifted it up.

"I can't read any of it," he whispered, as a man whispers in the presence of death. "The paper's gone too brown."

Donncha scuffed on his knees closer to the box. "It might as well have been left blank; there's nothing here to see."

"Let me," said Áine, scooping a lapful of straw over her apron. "I'm close to the lantern, here."

Áine took the thin manuscript on her lap, like a hen for plucking. She bent down over it. "What a shame. That someone cared so much to save it, and now it's as though it had never been."

Anraí squatted down with crackling knees. "I doubt it would have done us much good, after all this time. It's not as though there has been a change in the government, to make old claims good again. It's more likely a parish registry, hidden so that some old Catholics could deny their faith."

"Then it would have been burnt, not buried," said Áine.

An idea occurred to her, and she glanced down at dirty Ruairí. "Can you read this, lad, with your fairy eyes?"

He shook the dirt out of his hair. "My fairy eyes can't read anything, a Áine NíAnluain. Because my fairy brain has never learned the art of it."

Anraí stared at him over his wife's knees. "Not at all? You've had time enough for practice."

Ruairí giggled. "I do well enough as I am. I found the box, didn't I?"

"Indeed you did." Áine slipped a chiding glance to her husband. "And that art could be worth more than reading, to a poor man."

"It was no art beyond racking my memory. I saw them put it into the ground, back when Gaels had things to hide."

Anraí's red-rimmed eyes opened round. "Where? And when was this?"

Ruairí rubbed his wet face with his sleeve, leaving a new streak of dirt. "In the far east—almost to Galway it is—and in time . . ." He counted on his fingers, moving his lips, and then bent his fingers at the first joint and did it again. Then he counted with his eyes closed, using no fingers. "Two hundred years," he announced.

There was silence in the barn.

"And you remembered this? The digging of the hole? The planting . . ." Donncha's sentence trailed off.

"I did. After some thought." Ruairí's pleasant, square countenance turned from one to another. "You see, I'm clever enough in some ways, though not learned."

"Of course you are, Ruairí. Please God, sometimes I forget what you are," said Áine. "I think you're one of us."

"Aren't I?" asked Ruairí, and when no one answered him, he laughed loudly and began to rummage the box alone.

There was a satin cloth, dyed bog ochre and wrapped around a bundle, which he picked up and put down at Áine's feet. With delicate fingers she caught the corner to lift, and the cloth fell into pieces as she laid it in her lap.

Within the satin was a little dress, doll-sized and very perfect. It was of silk and dotted with pearls: both fabric and pearls the color of amber. "What is it?" asked Donncha, and he was abashed, for he felt his voice too loud for the little dress.

"A rich playtoy?" ventured Anraí.

Áine chuckled, but wanly. "It's a baptismal gown, Donncha. I'm sure it was white as snow. Poor babe."

"Not too poor," said her husband.

Something black fell out of the bundle and landed at Ruairí's feet. He lifted it and it made a noise. It had shiny sparks on the two bulbs at the ends and was about four inches long. "A rattle," said Áine, taking it. "A silver baby's rattle. With jewels. What a shame."

"I don't see the shame," said Anraí.

"The poor babe never had the use of it."

Her husband growled and leaned against a stall door. "What use does a child get out of such a bauble? I doubt he'd ever have been allowed to touch it."

Ruairí, having no interest in rattles, delved deeper in the box. "Here we go, my dearies." He pulled out something long and shining.

It was of gold and garnets, or perhaps rubies, and neither time nor the bog had had power to dim it. In its middle hung a single tear of cherry red. Smiling at Anraí, he placed the thing against Áine's worn forehead, with the drop above her eyes.

"Dear me, let me look at that," she cried and grasped it. She let out her breath in a long, quiet hiss. All in the room stared, even the horses, and Anraí squatted down beside his wife. "There is your house roof, Ruairí," he stated. "Your slates and your plaster and your hand-painted wallpaper, and whatever else will please your own lady."

Ruairí's smile was tentative. "I don't think so."

"But it's true. Even in Galway such a thing will sell for a very dear price, and in Dublin . . ."

The fairy rose up with his hands in his pockets. He danced from foot to foot in a thoughtful manner. "I think, Anraí, that the jewel makes a better ornament for Áine than it could make a roof."

Áine, alarmed, balled the necklace in her fist and shoved it away on the straw. "I couldn't, Ruairí, thank you. But I would not have a place to wear it. It would look a mockery on my old neck, and drive all the women of the parish to hate me."

He set his jaw. "If you won't have it, then the earth will have it again, for I've set my mind that it will not be my slates, regardless."

"Oh, don't be proud, lad." She struggled to express the absurdity of the wealth in her lap. "There's the tax man to consider. The last thing anyone in the county wants to do is to sport jewels and wealth suddenly, for there's a tax on everything, and the government would want to know where you got it."

"Well, then, I'll tell them. What's the harm in it?"

Donncha chuckled and Anraí cleared his throat. "I doubt they'd agree that it's yours, Ruairí."

For a moment the black eyes under the fall of silver hair shone with a hard light. "How, when I found it myself?"

Once more the door began to grind, and in puzzlement Ruairí watched his friends and protectors spring into action. Anraí snapped shut the lid of the box and sat on it. Donncha, in a leap, was in between Áine and the door. She herself piled the straw over the little things in her lap.

It was Seosamh, looking in expression much like Anraí. Behind him was the black Thoroughbred of Anraí's, already saddled. There was a sprinkle of rain on Seosamh's hair.

They watched him in frozen silence. "You can have your house back," he said. "I'm going out."

"It's raining," said Áine uncertainly. "When—when will you be back?"

He stared from his mother to his father, to Donncha, and at last (in surmise) to Ruairí. "When I please to. Not before morning."

"Be careful of that horse," called Anraí, but his words were lost in the grinding of the door.

There was another moment of silence, as Ruairí looked at the straw on Áine's lap. "Why did you cover all the treasure from Seosamh's eyes, Áine? Is he the tax man you were talking about?"

Áine's face twisted. She hugged the straw and the treasure to her bosom and began to cry.

*   *   *

The next day Seosamh had not returned, and Ruairí consented to give Áine the silver rattle rather than the necklace, though he thought her choice very odd. Anraí took upon himself the task of selling the necklace, for Ruairí would on no account travel as far as Galway for the purpose. And the old man did go, driving the cob in the gig, but not before having a rousing go-about with James Blondell on the subject of the chestnut stallion.

Blondell was not in a good mood himself, but he had started conciliatorily enough, at least in his opinion. "You've done wonders for that beast, Anraí."

"It was Ruairí, here," mumbled Anraí through a rotten headache.

Blondell had come to supervise the return of his stallion, but when he saw how biddable it was, he decided to ride himself. Donncha tacked it up, keeping his tongue firmly between his teeth, as though it might get away from him if not suppressed.

"Whoever it was, they've turned him from the best race horse in Connemara 'in potentia' into the best in fact!" He added, " 'In potentia' means 'in possibility.' "

"I know my Latin," answered Anraí. "And he is a fast horse."

"There's none that could beat him." Blondell, like many insecure people, watched faces closely. "You don't agree with me? You, who have trained him?"

Anraí squinted away from the sun and wished the man would take his beast and go.

"I don't mean any insult to him at all. But I've seen so many horses in my time . . ."

Blondell nodded amicably. "In your time. I suppose you have, old man. But here and now, there's none that could take him on."

Anraí, who was about to grant that much, suddenly found his mouth would not do it. Blondell's eyebrows shot up and the stallion beside him flicked its ears nervously.

"You don't think that colt of Ó Cadhain's . . ."

Lounging in the shade of the barn, Ruairí MacEibhir was watching and grinning, with his hair falling over his right eye.

Anraí shook his head, which action hurt considerably.

Blondell pressed him. "Not your black? He's a good horse, I'll grant you, but he's never seen the length of a track in his life."

"God be thanked," whispered Donncha to Ruairí.

Anraí's face pulled together like that of an old, unhappy baby. "It all depends on the length of the race, Mr. Blondell. And the terrain it covers."

Mr. Blondell hated to be called so by stablemen. "I'm talking about a distance, of course. Not any mile track. And if you think your black can do hills better than my chestnut . . ."

Ruairí spoke up, bold and brassy. "Not your black, Anraí. That grey stallion you keep on the mountain."

Anraí blinked over at him in complete confusion. Donncha stood still and whistled through his teeth. Blondell was interested, though not happy.

"Grey stallion? What's this? I didn't know you kept any more blood horses than your black and a few mares."

Ruairí's intent seeped into Anraí over a matter of five seconds. He found those unbroken black eyes holding his, and he was nodding, mouth open. "It's . . . it's not a Thoroughbred at all, Mr. Blondell. It's a fine native pony. Large."

"A pack pony?" Blondell's face was spherical in his disbelief. "You think a little draft horse can win a race with any blood horse, let alone my stakes winner? You're drunk, man! Or mad!"

"From An Cheathrú Rúa streets to the yard here," said Ruairí, calmly, as though he had not much interest in the matter. "I think the old grey might take him at that distance."

Blondell sputtered, half in laughter.

Anraí found his headache relieved, swept away by the heat of challenge. "All right, then. I've never been one to deny a man his amusements. If it's so funny to you, Blondell, we'll race your English stakes winner against our Irish pony. From my front door to An Cheathrú Rúa. At your convenience!"

At the words "English" and "Irish" all the good humor went out of Blondell's face. "That again! Goddamn you, Raftery, you're no different from the rest of them! This horse" —and he swept his hand at the chestnut, which was becoming momently more agitated—"is Irish for at least five generations! Does a thing have to be poor and defective to be called Irish?"

Donncha whistled low. Anraí was too angry to speak. Ruairí laughed. And Blondell began to understand what he had said.

"I meant . . ."

"We'll see," said Anraí, cutting him off. "Whatever you call your tall red bounder, we'll see what he does against a horse of the hills. From An Cheathrú Rúa to Knockduff, anyhow they can do it. On Midsummer's. Right? Right?"

Blondell had opened his mouth to speak, but found he had no idea what to say. "Right enough," he answered Anraí, and he swung himself up into the saddle. He gave the stallion the same firm nudge he would have given his red hunter and had a memorable, if not enjoyable, ride home.

Ruairí and his little black king were grading the large ring with a log harrow when Seosamh came wandering up to him. Young Ó Reachtaire was looking left and right, up and down, as though comparing times past and times present. He was wearing one of his father's báinín shirts, which was too short for his arms, but he still had on his soldier's trousers.

The pony snorted and rolled his eyes at Seosamh's approach, but that had little to do with any essential characteristic of the man; it was just the black king's way. The white showed at the corner of Ruairí's eyes also.

"So you're the new man."

"I feel old enough today," replied Ruairí, for all his bones remembered hauling the wooden box across thirty miles, and that in the same week as raising a house.

Seosamh glanced at him sharply and noticed his eyes. Ruairí, feeling the interruption over, clucked the pony into motion again. Seosamh followed beside, staring.

"We didn't used to need another pair of hands, when I was home before."

The brown eyes fixed on his. Seosamh could not read them. "Your father wasn't sick, before." Ruairí reined the pony in, murmuring apologetically to it for the confusion.

It was a perfect, fair day. A scarlet bee buzzed around the horseman's pale head, unnoticed.

Seosamh had soft lips, which tightened as he said, "I wonder if you're worth your keep, Ruarí, let alone what Father pays you."

An expression of delighted idiocy lit Ruairí's comfortable features. "Do you know what your father pays me?"

Without blinking an eye the other replied, in English, "Yes. He told me."

"And you are concerned I'm not earning it?"

"My father is a very easy man."

Now Ruairí's grin was dazzling. He piled the lines on the black king's back and stepped to the pony's head, which he stroked slowly. "Perhaps you'll want to see me ride a horse, and judge."

Seosamh had no difficulty reading the tone of voice. "Oh, I'll certainly do that. But it's your attitude we're going to have to get through, first. You are forgetting that my name is Ó Reachtaire." He braced his legs in the sand and ground turf, standing foursquare against the other. His hands were in his pockets. The two men were of equal height.

Ruairí giggled in his nose, exactly like a bad schoolboy. "Dear me, a Sheosamh son of Anraí, there are some who wish they could forget that."

Seosamh colored up just like his father, and the fist he pulled out of his pocket had the broken head of a hammer in the center of it.

Ruairí MacEibhir didn't bother to duck. He raised his left arm and smacked the loaded fist aside. He was still grinning. His right hand came up from his side, without windup, and sent Seosamh's chin sailing eight feet in the air, with the rest of him following. Young Ó Reachtaire landed like a sack and measured himself on the soft, sifted ground of the ring.

The black king put back his ears and made disapproving noises. Ruairí found it necessary to turn and comfort him, and then Donncha, who had been in the far barn, came panting up.

"What is it? Was the fellow still drinking, please God, or was it . . ."

"It was his turn to be kicked by a horse, Donncha, as happens to all of us," said Ruairí. "I think he isn't dead." Nickering very affectionately to his pony, he put the log harrow into motion again.

"You *think* he isn't dead, you frozen-hearted fish?" Donncha went down on one knee by Seosamh, whose breath was coming in great, painful gulps. Next to him Donncha found the broken hammerhead.

"Is this what you fell on, Joe-ín? No wonder you look so green. It's an ugly thing to hit a man on the head. I wonder how it came to be lying in the ring?"

Seosamh crawled up onto his elbows, mewling. With difficulty he focused on Donncha. He tried to call him a bloody bastard, but his mouth wasn't working, except to vomit.

He stood up and brushed himself off. He left the ring and walked the path to the house and past. He went down the road that led around Knockduff and toward Carraroe, and he did not come back to his father's stables for a long time.

CHAPTER TWELVE

Visitations

It was now June: the month of the year when it rains least in Connemara. That is not to say that it doesn't rain. The grass was almost as lush as it is supposed to be in Ireland, and the hills in the distance were green instead of brown, and lavender instead of grey. Even with such a wet spring behind, most of the bogs were firming, and the first piles of turf were being cut against the use of next winter.

The days were fantastically long, because Ireland is actually a country of the far north, though surrounded by waters risen near the Gulf of Mexico. The people of the seacoast rose early and went to bed late and very tired, for the unaccustomed sun spurred them through the days and even in the evenings would not let them rest. The potato beds were weeded and turned and last autumn's loads of seaweed dug in. The beasts were all shed out, almost. The soft mats of winter pony coat lined all the nests of the birds of Connemara, and there was still plenty to roll over the ground and stick to Áine NíAnluain's wash.

All over the pastures of Anraí's holding were the loose horse droppings caused by the watery grasses of spring. But the horses themselves didn't mind; the new shoots were soft enough for the babies' erupting teeth, and there were few flies yet to make trouble.

Seán Standún was walking again without a cane, and his older daughter was as silent as ever. She saw Father Ó

Murchú only at mass. Eibhlín was having the best spring of
her life, so far, seeming more fresh and glowing every day,
and there were two tunes and one poem with her name fixed
to them traded about at Maurice's hostelry.

Seosamh Ó Reachtaire was staying with his friends outside
of Carraroe, and where he got his money to live, his parents
did not know. He was discovered to have a pretty way with
poetry, which he expressed in the evenings at Maurice's. His
satiric ode upon the 47th Irish Fusiliers was pronounced
excellent. Once a week or so, Ruairí MacEibhir put his head
in the door, to see whether all were tired of trying to get
him drunk yet. On these occasions he did not speak to
Ó Reachtaire, nor the young man to him.

On a flawless morning, very early, Ruairí was painting his
parlor. He had been shown the rolls of linen chinoiserie and
the satin-finished cabbage roses and decided he could do
better himself. So the house was plastered white in the
common fashion, and Áine had been commissioned to pick
up an assortment of pigments on a trip into Clifden.

He was a careful painter and enjoyed his work. He liked
the colors of green and yellow, and perhaps gave too much
attention to the structure of the individual grass blades of his
landscapes and not enough to the faces of the people. Vines
crawled around every doorway, and through some of them,
with fruits depending from them that were not what the
neighbors grew in their gardens.

But he had not disregarded the popular taste in all things,
for Ruairí never forgot the purpose for which he was building. He had painted in a little arched bridge on the parlor
wall, with a small boy with a conical straw hat and a lady
with a parasol. Because of his lack of experience, however,
Ruairí made the parasol to resemble a sturdy Dublin umbrella, and then to add verisimilitude, he painted in the rain
over all.

He was cleaning the cobalt oil off the brush at the moment, stirring it vigorously in turps. He held the pot firmly in
his other hand, for he had already broken one in his enthusiasm. He was whistling as he worked, for he was very happy.

Yesterday evening he had convinced Máire Standún to look
at the house, which is a thing she really ought not to have

done. She had been made speechless by it: the size, the heavy rise of the walls, and the very perfect and professionally laid slate roof over all.

But it had been the paintings she had liked best, he told himself. At least she had kept staring at them. Or perhaps the presence of the black king in the hallway had been most impressive. At him she laughed outright, especially when he made his grand bow to her.

Had the paintings been more like the roof—strong, unobtrusive, professional—she would probably not have stared so long at them. She would probably not have blushed and blinked so often, nor have let him squeeze her in his arms for just a moment. Ruairí MacEibhir, in his own way, was not stupid at all.

He was grinning with all his teeth as he shook out the brush and dried it in a piece of moss. "She won't marry me, will she?" he sang to himself. "There's no one else she'll have, after knowing me. I know the woman that well!"

In a louder voice he added "I'm not speaking to you, Tob-ín son of James, so you needn't skulk to hear me."

Tobias Blondell crept around the doorsill, careful of the paint. He stared, mouth open, but unlike Máire, he did not blush or blink. "I wasn't skulking, Ruairí. I was . . . Say! This is smashing! Like the Italian villas, where the pictures on the walls go on and on, from the walls to the ceiling and back again."

"I thank you!" Ruairí bowed low and gracefully to the boy, with a peculiar gesture of both arms.

Toby giggled, and then the sound died in his throat and the light in his eyes. "Ruairí," he said, "they want to send me to school. In England."

Meeting the boy's eyes, Ruairí's own eyes went somber. He put his brush into its slot and he closed the case with a final-sounding click. He sat himself down on the boards of the floor, cross-legged, so that his face was below that of Toby.

"It is what happens in the life of a man. I am told it is very necessary: that every man should leave his home behind at least once, if he is to know what home is."

"I already know what home is! Home is here!" Toby's resentment died in the face of the complete attention in his teacher's face. "I . . . it's not just that I'm afraid to go. It's that I know I won't come back again. Not like I am. My mother, you see . . ."

Toby's eyes smarted and he knew he was about to cry. It made him furious and hopeless. "Remember what I was like, Ruairí. I couldn't ride. I had no Irish, no friends . . ."

"You won't be like that again," Ruairí slapped his hand on his lap. "For your mother cannot turn time back on you. Even when it is ill fortune and tragedy that has come, no mother has been able to peel it away from her children. You cannot forget how to ride, though you may grow sloppy. You may not hear the language of these people living about us for years of your life, but it will come back to you. And for friends . . . I say to you that you will not forget me, Tobias Blondell."

Toby, though his vision was swimming, had to giggle at Ruairí's swagger. "I doubt I will. But . . . I don't want to go, Ruairí. If it was right for me, I would know it."

"I hear that from every foal, at weaning. They would know it was time to stop suckling when their own babies had babies."

Suddenly Toby was offended: angry at this man before him, sitting complacent in his new house amid his old home . . . No great loss coming to him. He could laugh and make jokes. Toby wasn't to forget him, but Ruairí would forget soon enough. What was he, Toby, but a boy he taught for money?

Toby's small face set in a sneer. "Maybe this one won't be 'weaned.' Maybe I have some say in the matter, too." He turned, took two dignified steps away, and then ran helter-skelter through the door. The black king whinnied after him from his position by the door, but Ruairí sat without moving, with the paint box on his lap, long after the pelting footsteps died away.

As Ruairí was about to go under the shadow of Knockduff to the stables, Tadhg Ó Murchú trotted up on a borrowed pony. He had his crucifix-shaped ointment box with him, for he was returned from giving the last rites to a woman at the edge of the parish. Ó Murchú had not seen the round house before, but he had heard much about it. He slipped off the horse and lost his knees for a moment, for the pony's trot was hard and the priest not used to riding.

"God to you, Father," said Ruairí, and Ó Murchú cast a very sharp glance. "Are you making sport of me, Ruairí Léith?"

"Is it making sport of you to be polite? That is the greeting which Áine has told me is proper for you."

Ó Murchú grunted and looked up, up at the rise of the wall. "It's a fortress! How did you do it, Ruairí? This looks like the old stonecraft."

"I had help."

The priest's glance went even sharper. "I'll bet you did!"

It was an odd, uncomfortable visit, for though the priest was clearly taken by what he saw as they strolled through the two floors with their smooth plaster and bright paint, his eyes moved more like a man thinking than a man looking. He kept his crucifix in his right hand, against his chest.

"And how are the affairs of the nationalists, Ó Murchú?" Ruairí asked, as both stared out of the bedroom window, which faced south toward the blue water.

"Don't speak that word!" The priest started, and his voice was too loud.

Ruairí stood mildly beside him, his hands in the pockets of his canvas trousers. "You are safer speaking with me beside you than by yourself in a dark wood, Priest of the Parish. You can be certain there is no other ear about, if I tell you so."

Ó Murchú glared at him, uncertain. Then his eyes moved left and right, unfocused, and his lips twitched. "Affairs are tight and very strained, both in Galway County and in the east. And in my own house also, for the bishop doesn't like me." Once again he glanced at Ruairí. "He'd like me even less if he knew I had baptized you, púca!"

"A shame! He has never met me, or he'd change his mind."

Ó Murchú put his crucifix down on the generously broad windowsill. His intent, severe face did not change expression as he asked "Do you see much of Máire Standún these days?"

"As much as she'll see of me. Don't you?"

"Of course not. Why should I?" Ó Murchú let his attention slide to the window again. "Dear God, what a summer it will be!" he whispered. Ruairí was content to look at the priest for as long as that one gazed out the window. Flies tapped the glass.

"Ruairí!" He broke the silence. "I hear that Máirín NíAnluain brought you a sick baby and that you put a sign on it. Is that true?"

The fairy's quick grin broke out. "Who told you that? Not Máire herself, certainly."

"I . . . cannot tell the source." Ó Murchú folded his arms in front of his breast.

"Then I cannot tell the answer."

Ó Murchú's neat, dark face heated with his irritation. "You have not the power to bless children, lad."

"You mean I have not your authority, I think. The power to put a word on a beast or a child, that I most assuredly do have, and you know it."

The priest's folded arms started to come apart from each other, like an unsound argument. His anger shifted, became calculation. "Can you heal, then?"

The sun through the window shone on Ruairí MacEibhir, making him look shabby and half asleep. The shadow of the crucifix was across his middle. "I can heal. And kill. And work at trades, Ó Murchú. As you can. But I am perhaps better at a few things."

Now the arms fell down at Ó Murchú's sides. He began to walk the length of the empty, white-lit room. "Anyone can kill! A stray dog can do that. If you have the power to heal, fellow, then you must do it. These people have few doctors and no money to pay those who chose to endure it here."

"Why should I care?" Ruairí stood on one foot, scratching his other calf with his bootsole. His smile had gone mocking.

"Because they are your brothers and sisters," replied the priest carefully.

"I'm no Gael."

"You are a Christian. You took that willingly, and there is no greater vow."

"So. How does that mean I have to become the village leech?"

" 'Love your neighbor as yourself.' "

Ruairí continued to scratch, for the heavy canvas trousers were uncomfortable in the heat. But his face went wary and then confused. "If I promised that, in truth, then I promised my life away, for there are neighbors endlessly in An Cheathrú Rúa."

"*You did!*" Tadhg Ó Murchú spun on his heel and pointed his finger at Ruairí's face. "You did that, lad, and so did I, and I promise you, it will never let us go! Not past the bitter end."

He was shouting. His voice broke and he caught himself, with a sort of sob. Ó Murchú passed a hand over his eyes and mumbled. He went to pick up the crucifix, and then he stalked across the floor to the stairs.

"It isn't just An Cheathrú Rúa, either," he called over his shoulder. "It isn't even Ireland, worse luck. In fact," he craned his neck to peer upward at Ruairí, who leaned over the landing on the first floor, "there is no man, woman, or child on the earth who is not your sworn concern."

Ruairí stood and puzzled this, his black brows over his brown eyes and his pale hair hanging over all. "But . . . but am I *their* sworn concern as well, Father Ó Murchú?"

But the priest was hauling himself onto the borrowed pony, and he was mumbling to God or to himself too loudly to hear.

It was in the middle of the day and Ruairí was in Carraroe, buying soap and nails, when he saw James Blondell on his hunter, standing in the middle of the street. There was by him a small fellow with a large beaver hat, which shone like few hats in Galway County. This one was riding a restive half pony and shouting up to Blondell.

Ruairí had a handful of long-stemmed flowers, which the eldest Mrs. NíChonaola had given him, not telling him why. He was knotting them together, and his teeth and hands were stained green.

He had no objection to listening to the dispute, which seemed to concern Toby Blondell. Ruairí was very interested, though one couldn't tell as much from his face or from the slack way in which he sprawled in the gig. Both men were angry, but it was difficult to say whether they were angry together or at each other. Ruairí was forced to climb down to the dirt road itself, so that he could understand the English. But the conversation made no more sense, for the small man was speaking of rebels and the large one about his wife. Again and again Ruairí heard the word "seditionist" and wondered what Toby had been up to.

He wasn't forced to wonder long, or even to force acquaintance with any of the locals who happened to be standing closer to ear, for Blondell himself left the other and trotted his horse over to the black gig. Over his shoulder he called, "It is his own handwriting, and there's no need to look any further for cause!"

Ruairí tied a knot with his two hands and his teeth, and he glanced from under his eyebrows at Blondell. He was the picture of a man who didn't want to be bothered, and so Blondell began by apologizing quite sincerely.

"But it's my son. Tobias. He went away on horseback this morning, and now the horse has come back with the reins tied under his chin."

Ruairí's head came up. He wiped the juice off his lips.

"Toby's lost a horse? Well, that's an embarrassment, certainly, but he wasn't thrown, as is shown by the state of the reins."

Blondell's eyes flickered and he edged closer to Ruairí and further from the street's many ears. "He didn't lose the horse. He sent it home. There was . . . there was a note that we found."

Ruairí stared at the man hard and then harder. At last he said, "Oh. You mean he's run off."

Blondell sighed in relief that it was said. "Into the mountains."

As the two spoke, the big red hunter paid his courtesies to the dun cob in harness. It chose to resent this, and there was a moment for Ruairí to think about things.

"He didn't want to go to school, did he?" he said to Blondell, when the horses were quiet again.

The big man's eyes flickered. "No, he didn't. Did he tell you so?"

Ruairí stood with mouth open, weighing his loyalties. "I remember that he said as much, one time. Are you out to look for him now?"

Now Blondell looked baffled and a little sick. "Yes, of course. But I've got this man from the government, you see. It's very inconvenient. I don't know what to do with him."

Ruairí smiled. "Send him searching himself. Or send him to hell. It's all one."

"I'd like to do either, but I can't." He turned his horse's head. "If you see the young imp, Ruairí . . ."

Ruairí nodded very agreeably and said nothing, watching Blondell return to his government man.

Leaving the cob untended, Ruairí strolled across the street, weaving stems as he went. He stopped at the Ó Conaola door again, where Nóra was leaning against the jamb. Into her hands he pressed his piece of work, a heart shape of green flower stems, with the blossoms themselves ranked at the edge. "Here's a charm for your wall, a Nóirín. It will keep the . . . the government men away from your children."

She took it, and her lips were tight. "If it will keep that one away, you can have the first milk from three cows. He's come to put a rope around someone's neck, surely."

The brown eyes went very wide, showing white at the corners. "A rope, is it? Why is that?"

She sniffed. "James Blondell called him on us poor Gaels. *Mister* Blondell has had his feelings hurt by the Land League, I think!"

Toby had gotten himself lost very easily, though it would seem difficult in a countryside without trees. The round, rolling mountains that spilled from the north to the seacoast all looked alike, and his plan of heading for Mám Cross took him straight in among them.

If he had stayed on the road, it would have been an easy march. But if he had stayed on the road, he would have been also easy to find. So he had tried to keep one row of hills between himself and the straightaway.

The endeavor had succeeded too well and now there was no road to be found, but only the bald hills with heather and a green fuzz of grass, rolling on to Toby's nausea.

The plan was a child's plan: to sleep in a barn and to find work. The natives would not suspect him of being Toby Blondell, the gentleman's son with an English mother. He could speak Irish now. Better than Father. He would be respected. He would have horses, which he would train. He would return a grown man, sitting a stallion he had trained himself. His father would be impressed. His mother would be sorry. They would laugh over the idea that they had wanted him to go to school.

But there had been no barns to creep into, not barns like the great, pleasant-smelling hay store at home, or like the warm stable where Donncha and Ruairí slept. Upon these damnable, rippling hills he had found only a broken byre, roofless, and a stone poultry house, which was wet inside and out and malodorous in the extreme.

He had also found bogs, covered by heavy dry turf but soft within, into which he had fallen twice, and now his trouser legs were brown and wet and fiercely cold. It was not supposed to be cold in June.

If he went far enough astray to the east, then he would see the land change, from the bones of granite to the rich lime soil that covered most of Ireland. There would be trees and high grass and many more people. Toby gazed dully about him and decided he had not come so far east as that.

If he had reached the level of Mám Cross, then he would have struck the main road that runs to Clifden on the coast, and he had passed no road. If he had come in circles, southward again, then he would see Knockduff and eventually the water. And west was the road he was traveling. Very close it should be.

He sat his wet bottom on the cold ground and faced what he assumed was west. For a while he did not think at all, and then he heard cries in the distance.

It must have been his father coming to look for him. His chilled fingers demanded that he answer, but his mouth clamped shut. He was not giving up, but only tired. And cold. The cries continued, until Toby was on the point of tears, but he held out, even as they came closer. He looked for some place to hide, but there was none closer than the poultry house he had left behind hours before.

Then the criers of the cries came into sight, and they were a flock of ewes, being butted into movement by the ram. Toby watched the sheep go by and was filled with the rage of betrayal.

He wouldn't make it to Mám Cross. He wouldn't find work. He would die of cold and weakness on this raw, empty mound of stone while Ruairí MacEibhir and Donncha MacSiadhail laughed amid the warmth of the horses, with bellies full of potatoes and buttermilk and likely whiskey at their elbows. They would not think of Toby, or if they did, they would make a joke of him. Those people were great for making jokes.

Toby felt such a potent jealousy of Anraí Ó Reachtaire's grooms that he himself cried out, much like a sheep. His rage balled in his stomach and ached in his head and stirred his whole small frame without succeeding in warming it. "It's not fair!" he shouted, but he heard his own voice weak and piping over the bones of the hills.

The sky was now purple and clear, and glancing upward Toby knew he should appreciate the beauty of it, but the west wind was springing up and he began to shake. Shadows covered the east side of each hill, making a bold, inhuman pattern. Now that the sheep were gone, there was nothing moving to be seen. No birds in the sky.

Was this the place he loved so dearly he would leave his family, his pony, and all else he had for the sake of it? It was a cruel landscape which would not be loved. It was killing Toby with cold, and as he grew colder he began to weep, for there was no one and nothing which could hear and make him ashamed.

Toby stood up and walked to the top of the hill, hoping there would be the lights of a cottage on some horizon. But there was not even moonlight.

The stars, however, were growing more brilliant moment by moment, as the wash of purple ran to the edges of the sky and left black behind. At last even the rim against the earth was of indigo color and the stars were thick and silver. They, too, were inhuman, and Toby found them baleful. He turned in a circle and found he could guess which way south was, by the strip of ocean that reflected the light. It was exactly opposite of where he had expected to find it, and even now he wasn't certain.

He shivered uncontrollably and wished he could hide from the stars as much as from the wind. He felt his father's old pain, of being an interloper and unwanted. But he knew better than his father; it was not because he was of English descent. It was because he was human.

The black and the darkness made him dizzy, but the

ground was too cold and wet for him to sit down. And there
was a noise in his ears. A pounding.

It was heavy hooves pounding, very fast, as though on a
road. Toby turned in wonder and complete confusion, and
lost his directions again. He reeled and fell, sitting, and the
stars seemed to fall around him.

The horse on the next hill was white and splashed with
starlight. It bore no rider, and its breath grunted and labored
as it came on. It was impossibly large on the blank hill and
under the blank sky, very unlike the sweet-breathed servants
that carried him under Ruairí's direction. Toby's neck hairs
all stood on end as the horse leaped the stream that divided
the two hills and sprang toward him, heavy but very, very
fast.

It was up beside him, breathing like a bellows and with its
nostrils swollen in passion or sheer effort. That shining, huge
head was high above his, and there was nowhere Toby could
run, even if his legs would carry him.

In the middle of his shock and terror it came to Toby that
there was something familiar about the horse. Its mane was
neatly trimmed for braiding. Its nose was black at the end of
the white face. The eyes, more black against the white softness of lashes . . .

Toby opened his mouth to say, "I know you," but all that
came out was a groan. Then the horse reared up, and the
wide, round hooves hung above Toby's head, and he was
about to be trampled and smashed. Toby fell, but instead of
crashing down, the black hooves went up and up and the
white body rippled like a sheet or the flame of a candle in
wind and shrank down into itself. Toby began to scream.

"Toby! A Thóibín! Stop it now. That's plenty." Ruairí
picked the boy up and with his square right hand he smacked
him lightly across the face.

Toby stopped his noise abruptly. He stared at the shadow
outline of the face of his friend and teacher, and it seemed for
a moment he would forget what his eyes had seen and his
ears heard, in order to make sense of the present. But Toby
Blondell was neither so young nor so cowed as that. He
stepped back, wrenching his arms free, and again he stumbled.

"What . . . Who are you?" he shouted, and made small fists at his sides.

Ruairí straightened. "You know me, Toby."

"I don't! Or not until now. I saw what I saw, Ruairí. Don't tell me I didn't. You were in the shape of a horse, and then you changed in front of me. You're not a man at all."

"I'm not human, Toby, but you mustn't say I'm not a man." Sighing, Ruairí squatted down in front of the boy. Because of the slope, his head was at Toby's level. "I think my kind would not exist but for your kind. We are kin, you and I, though not quite the same."

"Who are you?" repeated the boy, flat voiced, though his body shivered.

Ruairí paused for a few heartbeats. He looked at his hands and then up at the stars, which shone in his silky hair. "I am the son of Granite and of Wind. Among these people and in this year I am called Ruairí, which is a good name. I have other names, too." He spoke softly, as though he were talking to himself.

"I am the horse that bore you over your first jump, a Thóibín. I am the hauler of the stones for the walls hereabout. I eat the paltry grass and the flowers and I wade in the sea. I steal men and women, if I might love them, and I carry them off. I am the púca, and my riders come off me different people than they went on." Then Ruairí giggled like a girl. "Or that is the idea. I would be a more formidable fairy if I were more clever.

"I am broad back and bone, stones and flowers, long work and green idleness. New things come slowly to me, but I have been here a very long time and I have seen too much change to be bothered anymore." He dropped his gaze from the heavens and touched one gentle finger to Toby's chest.

"I am Connemara, Toby Blondell. The country where you were born. So I am mother and father to you and I will call you my son."

Toby stared, half in astonishment and half in distrust, at the white and black face below his.

"And I say to you that you are bone out of my stones and blood out of my little rivers and bogs. I name you prince of this kingdom in which I am the sleepy, old high king. It cannot be taken from you."

All this while Toby had sat silent while Ruairí spoke, and he was silent now as the stars ran like watercolors over his blinking eyes. Ruairí's words, which he only half understood, made his eyes smart, and once he had time to think of them, he suspected he might cry outright again. He wrapped his knees in his arms and rubbed his eyes against the knuckles of his thumbs.

With his vision so disarrayed, he was not certain what sat before him, white and shining under moonlight. "Can you teach me to be a púca, too?" he asked.

Ruairí's white teeth shone like a glimpse of the moon. "Only a púca can be a púca. It is not such a great destiny, my friend. I don't think you would be happy swatting flies for days on end, with your mouth against the soil."

Toby sighed, though his shivering had almost stopped. "It's better than being a boy and going to school."

Ruairí gave this full consideration, as he scooted his seat over the wet soil until he was behind the boy, and he put one of his canvas-covered legs to either side of him. He chafed the thin, cold arms. "It may be so. And if you like, my son, I will hide you in the mountains where they cannot find you until you are grown."

Toby twisted around until he was face to face with Ruairí. "You would do that?"

Ruairí smiled again. "I never quite lie, boy. I will do it; it is your choice. But for the space of ten years, you must shun the company of men and women and remain with the cows and horses. I will teach you the names of the grasses and herbs, both in Gaelic and in an older language, and you can *try* to teach me them in English. But good luck to you in that endeavor . . ."

Toby broke in, "Shun the company . . . for ten years? That's . . ." His working mouth sought for a word to describe a thing that was both ill-advised and completely impossible, but he didn't know one, either in Gaelic or English. "I can't sit on a bare hill for ten years. I wanted to go to Mám Cross and fit in as one of the locals."

Now it was Ruairí's turn to be incredulous. "And pass as one of them? Never, a Thóibín. Even I can't pass as a native here, and I have had the language for fifteen hundred years. Don't gawp at me, I said fifteen hundred. But the tongue changes too fast for me, and *you* can't change fast enough in a few months . . ."

"You're that old?"

"I was born on the day that the Welshman Pádraig landed for the second time on Irish shores."

Toby used Ruairí's large shoulder as a brace by which to scrape himself around so that he could look the fairy in the eyes without straining. "If you are that old, Ruairí, you ought to be very wise by now."

It looked as though Ruairí would be offended, but then he burst out laughing. "Ah, but then I've never been to school, you see. I hadn't the advantages."

At the Blondell household James and Hermione kept vigil, and most of the servants did the same. There was a lot of weeping belowstairs and some in the library, where the Blondells were picking over the last of a midnight supper.

James Blondell had a glass of Madeira in front of him, and the rest of the bottle was set beside. He wanted to finish this glass at a gulp and fill it again and again until his hands would not obey him, but he was also in terror that they would bring in to him the body of his son and find him dead drunk. So he stared at the glass with its dark-oak liquid, and occasionally he made honey-brown swirls along the sides.

His wife drank tea with a shaking hand. "Hermie," he said. "If you keep drinking that stuff, you'll never get to bed."

"I'm not going to go to bed, James." Her voice was in excellent control. Delagardie. "I'm going to wait for Toby."

"He's undoubtedly asleep himself, holed up somewhere. With locals or in a barn. It's not cold out tonight," he added, though he felt that part, at least, was a complete falsehood. He had been out searching until eleven and had seen his breath under the starlight.

Hermione stared out of the tall library window. She spoke to it, as though she were speaking directly to James's face. "I don't think you take Mr. Grover seriously enough in this matter, my dear. He expects we will either receive a ransom note, or . . . or . . ."

James, who was sitting behind her, stood up. He placed the glass on the end table and walked toward his wife. She lifted her head but continued to stare into the window.

He felt it hard, this one more rejection: that his wife of fifteen years refused to meet his eyes. She blamed him that much.

But then his own eyes strayed to the window, and Blondell noticed that the lamplight had turned the surface to black glass. A looking glass. As he gazed straight into it it showed him Hermione's face perfectly, and she must have been looking at him all along. Indeed, now that he was beside her, she turned her head as much as she could in the wingback chair and reached for his hand.

He kissed the side of the Delagardie nose. "Oh, Hermie! Sometimes I misunderstand you so!"

"And I, you, James." She lowered her lips to his hand, thinking how it reminded her of her son's short-fingered, child's hand. "But about Mr. Grover . . ."

James Blondell groaned. He felt very embarrassed about Mr. Grover, who was at this moment in the sleeping part of the household, preparing for another day of nosing out nationalists and driving the people of Carraroe further away from Blondell. He had expected more subtlety out of a Crown man, and more intelligence. "Mr. Grover is a detective, darling, and he interprets everything that happens in terms of his calling."

Hermie sniffed and dropped his hand. Blondell froze in place, with his hand over her lap, because he was listening. He stood.

"I hear doors. Feet." He threw open the library door and leaned out into the passage. Hermione remained in her chair, with her eyes closed and her back braced against bad news.

Along the passage came Toby, with a shirt of báinín over his clothes and roped with a bridle rein at the hips. This outfit turned his slight figure into that of a medieval serf. He marched firmly and alone. With difficulty, he looked James Blondell in the eyes.

"I have come back, Father, and I am prepared to do whatever it is you want of . . ." Here his mother's voiceless shriek broke his concentration.

"Oh, Mother," he said. "I'm sorry. I . . ." and he bowed his head for her coming.

Her hugs and her cries and reproaches were everything he had expected and he endured them, knowing they were deserved. His father stood over the scene and observed it, missing nothing in his son's expression. When Toby had the opportunity to look at his father again, he found Blondell's face very peaceful, and Toby's father nodded to Toby and smiled.

"Who brought you home?" he asked, and Toby told him.

So Ruairí was brought in and made to tell where he had found him and how they had returned all that way to the estate. He spoke, of course, in Gaelic. Toby noticed that Ruairí never lied, quite.

Hermione didn't understand more than five words, but she smiled graciously and stroked Toby's hair. Blondell shook Ruairí's hand very honestly and thanked him in both Irish and English. He did not offer him money, but instead invited him for dinner.

When he had departed, Hermione sank back into her chair and wiped her nose on a hankie. She gave a little laugh and a moue, pointing at the Aubusson carpet. "My, that ploughboy had dirty brogues."

Blondell glanced down at the mud, and his jaw clenched in happy belligerence as he messed Toby's hair, which Hermione had straightened. "Maybe he'll scrape them when he comes to dinner Sunday," he said. But they were both too weary to make an argument out of it.

CHAPTER THIRTEEN

Consequences

It was the next day that Ruairí caught Eibhlín hiding under a tall gorse bush by a culvert on the Cois Fhairrge Road. It was a corner of her red petticoat that alerted him, as well as the sound of her breathing.

He leaped the culvert with surprising lightness and crept down the back on the other side of the blooming gorse bush, bent low away from the thorns. Her back was to him, and she was watching up the road through the dead lower branches of the bush.

Ruairí put his hands very lightly over her shoulders. She gasped and then turned to him, her pretty face radiant.

"God to you, Eibhlín," he said, as a good Christian ought, and at the sight and sound of him, her mouth went from a smile to a shock of fright. She sprang back from him, impaling herself upon the thorns of the trunk itself, and her eyes filled with painful tears.

"Rory MacEibhir, what do you mean by this?"

He laughed at her and didn't draw back an inch. "A man might be curious, seeing something so odd as Eibhlín NíStandún squatting in a ditch, and not to pee."

Again Eibhlín gasped, this time in anger, and she raised her hand to slap his face. Ruairí did not move, but she laid her hand down again. "I . . . I had a cramp in the leg, that's all."

He made no answer and did not look obviously disbelieving, so she pulled herself away from the gorse: first petticoat, then tangled hair, and lastly the shawl that had suffered most from the contact. Ruairí helped her with the thorns and she made no objection, though she was stiff as the gorse bush itself beside him. "Now you must leave me to rest, for I wouldn't have you seen here in this concealment," she announced firmly.

"I know it. The people around here don't like to see a young man and woman together under a bush!" He grinned and backed out awkwardly, with much waggling of his hind end. Once standing on the bank of the stream, he leaped up to road-level easily and stood looking down at her, a dark outline against blue sky. She hugged the corners of her shawl and turned away.

"Eibhlín," he called down again. "I know that a foal lives well on milk and grass and has no need of a father at all. We are not all so lucky. Be careful."

By the time she turned to him in both fury and fear, he was gone. No sound.

It had been hard work, even with all the help, but it was complete. Ruairí sat himself on a rock beside his black king and surveyed his house, trying to pretend he had never seen it before. "It is handsome, isn't it? Not so lovely as a hilltop at night, nor so comforting as beech trees, but after the manner of its kind, very handsome."

The king, who had been in and out of it, up the stairs and down, gave him a supportive snort.

"It has floors and a ceiling and all the walls are painted. There are doors that open and close, and glass in the windows, for the birds to strike their heads against. Now only two things remain . . ."

The king lifted his head at the sound of hooves coming down the road, a few acres behind them. He was like a dog that way, lacking only a growl.

". . . to persuade the stream of the hill behind to dip under and send us a tap into the kitchen, and to persuade Máire my queen to come and dwell in it. Either or both of these might have been done more profitably before the house was built. But that thinking is for clever folks."

The pony gave out a whinny like trumpets and stamped

his round hoof on the sod. Ruairí turned his head only as much as necessary, to see who was coming.

It was the little man with the tall hat, bouncing along on—of all mounts—that chestnut filly which had spent the winter and spring in Anraí's barn. He was making rough work of it, too, for she was still a willful girl, though that was no excuse for bouncing. Not on a Thoroughbred.

Ruairí sat and watched him pick his way over the boggy ground, with reins so short the filly could not see to place her feet. Instead, he leaned heavily over her right side and squinted at the soil himself.

Ruairí MacEibhir greeted him composedly. He straightened as he yanked the filly to a star-gazing halt, but he did not dismount. "Mister Blondell tells me that you speak decent English."

It was hard on the neck to look up so far at the man's face, and the sun was behind him, so Ruairí merely looked at the horse's belly. "I make my wants known," he said, stroking the ground as though it were an animal as he spoke. "Sometimes."

The small man had a large head, to fit his hat. His hair hung in two curled sideburns of dark fox color, and his chin was shaven so that it shined like the beaver. "Don't have anything to do with your time, hey?" he said, as the filly shook her head and made the bit rattle. He yanked again.

Ruairí stood up. He put his finger into the horse's mouth, between the corners of her lip and the bit, and he whispered nonsense to her. Her ewe neck lowered in relief. It occurred to him that Blondell didn't mount this fellow on the filly out of his great friendship with him. Ruairí grinned and stroked the nervous chestnut brow. "I'm a little tired this morning, because I was up half the night taking Toby home. And I was looking at my new house."

The small man glanced up at the tall, curved wall of stone, roofed in slate and with the morning sun glinting on each new window. He had not connected the structure with the man in báinín and canvas, squatting on a stone in front of it. "That's yours? I took you for a native."

Now Ruairí looked straight at him, regardless of the sun. "I am. No one more so."

Thinking he had made a mistake in words, the man added "I mean a Papist. A Catholic."

"I am that, too. I could hardly forget my baptism so soon.".

Confusion in the hazel eyes gelled into suspicion, mixed with a good dose of rancor. "This I have to see," he said, and put heels to the filly's side.

Part of the horse's problem, besides the poor quality of her rider, was that she was in season, and so young as to scarcely know what that meant. But as she passed the black king she knew very well that the pony was a stallion, and he knew everything about her he needed to know. He made a suggestion she found outrageous and delicious and her response was a single squeal and a hop that left her rider crumpled on the ground at her shoulder. This was so frightening she ran away, dragging the reins, and the black king would have gone with her, but for Ruairí's restraining presence.

He stepped over to the man on the ground, not hurrying very much, and lifted his head and shoulders off the wet, boggy soil. The tall, shining hat was a loss, and he tossed it aside. "Too bad," he said. "She isn't a bad horse; her gaits are grand, but she's very green."

Grover came to his feet, his teeth chattering in anger. "And you're not, I guess!"

The fairy lowered his white lashes half over his strange eyes. "Green? Not by many, many seasons of experience," he said in puzzlement.

"That's not what I meant by 'green' and you know it."

"I do?" He laughed at the little madman and leaned indolently on his pony's shoulder.

"Damn well you do." Grover looked about him for his hat, and went partway to picking it up before he lost hope of it. "I know very well you made the beast do that to me, by what you put in her mouth."

"Then you know more than I do, man. What I put in her mouth was a finger, to save her from those torturing hands of yours. And I'm thinking we should go find her now, before she breaks her breedy neck with those reins, rather than . . ."

"I'm sure you would rather, *Mister* MacEibhir. But I am a servant of the Crown, and I am not going to chase crazy horses up the mountains when I see my work before me."

And he made for the front door of Ruairí's house, limping as he went.

With a last look at the road down which the filly had disappeared, Ruairí followed Grover. With a last, regretful sniff of the air, the black king followed Ruairí.

At the front door, which was of oak with a little pane of glass, Grover stopped and whistled. "This is almost a manor."

"It is as big as Seán Standún's house outside An Cheathrú Rúa," said Ruairí equably. "I had to make it so, so that his daughter would not feel too close here."

Grover gave him another hard look. "John Stanton's house I have already been to. He's a respectable man and has an excuse for a house this size." He put his hand on the long latch, and since there was no lock on the door, it opened to him.

"You are not welcome within," said Ruairí, still very calm.

"I don't have to be welcome with such as you," answered Grover, stepping into the white hall. "Agent of the Crown."

He walked up and down in the house and to and fro within it. He opened every door, including that of the pantry, which was already dusty. "Good carpentry," he grunted.

At last he came out into the sun again, where Ruairí was waiting. "All right. Where did you get the money for this sort of construction?"

Ruairí was leaning against the warm stone wall, one hand in his canvas pocket. He was long prepared for such a question, having been coached by Anraí. "There was very little money involved. The walls I put up myself, with the help of my kinsmen. In the carpentry I was aided by Turloch MacMaighion and his son, but I did not pay them in gold; rather, I am training their teams for them. The roof slates alone were bought by money, and that was something I inherited."

Grover glanced out the window at the long eave of slates. "Poppycock you inherited it. You're the servant of a little native stable keeper, and you're a nationalist."

Ruairí laughed aloud, as though there were no such thing as insult in the wide world. "I'm not sure that I am and I'm not sure that I'm not, for I have only the lightest idea of what a nationalist is. But Anraí Ó Reachtaire is not a stable keeper, and I am proud to act as his servant, for a while. That has no bearing on my own wealth or poverty."

"Raftery," mused Grover, and he scratched in his sideburn as though after a flea. "There's a man we have evidence on. Him and the Popish priest."

Ruairí put his weight evenly on his feet now and took his hand out of his pocket. "Who could have a thing to say against Anraí?"

Grover chortled. "The man's own son. Signed statement. What do you think of that?"

Ruairí erased all emotion from his face. "I wish I had him here."

"Oh, I'll bet you do. But we'll take care of him, don't you worry. We have a long arm to protect those who help us in our cause." Grover looked almost merry, and he slapped his hand against his thigh. He peered up from under his foxy hair at Ruairí, and there was new speculation in his eyes.

"Stanton has agreed to be helpful."

Ruairí frowned. "Do you think *he* is a nationalist?"

"No. But he has boats and that fine house of his. It's very hard to collect the tax in a primitive place like this, where half of all dealing is by barter. But it can be done. It *will* be done, but not in his case.

"You, too, could keep your house," added Grover, with an almost kindly smile.

"I expect to keep it."

"Then tell me about Raftery."

Very quietly, as though to insure secrecy, Ruairí stepped up to Grover as he stood in the doorway. His hand struck upward, and the force of his slap slammed the little man into the door, which rang.

Grover was stunned for the second time. He remained flattened against the door, with his eyes fixed on Ruairí, and his face was pale as a squid. "You fool," he whispered, and he put his hand to his broken lip. "You utter fool. Now you'll spend the rest of your life in chains, if I can't get you hung."

"For hitting you with my open hand?"

"Yes! An agent of the Crown." Grover sidled away and turned his face south, seeking his errant filly or other aid. The boggy fields were green and empty, with a gentle haze rising into the air. No one was along the road.

Ruairí's face was knotted in thought. "A life in chains for me and prison for Anraí and the priest, too? That's too bad for us. I prefer it to be too bad for you."

And as the little man glanced back in new alarm, he was grabbed by his fox-colored hair. Around each of Ruairí's brown-black eyes was a ring of white. He dragged Grover's head down to the level of his own belt and he raised a fist like a stone hammer above his head. He broke the man's spine and dropped him in a pile at the doorway. Then he stood still, staring at what he'd done.

The black king went up to him and nuzzled, wondering how Ruairí's face came to be sweaty. Ruairí leaned against him with his whole weight. "My friend, I fear that I have broken a vow," he whispered into the pony's ear.

In this season the water was very low, but there were still spots of open bog amid the drying turf. Ruairí MacEibhir, bearing his burden, came to a ruddy, acid pool, surrounded by clarkia and green violets. It reflected the sky as white, and made Ruairí into a giant. "Take this," said Ruairí. "Take him in and never give him back to the sight of men." He flung the limp body easily into the center of the water, for Grover was not heavy.

The white mirror broke with a splash, and Grover floated for a moment on his back, his slack face upward and his hazel eyes staring sightlessly up at the sun. Then he sank beneath the surface. Ruairí tossed the hat in after.

There was a sliding noise and a disturbance beneath Ruairí's feet, and then the mirror of day formed once again, and he stood beside the empty pool.

Tadhg Ó Murchú sat stunned, his head between his hands. "Dear God. Dear, dear God, it can't be true. Not murder."

Ruairí stood before him in the small, very private back parlor. "It was murder and my fault. This morning, it happened, but I couldn't get to see you until now."

Ó Murchú had heard the story in a hundred or so words, but he still shook his head against it, and his hands were over his ears.

"I have broken my vow, which I took only a few weeks ago."

Pain and puzzlement wrinkled the priest's smooth, round forehead. "Vow?"

"Not to kill. One of the ten."

Ó Murchú looked into the earnest, pleasant face across the table from him, and he tried to understand "murder." It seemed that could not be done. "You mean, you had a fight with this man Grover, and he died of injuries."

Ruairí almost smiled. "You might as well say I had a fight with a rabbit and it died of the injuries sustained. Grover was a little rabbit, or weasel, perhaps. I killed him to prevent his bringing trouble to all, forgetting I had vowed against it."

Ó Murchú sighed and sat upright, forcing his hands into his lap. At this moment he looked like a very old Welshman. "Trouble for whom?"

"For Anraí, and for you, and for myself, and even Seán Standún, whose foot . . ."

"Spare me!" cried Ó Murchú, slapping the table with his hand. "Spare me hearing that you murdered a man to save me trouble of any kind."

Ruairí shrugged against this blast. "I didn't. I wasn't thinking of you at all, Priest of the Parish, but of Anraí, who should not die in a black prison."

Ó Murchú flinched. "But . . ." His nails scratched across the varnish of the table. "What could Grover have had against Anraí?"

"A statement by his son that he was a nationalist criminal."

For a moment Ó Murchú just stared, and then he came to his feet in such a rush of fury that his chair spun backward against the hearth and cracked into the fireplace guard. His eyes were black slate. "Seosamh gave him that?"

"Not for free," replied Ruairí, and then fairness compelled him to add, "At least that is what I was told, by the weasel man. Usually I can tell if a man lies to me, but this one . . ."

Ó Murchú walked the confines of the little room. "And who else was mentioned, besides myself and Anraí and John Stanton?"

Ruairí scratched his neck and ruined his face with thought. "I remember no other names. It was not a long conversation." He watched the priest around the table.

"And the paper itself, that he had been given by Seosamh. Where is it?"

Ruairí's brow cleared. "I don't know. If it was on him, then it is now hidden in bog water, where it will not be found again."

"It wouldn't be on him." Ó Murchú returned to the table and sat down. He put his hands together and hid his face behind them and was quiet.

"What am I to do to redeem myself, if that can be done?" asked Ruairí.

"Sit down, for now. I don't know."

Very respectfully he did as told, for he knew the priest was talking to God. Ruairí himself had never spoken with anyone more exalted than the Dagda, unless it were the Tinker who had ridden him that once, and neither of these had been the sort to make him timorous. He folded his hands on the table, but if he prayed, it was only the prayer of patient waiting. He could hear the eight-day clock ticking above the mantle, very loudly.

When Ó Murchú took his hands away, his face was almost peaceful. "Ruairí," he said. "It may have been my fault. I baptized one who was not made for baptism, and put you under constraints you cannot understand."

"I know what it is to break an oath, Father."

"Hmm. But is that only a breach of honor, or do you feel a true horror at having taken life away from a man in the midst of his sin? Now, though you repent, how can he?"

The fairy groaned heavily. "It's true, Ó Murchú. I've known very few dead men who felt any repentance at all."

Ó Murchú shivered. "Have you known many dead men, then?"

Ruairí lifted his innocent, animal eyes. "Oh, certainly. Fairies and ghosts, you know, are much the same. For they die once and we a hundred times—we are taken back into the earth, but the earth spews us out again. It is our nature. But on the other side of the black door we are much alike."

"Other side of the black door? Do you mean heaven, hell, or just the grave, Ruairí?" Ó Murchú waited intently for the answer.

But Ruairí's unaccustomed soberness slipped off him. "None of these, Priest of the Parish! On the other side of the black

door is a world like this one, but in a mirror of the mind.
And like this one, it is not forever. My people die back, and
yours go onward. You know more about mine than I about
yours, and that, I think, is because yours came first."

Ó Murchú allowed himself to be distracted. "Yet yours are
called 'the ancient folk,' and it is you who live so long."

Ruairí smiled sweetly and sadly. "So I was taught, as a
rowdy boy, by a father high in pride of his lineage. But I have
run over the grass of this world a long time, and I believe
that you are the older and that we were only the mists given
by your dreams in the night."

The priest leaned over the round table and set his hand on
the other's. "You are not a mist, Ruairí."

"Hardly!" Ruairí sighed. "I am a Christian and a fool, and
what can I do to redeem myself from th murder? Shall I
give myself over to the Crown of which ˙his man was a
servant, and submit myself to their torments?"

Ó Murchú was not certain whether Ruairí was joking by
this offer, but his broad face, for once, had no shadow of fun
in it. "You should not, for it *would* be torment you received,
and you could not be sure you wouldn't break under it and
be used to convict your dearest friends."

"I wouldn't do that. I have been in the hands of my
enemies before, Tadhg."

"Forget it. Turning yourself in will do no one any good.
They may take you anyway, depending upon what this agent
has left in the way of evidence.

"Ruairí, I have prayed for guidance and I think I have
gotten it. I have a great penance for you, and it will take all of
your life—or at least a human life—to fulfill it. I know you
feel nothing toward the Gaelic people . . ."

"I feel no anger, anymore, at least," Ruairí interrupted.
"Though they burned my mother so bitterly she will not
come back to our birthland, and turned my father against the
world for these thousand years."

Ó Murchú touched his hand again. "I am sorry for that.
But those who killed her are dead and beyond dead, if I
understand you correctly. These folk around us now, in An
Cheathrú Rúa. Have you no feeling for them at all?"

Again the grin came up. "I like almost everybody I know.

And my Máire is half of their kind, too. How should I not like them?"

"Good. Then this is your penance and your redemption, Ruairí. I name you shepherd to the entire flock of them. With your knowledge, your back, and your courage, you must attend them and take care of them."

Ruairí braced his head on the heel of his hand. "Do you say again that I am to be everyone's dray horse in the parish?"

Ó Murchú smiled grimly. "At least that. And their teacher and their consolation, also. Father and mother to them all."

Ruairí remembered his own words to Toby, not twenty-four hours previously. "But isn't all of this what you are to them, Priest of the Parish? Would you have me wear a black cassock, like you?"

"White báinín will do," answered Ó Murchú, dryly. "And I will not be here to continue as mother and father to An Cheathrú Rúa much longer, I suspect. It is best to have another in training."

"And . . . may I have no life of my own, Tadhg? Must I sleep in the barns of others for forty years?"

Slowly Ó Murchú stood. This interview had tired him, and his laugh had an edge on it. "You mean Máire. Can you ask her to share her life with you, when you might be hauled in irons any day from now? For the man Grover was not such a fool . . . Who would care for her and for your babies, if you were hung by a rope? Could you issue out of the earth the next day and return to your duties as though it hadn't happened?"

Ruairí shrank into his chair. "I could not, in truth. Oh, woe! But in time this Crown shall give up sneaking around here and go home to England, or Dublin, or wherever it lives. Won't it?"

"I pray each evening that it will," said the priest.

After a fortnight Máire stopped wondering when Ruairí would next wait under her window, and then she began to get angry. She had known it, she told herself, watching the wind blow the moonlit curtains about her face. From the beginning she had made it clear to him that she understood he was only sporting with her, out for what fun he could find. It had been difficult, with his antique accent and his flights of poetry and his protestations of lasting love. But she must have understood him, inside, for she went on repulsing him when most of her soul wanted to give way to him. She herself had thought it her incurable sullenness, but in the end her sullenness had been proved right. Now she could enshrine that slimy, cold knowledge within her bosom. She had been right. Been right.

And where was he now? In the local, perhaps, playing the clown like young Seosamh Ó Reachtaire. Ó Reachtaire batted his blue eyes toward Eibhlín, and the girl was enough of a fool to bat hers back. Máire gave a glance toward her sister, who slept whole and blossoming and undisturbed. More beautiful than ever.

Máire lay down again and wrapped the thin quilt over her. She felt ugly and large and that people were pointing fingers at her.

Maybe he had found another girl to court and was standing as staunchly with his soft voice and broad shoulders in the shadows of *her* window. Telling her she was of fairy blood herself. (Was that a lie? Máire moved uneasily on her pillow. If one has to be a bastard, it was more pleasing to believe her father was a fairy than a butcher, a chandler, or a tramp.)

Or perhaps the fairy man was out over the meadows in horse form, dancing under the moon. Perhaps he had found a mare he preferred to Máire. He did so respect broodmares. This thought, which had begun as a bitter flight of fancy, swelled in her mind into horrible possibility.

She ought to confess the whole thing to the priest, except that the only priest around was Tadhg Ó Murchú. She would dearly have liked to tell Ó Murchú, too, but not at confession, and he would hear her at no other time.

What a terrible fate she had just barely escaped, being wed to a cheating fairy. An incubus! And how happy she should be that the temptation had at last passed her by. Máire hugged her happiness and her pillow to her breast, weeping soundlessly.

If James Blondell had no idea what had happened to Mr. Grover, Hermione had scarcely a doubt that seditionists had carried him off. She wrote as much to her sister in Kent, who was quite flurried by the news and pressed them all very strongly to come home for the duration of this unpleasantness.

She could not understand her husband's reluctance, considering that it was all their lives at stake. He, in turn, could not explain that a bailiff could not be expected to maintain the affairs of an estate of nearly five hundred acres, through the heart of summer and into autumn harvest. He could not explain as much to Hermione because bailiffs *did* maintain most of the Irish estates in much this fashion. But the thought of deserting his place and his people for so long made Blondell's heart beat erratically.

Besides, he was sure the filly had broken the man's neck. She came home looking the image of a horse that had tossed its rider, with reins snapped off under her feet and her saddle hung over her left shoulder. They had had to put her out to pasture again, for she was not ridable.

And besides again, James Blondell had a race coming.

A major had come with eight soldiers to investigate Grover's disappearance. They had destroyed the peace of Carraroe and gone again. One of them had been accused of trying to force a girl on the main road, and that had been a day's wonder and fury, but no lasting harm done. They had not found anything to account for the disappearance, or if they had, they hadn't told Blondell.

But two weeks now, and no one had found the body. Blondell thought about this all during breakfast, and afterward wandered up to the room where Grover had stayed, the two nights he had been with him.

It was a very nice room; Hermione had chosen it and supervised the readying of it herself. It was sparely furnished, with post bed, dresser, and desk of mahogany, but the wood was very good and the outlook was east, toward the ha-ha and the birch copse. One could see sheep. A man's room, and very pleasant in summer.

He sat himself in the light chair and looked out at the sheep, which was very restful. Why had he been so sure they in Dublin would send him a gentleman, a man he could speak to frankly and who would understand what one could do in questioning the locals and what must never be done? Of course it wouldn't be a gentleman doing this Paul Pry work for money. Grover had been (Blondell was certain he was dead) the sort of tool shaped to the purpose, but it was not an Irish west coast sort of purpose. Now the whole community was shut like a clam, against Blondell as much as Grover. He could not even be angry about it, but only very low.

He opened and closed the desk drawer idly, wondering that the man had left nothing behind him but his toiletry bag and a few shirts. Surely he had kept a notebook, for the bits of dirt he dug up.

Of course he had, and Blondell remembered seeing it in his coat pocket. It smacked against his side whenever he tried to sit the trot, and more than once his pencil had come popping out, to the terror of the horses. But that notebook and that pencil had vanished with the body.

If he were a detective, he considered, and he felt he were surrounded by danger, he would not carry all his information around with him, but would keep it in a place of safety. Insurance for it and for himself. Blondell cast an eye across the light-papered walls of the room.

Major Hous had looked already, with a pair of his men. But that didn't mean James Blondell couldn't look also. It was his house.

He searched the desk for hidden drawers, though he knew there were none. He turned the mattress and examined the pillows for rips. He pulled up the carpet. Annie, the upstairs maid, came to the door to ask him if he needed any help, and quite genially he sent her away again, locked the door, and returned to his treasure hunt.

While down on the floor, quite winded and with his hands smelling of mouse droppings from the carpet pad, Blondell noticed a black stripe on the wallpaper that was not part of the pattern. It was under the bed, and so he scuffled in after it, to find that a foot-long vertical section had been slit with a knife.

"Bastard!" he whispered, "ruining the paper in my own house." He wasn't angry, really, but as enthused as a boy.

He had to rip the paper slightly to get out what was stuffed under it. It was three sheets from the little notebook and a heavier sheet of foolscap. Blondell wiggled out from under the bed and returned to the desk, thinking as he brushed dust and cobwebs out of his hair that he had a perfect excuse to chide Annie about the state of things in the nether regions of this room. He would not, though, after having such fun poking about.

The notebook sheets he put on top and the larger sheet beneath them, face down, as a sort of sweet for the end of his reading. He held the notepaper against the direction of the light and bent his nose to it, for Grover's writing was very bad.

It was a list of names—surnames only, and spelled with originality. Cannaly, Mayon, Kelly, Raftery, Murfy, Handlin, Faygon, Maccrody, Stanton. Blondell read it again and then stared fixedly at the sheet, as though persistence would give it meaning.

Was it a list of people for questioning, gathered at random, from shop signs perhaps, or was it the heart and brain of the nationalist cabal that Grover had come to break? If so, it was useless as it stood, for there weren't so many surnames in the parish; he'd gotten at least half of them down here, and each name had a dozen or a hundred whole families under its aegis. Blondell bit his lip and put it aside.

The next slip had only one phrase scrawled on it, and it was difficult to read. "Priest to the Droylin, Kerry and France," it seemed to be.

"Droylin" would be "dreoilín," or "wren." But capitalized. Grover was an erratic penman, but Blondell remembered that James Stanton did have a hooker named *Dreoilín*. And France. That didn't sound good. Not at all.

Everyone knew that some of the agitators slipped in from France, and more than a few wanted men headed west as the first part of their escape from the authorities.

By priest, Grover could not mean Reverend Palmer. The notion that the Church of Ireland rector was helping spirit criminals in and out of Ireland was idiotic. The Catholics, since the death of old Father Mullin, had only Ó Murchú.

Blondell lifted his gaze out of the window, but he was not seeing the birches, or the backs of the drifting sheep. He remembered that closed, dark neat face listening and nodding and saying nothing. He had gone to Father Ó Murchú just this spring, when the mood in the town had begun to go sour. Had the priest been more help, he would not have been reduced to calling in a hound like Grover.

Blondell grunted and rapped his fingers against the beeswaxed surface of the desk. He went on to the third sheet and turned it up.

"I, Joseph Raftery, late of the . . ." and here something had been crossed out in black, "son of Henry Raftery of Knockduff by Carraroe, state that to my own present knowledge, my father has advocated the overthrow of the British government in Ireland and has both conspired and committed crimes in the interests of this cause."

Blondell read that much twice in astonishment and then sat stunned. Anraí, a green nationalist? And Blondell had not even known young Seosamh was back in Ireland. Or had Grover brought his paper with him, using Blondell's letter of request as pure pretext?

But the writing was identical to that on the notebook slips. Seosamh was not illiterate; why should he dictate to Grover, rather than write himself? Blondell continued reading.

"In the kitchen of the house I witnessed many times meetings in which the violent overthrow of the government was projected and means to that end discussed, as was the murder of certain prominent citizens . . ."

The words "certain prominent citizens" Blondell read again, and he felt his fingers growing cold. But no names were given.

"Present at these meetings were Tim Murphy, Catholic priest of the parish, Rory MacEever, and Donald Sheel, grooms to my father, and sometimes others, such as Timothy Keene of Maam Cross and Bert Shannasy, tailor of Carraroe.

"My mother, Anne Raftery, was not in any way involved."

This line was scrawled in between two others and in another, broader hand. Blondell smiled in scorn, and aloud he said, "Where was she then, Joe—hiding in the barn? Your house is not that big."

It was not a long document, as betrayals go. It only covered one side of one page. The signature matched the line that had been squeezed in, rather than the body of the writing. It might well be Joe Raftery's.

The document didn't mention any murders, but then of

course one couldn't expect Grover to predict or design his own. If he was murdered.

If there was a word of truth in the lot.

Blondell slipped the papers into the drawer of the desk, and he tried to think. He thought about Anraí and the image of two horses came to him, a red one and a grey one. He thought about Ruairí MacEibhir and he saw Toby's face and nothing more.

Blondell closed the drawer and locked it. He rose, moving very stiffly, and he left the room, locking that door behind him also. He took both keys with him.

CHAPTER FOURTEEN

A Great Victory and a Great Loss

Though it was high June, it was raining on the day that Blondell sent his red stallion back to Anraí's stable, to make ready for the challenge race. A small and very active man by the name of Colm MacCadhain came with it as jockey and to care for the horse for the day and a half before they were to run.

"Does he think we'd damage him?" asked Donncha, with a disgusted twist of the mouth.

"I don't know," answered Ruairí, who lay flat out on the hay with his eyes open, a position in which he found himself very frequently of late. "Would we?"

Colm had a similar cause to be offended. "Do you think I'd do your fellow some harm, like put a pin up his sole or blow opium up his nose, that you have to hide him from me? Here's the Imperator for all to see, and I've never glimpsed the hide of your racehorse."

Anraí smiled indulgently as he stroked the chestnut's neck. "You have at some time, Colm. I'm sure of it. But he's being kept on the mountain and won't be down till Donncha brings him tonight. Then you'll see."

"You'll race a horse straight off the grass? Anraí Ó Reachtaire, you're too old a hand for that. You're pulling a trick."

Anraí was instantly offended, since in a sense he *was* pulling a trick. "You'll have to wait and see, Colm MacCadhain. And don't worry, for you'll have a good sight of his back end all the way from here to An Cheathrú Rúa."

*   *   *

Anraí, Donncha, and Ruairí strolled out that early evening, after the rain had stopped. The grass was high and silvery, and stepping on it filled the air with green scent.

"What have you been doing for training, Ruairí my son?" asked the old man, slapping Ruairí in a proprietary manner. "Short bursts? Have you been practicing the course?"

Donncha chuckled. "Almost every night he flings himself into An Cheathrú Rúa and back. What could be better practice?"

Ruairí yawned. "I haven't done that for quite a while, Donncha." He rubbed his face with both hands.

Anraí's easy confidence began to shake. "But they've been running the red on sand and road surface every day for weeks. Do you expect to go against him without conditioning?"

They were over a hill and hidden from house and barn. Ruairí sat himself down and yawned again. "I've been training by piling stones on fence walls. By digging holes in the earth. By creeping into cottages without waking the inhabitants."

Donncha looked at him without expression. "I think, Anraí, that this one has suddenly remembered he's a fairy. But he's supposed to knock down the walls, not build them up."

Ruairí laughed. "It would be easier. But it's something I promised the priest."

He glanced at Anraí. "Shall I run from here to An Cheathrú Rúa and back right now, to please you?"

Anraí cleared his throat. "Too late for that, boy. Either you're in shape or you're not. But you seem certain enough you can beat the stakes winner."

"I am. No horse will pass me unless I choose him to."

Anraí started. "Unless you . . ." He fell on one knee in front of Ruairí. "Are you telling me that you intend to fairy cheat this race, Ruairí MacEibhir?"

Ruairí blinked in surprise. "Well the fact that I'm in it makes it a fairy cheat, doesn't it?"

"But . . ." Anraí clenched a small fist between them. "But you will run it fairly and win it fairly."

Ruairí only stared. "Or lose it fairly," he said at last.

"Then so be it." Anraí sat down, for he was suddenly tired. "Only, I wish I had known you were uncertain before I bet what I have bet."

Ruairí nudged him. "I am, Anraí. I am certain. I was just sporting with you."

But Anraí wouldn't turn, and Donncha's face was doubtful. "Enough sport, Ruairí. The racing of horses is a sacred matter. Convert yourself now, so I can trim you, for I don't want to be riding a sloppy pony."

"You won't be," said Anraí, rising again. "For I'm doing the riding."

"He can't!" Áine dropped the bowl on the flagstones of the kitchen floor, where it broke into very small pieces.

"He will, he says," answered Donncha. "And I have no means of budging him, though I reminded him that Blondell has hired a jockey. He said only that it is Blondell's way to hire people and his own way to ride horses. And that he is smaller and lighter than I am."

"And older," said Áine. "Much, much older." She put her hand on the tin-topped kitchen table, to hold herself up. Donncha found her a chair.

As Colm MacCadhain slept beside his stallion, so Anraí Ó Reachtaire, in the far barn, spread a blanket on the hay beside the grey. He felt fine, in fact stronger than he had for months, but he could not find sleep. At last he opened his eyes to moonlight and found Ruairí, not the horse, leaning over the stall door and watching him.

"Tomorrow is a dangerous day for you, old man," said the fairy.

Anraí flung the blanket off. "I know that. I may be a fool, but I'm not a blind fool. But do you think I will be in any more danger on your back than standing at the line in An Cheathrú Rúa, straining all the tendons of my heart waiting?"

Ruairí shifted and settled his head on his arms. "I don't think you will be. But the danger is there, either way."

"I know it. Now go to sleep." He heard the sound of hooves on the clay floor as he wrapped himself up again.

It was bright but drizzly on the morning of the race, and ten degrees colder than it had been for all the month of June.

"Fast weather," said Donncha, as he put the light saddle on the grey horse's back.

Anraí glanced around a sparkling horizon of grass. "Weather to break a leg." Anraí's face was calm, and the wrinkles of ill health and weariness had vanished. His color was high and his blue eyes very clear.

Colm needed Donncha's help with the chestnut, for the nerves of the company had infected him, as well as the sheen of the silks Colm wore (for he was a professional, working on the Galway track). The short jacket was orange and green, Blondell's colors, and so rarely had it been used that it bore a phantom checkering of bright lines, from the years folded.

Áine, holding an umbrella, stood in front of the picket fence, where her peas were now in royal bloom, and in her white and scarlet (Anraí's colors) she stood with the dignity of a queen, and no one, not even Donncha, knew she had been weeping half the night.

Maurice the hosteler stood beside her, for it was his job to start the race, and that would give him grist for the mill of his profession for weeks to come. He danced from foot to foot in the cold. Áine's gig with the dun cob was tied to a post, waiting for the two of them and Donncha to follow.

The grey horse stood still under his slight rider, while Donncha led the chestnut to the house drive, with a hand-kerchief blindfolded over his eyes. "God with me, I'm in trouble," said Colm cheerfully, patting the sweating shoulder. "I only hope I can turn his madness toward An Cheathrú Rúa."

Anraí pressed his horse as close to the other as he dared. "Lower your stirrups, Colm lad. You will need a deep seat with him more than you need to ride lightly. And don't let your firm hand become a restraint, for that one will not go forward without a free head."

The jockey burst out laughing. "It's likely I'll follow your advice, isn't it, Anraí? And you my only competition."

Anraí remained serious. "You should. I trained that beast, as much as he is trained, and it's my own back that ached learning what I tell you for free. And he will do best on the roads, for his action is very low and his strength is on the flat."

Colm now had two minutes of war with Imperator, but he rode him down very well and soothed him at the end.

"Whereas you will charge through bogs and up hills, Anraí?" he said, meaning irony.

"Likely I will." Anraí moved the grey, whom he simply could not think of as Ruairí, away to the line now, for he felt he had done enough for his opponent. But he was glad that he had spoken. His own magnanimity made him feel like a hero, and the clean wind was heady. He spied the ramrod shape of Áine, and he bent to her.

"Áine NíhAnluain, my love, look at me! Isn't it ridiculous, a bundle of bones like myself . . . ?"

"You look like Bonaparte himself, Anraí." And to his surprise and embarrassment she took his left hand from the reins and kissed it, banging his shoulder with the umbrella, and then she kissed the nose of the horse. "Go with God, my old man!"

"Now," said Maurice, when the two horses were even at the line scratched in the gravel. "This is a steeplechase (as though you could sight any steeple in An Cheathrú Rúa from here). So you may take whatever road, path, trail, stream bed, or bank of fog which will get you to the street in front of the Brown Pot first. For I have to tell you the priest has refused permission for us to use his church as finish line.

"What you may not do is interfere with each other or each other's horse in any way. And it is no purpose of this race to do a beast damage, and Diarmuid Ó Cadhain will be at the other end to look them over, and if there is mark of blood from the lungs or from the whip, you'll be disqualified and all the bets go to the other."

Anraí glared at Colm. "Don't abuse that horse!" he said rudely, for he was getting too excited to think about manners. Colm, who was innocent of such thought, sparked in answer. "Indeed, I think it's you who ought to have that warning, for distance at speed will drive that heavy pony of yours into the ground!"

"Enough," called Maurice blandly, though he enjoyed and memorized every acrimonious word. He wiped the increasing rain out of his eyes. "Save your energy for the ride; it's a long one." Maurice had worn a waistcoat so that he might draw out his watch from it and so he did. It lacked thirty seconds of ten o'clock. He put his hand up into the air and held it there.

"God keep you both. Or all four of you," he added. Fifteen seconds.

Áine's fingers on the umbrella shaft were losing feeling, she was holding to it so tightly. Donncha ceased from destroying his ragged thumbnail. Five seconds. Rain had turned the chestnut to a bay and the grey almost black.

Maurice's hand snapped down and hit his thigh. There was a moment of quiet, as though nothing were going to happen after all. As though the horses would sit there under their riders and the day would pass without sound or motion but that of the rain.

Then, together, the horses were off, the red with its head thrown to the sky and the grey roaring. Áine gasped, and the gravel of the drive scattered like a shower amidst the falling rain.

Colm was all amazement at the speed his mount was turning, for he had assumed that Imperator was a spoiled, retired horse of a few races. But he was only a jockey of the Galway tracks, and the red horse had run at Newmarket, and won. He was far more amazed, though, that the grey was keeping up with him. Anraí and he were together, like friends out for a Sunday canter.

"This isn't a sprint, you know," he called to the old man. "I think you'd better rate your horse."

"It's you who had better do that, Colm," answered Anraí, and he laughed. The grey was easy to ride, and Anraí gave him his rein. His rating was his own business, for Ruairí was no youngster. Anraí did indeed feel like a man out for a Sunday ride in good weather, for he didn't even feel the rain that hit his ruddy face.

The drive met the road south of Knockduff, but Ruairí had no intention of staying on it that long, for it added at least two miles to the distance. With a grunt of warning for his rider, he leaped the ditch on the right-hand side of the road and took off through what seemed to be all bog, toward a ridge of steep hills.

Imperator was thrown off his stride by this, for he knew what a race was, and in a race the horses run in the same direction. He whirled, and Colm was almost unseated. He cursed himself for ignoring Anraí's advice about the stirrups. It took him a minute or more to get the stallion moving in the direction he wanted. "Do I need to use the crop on you already, lad?" he asked aloud, and gave him a light tap on the flank.

The horse threw himself forward then, at full tilt, and after Colm was sure the fireworks were over he took a feel of the bit. "Oh, my sweet love," he whispered, for he might as well have been pulling against a post of iron. "Someone here really is in trouble."

There were no fences on the bare hills north of the bay, but the boulders and puddles of standing water made up for them. The horse settled into a strong canter as soon as he had left the road, and Anraí wondered whether the show of madness at the beginning had only been for the purpose of upsetting Imperator's delicate mind. He could not call that fairy cheating, however, for horses of more ordinary nature did it all the time.

The long water jumps were exhilarating, and Anraí could not resist giving the horse some help, if only verbal. "Don't place so close, lad," he called as close to the outstretched head as he could reach. "If you go down into the water it'll slow us remarkably. Nor do you need to arc as high as all that; water don't rise up to bite you."

Already they were down the slopes around Knockduff and climbing the ridges. The horse charged the first one, going half up as he veered around. Uphill was no slower than the straightaway for this horse, and the muscles of his very wide hocks shone round, dark, and shining under the rain.

"That was a waste!" shouted Anraí in disapproval. "One foot upward is worse than five feet on the flat. Go around next time."

Next time came very quickly, and obediently the horse kept to the low point between the ridges. But this was the bed of a stream paved in large, round rocks, and as Anraí chanced to look down, he gasped and closed his eyes.

The grey splashed and grunted and still he was galloping. As they left the stream bed he stumbled, very slightly, but Anraí felt it and he cursed the horse for a fool.

The next ridge was very steep and it sparkled with granite,

but it fitted neatly into round hills on either side, and having come this way, they had no choice but to go over.

The thrust of the quarters pushing the horse's body up and forward was so strong that Anraí was on the edge of losing his seat. He feared also that the saddle might slide, and so he balled the reins in his hands, grabbed two handfuls of mane, and leaned forward, laughing that an old hand like himself would stoop to this beginner's trick. And the horse came on almost as fast as on the smooth drive, but blowing and grunting with every push.

"Don't do yourself an injury, lad," murmured Anraí, for he began to worry about this. Never in his life had the old man ridden a horse to damage, and he was fond of this fairy, both horse and man.

At the top of the ridge the wind hit them and Anraí coughed. The way down was steeper than the way up, and in a few seconds the horse had begun to slide. Down it crouched on its hocks, and Anraí leaned far back, giving most of his reins away. Down the hill they came, sliding and hopping, and at the bottom the grey was covered up to the chest with spattered mud.

To the south and below them was the tip of Cashla Bay and the tiny town of Casla, with the road winding through it. The grey horse heaved forward again and galloped over churned earth and rock toward it.

As they came nearer, even Anraí could see the speck of red that turned into the chestnut stallion, with Colm on him. One glimpse and Anraí knew the horse was riding without control.

They leaped the road ditch once more, and Imperator was remarkably close behind. Only a hundred yards separated the horses, and as Imperator saw or smelled the grey horse again in front of him he screamed and charged forward.

"By Jesus, that's a sweet-running animal," said Anraí to the grey. "I am proud of my hand in him, and I hope that he doesn't fall dead on the road here or kill young Colm." The grey put his ears back and his gallop grew a bit rougher.

"But we're going to beat them, my son," added Anraí very quickly, and he smiled at the touchiness of horses. Or of fairies.

*   *   *

When Eibhlín had told Máire about the challenge race, Máire had had no doubts concerning the grey horse Anraí would be riding. Nor did she doubt Anraí would win. And a voice within her said that Ruairí had been in training, and was why he had not been to see her these two weeks. Now he would be back. She shouted the voice down, because she had a great fund of common sense, and she knew that training for a race from Knockduff to Carraroe does not prevent a horse running from Knockduff to Carraroe. Besides, it didn't matter. She was well rid of him.

But she never considered missing the end of the race. When the lookout rang the bell that meant that a horse had reached Lochán an Bhuilín, she was across the street from the hostelry, wearing her best petticoat and breathing hard.

Back on the road, Anraí felt no strain, nor did the horse under him seem to be suffering. The wind beat on his face, though, and at times it made him cough. He remembered Ruairí's full name: Rory son of Granite out of Wind, and he wondered that a body's own mother might blast against him in this manner. Better if she were blowing behind his tail.

But behind his tail was not wind but the chestnut stallion, and he was coming up fast and smooth, throwing his legs forward only an inch above the roadway and making pebbles scatter. A glance over his shoulder revealed to Anraí the red neck, not crested but stiff and straight as a board of oak, and the wire bridoon tearing unnoticed through the corners of the stallion's long, black mouth.

Anraí cried loudly, "Are you in control at all, Colm?"

"Not a bit of it," screamed the jockey.

Then the red's nose was even with the grey's long, whipping tail, and still he came on. Suddenly Anraí's soaring mood failed him, and he was in a fury that he would lose this race. "They're taking us, lad," he called to the horse, and he raised his empty hand to hit him, not having a crop.

That hand never finished the motion, for with a grunt more like that of a pig than a horse, the grey horse gathered his quarters under him and sprang low and long, over the ditch again and onto the very broken ground of the peninsula. As he ran he screamed like five stallions put loose into the same box.

Anraí was confused. He took a tentative feel of the mouth, to which the horse responded by bending his neck nicely, but not checking speed. "Ruairí, Ruairí, surely the road is the clearest and shortest way from here!"

The grey horse gurgled in his throat and bounded on over the scree.

Colm had ridden so long in vain effort to rate his stallion, that he hadn't the strength to stop him when it bellowed its answer to the challenge, shied off the road, and flew the ditch. Onto the rubbled ruin of the coast it climbed, and at its first step it hit a forehoof against a rock, stumbled, and almost went down.

Through this maze of sharp rock and sinkholes the grey horse cantered with all four legs bent and muscles bunching. The rain had let up, but the horse was blacker still with its own sweat. His head no longer stretched forward but was at the vertical, with the veins on its face like tree roots and its neck muscles pressed out against the slick hide. Anraí felt the steam rising from his horse's effort, and he leaned back in the saddle, so not to get in his way. It was not a terribly fast progress, for the horse placed every leg with care.

The cottages of the coastline appeared, with their stone-fenced acres stretching toward the bay and the ocean. The grey horse took the fences in the same rounded form, and Anraí did not try to interfere.

There was a child's shout as they passed over the garden of a cottage, jumping the beds. Ten feet from the door they passed, and Anraí had a glimpse of a woman's oval face peering out, with her mouth a perfect circle of wonder. Over the next wall, and Anraí could hear more shouts marking the passage of the red stallion behind them. He doubted that horse had thought to leap the potatoes.

Here, north of Lochán an Bhuilín, the cottages were clustered more tightly, and they had a rabbit's run, popping fence after fence. The grey horse shied once, much to Anraí's surprise, and a man rose up behind them from where he had been weeding, cursing them in a voice shrill with terror.

This was the same route he had taken on his first ride on the horse, which, like this one, had been out of Anraí's control. But this time they were running closer to the east and the road, for Carraroe was straight along. "What will you do now, lad, jump the whole lake or wade through it?"

It nodded its pony head, as though considering those alternatives, but at the edge of the water it turned left and ran the black rocks of the bank, shooting flint sparks into the air. It took the five-foot embankment smoothly and came back to the road.

Colm was aghast at how the chestnut was making himself suffer. The fences were no problem for it, but the stoney fields were deadly. They had stumbled a half dozen times and once gone down on one knee, but still the horse kept the bit and flung on. At the shores of the lake it slowed, scenting the air for its vanished opponent.

"To the road, fellow," shouted Colm, and he turned the horse and took the leap at the same place Anraí had, only seconds before.

And now the grey was visible in front, only fifty yards away. But there was no more than a quarter mile to go in the race, for Colm could see the church ahead, and milling people beyond it. He gave the stallion the second stroke of the crop that day.

"Dear God, they're catching us again," whispered Anraí. "That horse isn't human!"

The chestnut's legs were dark with blood and his lips dripped blood and its eyes were glassy. Too weary to scream again, it threw its long legs forward and came on.

There were so many people. There is no horse race in Ireland that will not draw a crowd, but Anraí hadn't suspected that his challenge to Blondell would cause such an event. That must have been Maurice's doing.

The gap was shrinking between the riders. On the road, the grey could not win. Anraí recognized this, knowing horses, and his eyes stung with love and pity for both animals.

"It's all right, my son," he said to the grey, and he stroked the hot neck lightly.

The horse made a spitting noise and Anraí was almost flung from the saddle by its bound forward. The advance of the red horse slowed.

Here was the first grocer, and the streets were lined with watchers who cheered, for whom Anraí did not know or care. There was one that looked like Seosamh, but Anraí paid him no mind.

Now passed the church, and Ó Murchú was there, small and neat in his black with his black hair. He lifted a hand.

Colm struck the stallion for the third time, and the two horses were neck and neck. Vaguely he noted then that the grey was a good hand shorter than the chestnut, and shorter still in the leg.

To the watchers by the line Maurice had stretched across the road, the noise of their approach was overwhelming, the pounding of the grey's hooves and the clatter of the red's shoes and the groaning, bellows breath of both. They cheered and whistled to make the sound more tolerable, but still all flattened themselves against the buildings as the horses galloped by.

Diarmuid Ó Cadhain, standing at the line with James Blondell and his son next to him, saw the nose of the grey horse and the nose of the chestnut pass over the line and not a shade of difference between them. An instant later, the great chest of the grey flew by in front of the chestnut, for the chestnut had the longer neck.

Ó Murchú stepped back, dark browed and thoughtful, for he was not certain if it had been a perfect tie or the grey had won. He heard the half-frightened cries of people vacating the street ahead, lest they be trampled by the backwash of the race. He heard a scream more piercing, and he lifted his head again.

The grey horse had obeyed Anraí's rein very willingly and was already trotting slowly, almost in place. Sweat poured from his forehead down his nose. The chestnut had run by, and with the competitor now behind him, he answered the rein with his ripped mouth. From a canter he stopped still, and all could see his heart pounding through his ribs, belly, and hide. Colm opened his hands with a whimper of pain, for his gloves were shredded and his hands as bad as the horse's mouth.

For only a moment the chestnut stood there, legs braced, and then it gasped, lifted its head to the sky, and crumpled. Its hind legs went first and then its front. Colm felt the collapse too late; he screamed as the horse pinned him to the ground.

Anraí threw his leg over and leaped from the saddle, whereupon he fell flat on the road. Crawling and scrabbling he climbed to his feet and ran with deadened legs.

Blondell was already there with two other men, and they heaved against the huge red back and worked the jockey free. "My leg," he said, teeth clenched. "It's just my leg; I'm all right. See to the poor beast."

But Blondell's stakes winner was dead on the road, the bit hanging limp on its swollen tongue. Blondell picked up the long, gaunt head and knelt before it.

"Oh, no. Oh, no, Imperator. You've killed yourself. You burst your heart on the race." No one else was meant to hear the words, but Toby was there and Anraí Ó Reachtaire knelt beside.

"Is he dead?" asked the old man. "Is the great fellow really dead, then?" Blondell glanced over to see Anraí's face, white and mottled, and his eyes swimming with tears.

"Alas! I would so much sooner have lost than that this should happen." He put his hand on the other man's shoulder. "You were right, a Shéamais. He was the grandest horse in Connemara, and mine is but a pony who outtricked him on the road."

Blondell turned his eyes away, though not out of anger. He found his son was crying like old Raftery, and he began to blink himself. "Colm, why did you let him do this?" he asked, in a whisper that grew into a shout.

"Hush, a Shéamais. It wasn't poor Colm's fault. It was Imperator's race and he took it. He couldn't be turned or rated."

"You might have been able to," said Blondell flatly. He closed the red horse's staring eye.

"Not me. Not even Ruairí MacEibhir. If pain will not turn them, a man's strength certainly can't."

Blondell winced, and he nodded, and he put the horse's head down. "What about your pony, Anraí? Shouldn't you be walking him?"

Anraí snorted. "Oh, he'll take care of himself." But he rose up, feeling very lightheaded. He walked back to the grey, who hadn't moved all this time, and he put a hand to the soaked shoulder. "Well, we won, my pack pony, my native horse." And the horse put his black nose to Anraí's forehead.

There was a small circle of people around Anraí, afraid to
cheer or to shake the man's hand while the dead horse lay in
the road with its master mourning beside it. Anraí looked at
them as though he didn't know why they were there, and
then Tadhg Ó Murchú stepped through, wearing his cassock.

"Sit down, Anraí. You don't look so good," he said. Anraí
tried to smile at him, but as the priest touched him he went
down like the horse and lay in the dirt with his legs under
him. A woman gave a long, warbling wail.

Ó Murchú's left hand was under Anraí's neck, and Toby
Blondell, at Ó Murchú's command, straightened his knees.
To the priest's dismay, Anraí's face was turning blue. Someone shouted for a doctor, as though one of the poor peasants
gathered round might suddenly turn into one. Ó Murchú
performed the sacrament for his friend, whispering, and without any oil. Anraí's floundering hand interrupted him.

"Tell Áine," he said, though he had no breath. "Tell Áine
that I would have waited for her if I could." Then he dropped
his hand on his chest and stared at the sky with his blue eyes
until the priest closed them.

Ó Murchú bent over his friend's face and kissed him. Then
he stood upright, neat, black, and secret, as always. "He is
gone from us," he said to the crowd. "Our brother Anraí is
gone. Give him your prayers."

When Áine drove in, she seemed to know before, and she
stopped the gig in the quiet street where none of the people
were talking, and she walked into the church where they had
laid him. "Oh, old man, old man," she said, and she sat
down on the pew next to him and put his head on her lap.
"Farewell to forty bright years," she said to the closed eyes,
and her own eyes were dry. "Never was there better sweetheart or husband along the coast than you, my angry old
man, and if it were mine to choose, I'd follow you now."
Then she reached under his shirt and took out a sweat-
stained halter of rope, which she slipped down her own
white blouse.

Outside in the street Maurice asked about the grey horse,
who, by surviving, had won the race from Knockduff to
Carraroe. Then all the bystanders looked up and down, for

when Anraí fell, no one had had an eye to spare. Máire Standún walked over to the last place it had been seen.

Down at the dirty slope of the street by the hostelry was lying the saddle, with the girth still buckled. The bridle was in a heap nearby.

Seosamh Ó Reachtaire sat at the deal table in Seán Meighian's house and wondered whether he was going to join his mother in the church.

It was a complex question, and in front of him was a mug of poitín to mull it over with him. Seán himself was at the hostelry, along with half of Carraroe, digesting in company the great race and the losses it had entailed. Seosamh felt a dull resentment that he could not join them, being the bereaved and therefore one of the most salient objects of discussion. He would wish to be alone, they knew. His circle of good friends (who never had been his friends before he went into the army and came out again) would be much happier without him to restrain their humors. And their speculation.

Rain beat against the shutters, and Seán's house was very damp. Seosamh filled his mouth with poitín and let the stuff sit there, so that at least his breath might be warm.

The church would not be warm, and the rainy walk of almost a mile would not be warm, and his coat of rewoven British wool would soak through. Báinín was better for getting wet, but Seosamh was long past the wearing of báinín. Or of uniforms.

Half the women of Carraroe would be sitting with his mother, just as half the men would be at the bar. Seosamh would feel like such a fool to be sitting with the women.

But if he went to condole with the old woman, then he could stop at the hostelry on his way back, for everyone would understand he would need bucking up after the ordeal. And once they heard where he had been, there would be no more talk about Joe Raftery's being heartless about his own family. The men who bet on his father's grey would buy him drinks.

Seosamh had watched the race, and he could not be his father's son without knowing something about horses. He had been surprised the stocky grey had taken the Thoroughbred, and could only attribute it to a hidden weakness of the horse that died. Or to gross mismanagement. Or . . . the chestnut had been stabled at Anraí's over the night, hadn't it? Plenty of time to do a damage to it, and who better than Seosamh's ugly little father to know how?

Another swallow of the liquor gave him a warmth of inspiration, and it came to Seosamh that the grey horse of his father's was *his* grey horse now. And so, for that matter, was all the stable, for he was Anraí's only heir.

This put matters on a different footing and warmed the air of Seán's cottage by at least ten degrees. Seosamh began to shift the gears of his thinking, from those suitable for a poor man to those suitable for one with funds.

It would be important to sell the grey horse quickly, while it still had its reputation as a miracle. The rest of the stock could wait for good prices, for he didn't want anyone in the county to suspect it was a desperation sale, to cover certain debts.

As would happen, if the men of his regiment found out where he was. But in a few weeks the regiment was leaving for Afghanistan (which was one of the reasons he had chosen to depart from it), and Seosamh would then have a good padding of time and space.

The black stallion of his father's he would keep, to ride—a gentleman's horse.

But what, his next swallow asked him, if his father had left the property to his mother or in her care for her life? Jesus, but it was cold in here. Well, Seosamh had always been much bigger with his mother than his father, and no doubt she would be glad to put the lines in his hands.

In that case, however, it would really be the thing to do to go to the church, and then tomorrow he would ride to the stable beside her in the gig, very officially.

Resolved at last, Seosamh put his hands to the table so that he might rise. So cold was it that he scarcely felt the board beneath his fingers. He stood up.

And then sat back down again, for his balance was totally gone and so were the contents of the mug.

"Sorry, old woman," he said aloud. "The cards fell out against you." He folded his arms and lay his head upon them. Just before he fell asleep smiling, he remembered that on another night, drunk as this one, he had signed a sort of document for an Englishman named Grover. And Grover was gone and no one knew where. Perhaps the document was gone, too. Perhaps not. Seosamh's mind was on this document when he did fall asleep, and he was not smiling.

It was the same evening, and James Blondell and Toby had returned from their small vigil with Áine and had stopped on the way home and had a drink with the men. They had gone in together, and Toby had downed his like a man in honor of his old teacher and (and this was what made Blondell very proud) the horse that had won the race. And Hermione had been sound about it, because she was sound at bottom, and had dismissed the importance of neither the dead man nor the dead horse, or even lectured about the unadvisability of putting drink in front of a young boy.

Dinner had been subdued, but very welcome after the trials of the day. He had glanced at his mail, including one more letter from Major Hous, and put it all aside unopened. Now Blondell took his humidor and smoking rack under his arm and donned a quilted robe with very worn elbows. Instead of going to his library with his treasures, however, he went up the stairs and unlocked the door of one of the unoccupied bedrooms.

In the drawer of the writing table he found the suspicious little sheets of paper and the larger, incriminating one.

He took a lucifer from the tall container on the rack and lifted out the amber glass ashtray. The document of Seosamh Ó Reachtaire he rolled into a cylinder, and he struck the lucifer against the roughstone inset on the rack. The light of the energetic match overcame the last rays of this longest day of the year and turned the window in front of him into a mirror.

In that mirror he saw himself lit from below: a sorcerer over his brews. A round-faced and thin-haired sorcerer, he qualified, who had drunk good port after dinner. He lit the cylinder and put it upright, torch fashion. As it burned down, he twisted it and turned it, and still he had to light two more matches before it was all ash, powdered over the glass of the ashtray. When that was done he took the list of misspelled surnames and made a tent of it and lit that.

CHAPTER FIFTEEN

The Game Is Up

Donncha was hauling grain out to the mares that ran out on the high meadows with their babies. This had not been done yesterday and he wished fervently that he didn't have to do it today, for he was sick tired and because of his work, would miss the wake tonight. As he walked he banged himself into the side of the cob repeatedly, for that animal was trying to go in circles, having more interest in the oat-filled sacks on his back than in the job at hand. Now he hit against Donncha's side so smartly that the man lost his footing for a moment and only kept himself upright by hanging to the cob's halter.

In his irritation he raised his hand to slap the beast back, but he thought of Anraí, with his bad health and bad temper, who never hit a horse out of anger. Never even felt the temptation. So Donncha put his hand back and felt very low.

One man could not do all this work. Where was Ruairí MacEibhir?

Donncha reached the fence of poles and wire, anchored into the old stone wall. They had heard him coming, and here were a half dozen tall mares with tall babies waiting in a row, and twice that number of ponies and their offspring in a circle around them. The cob greeted all that feminine beauty, but was ignored, for Donncha was quick to spill the grain onto the grass beside the fence, in a thin line fifty feet long, so the big ones could pig it all.

This was usually Ruairí's job, by choice. But the fairy was

gone like a ... like a fairy, and perhaps that was all the explanation necessary. Came with Anraí and went with him. By that Donncha had meant "went at the same time as him," but hearing the thought ring through his tired head, Donncha felt a shiver in his bowels. Went with him.

And what was to happen to them all now: the mares and the babies, the stallions and the hunters and the pack ponies, and Áine's cow and Áine in the empty house and Donncha himself in the barn? God with us all, thought Donncha, the kingpin of our carriage is broken. "Anraí Ó Reachtaire is dead!" he shouted to the mares. "The old man who kept us all is dead!"

The dun cob rumbled and danced sideways, and the mares and babies lifted their heads for a moment, for Donncha had spoken loudly.

It was such a lovely day. It seemed to Donncha MacSiadhail that it was always a lovely day after someone was dead, and the more mourned and valued the someone, the brighter the weather. It was known that the sea was as tender as a lover whenever it had taken men the day before.

"It isn't worth it," he said, leading the cob back down the hill. Now the problem was trying not to be run over by the beast as it worked its way down the slope with its empty bags. "I'll take our dirty Connemara weather in preference." He shook his fist at the glorious sky.

In answer came a circular, indolent wind that kissed his bitter lips and closed his eyes for him. Donncha sighed, and the cob shuffled to a stop.

Perhaps he could turn the stalled horses out until after the burying tomorrow. All but the black Thoroughbred stallion, who could jump too well for his own good and who would have to be either ridden or lunged every day. Donncha wasn't thinking any further than the burying.

Down below him were the two stables and the great paddocks and the hay barn, their damp slate roofs all shining in the sun. Beyond them all was the house. At this season, its grey walls were hidden behind masses of Áine's ragged robin and her yellow Chinese roses. Something was moving at the doorway. Not a horse.

*   *   *

Donncha loosed the cob in the near paddock and approached Seosamh still holding the halter rope in his left hand and with the pack saddle canted over his right shoulder.

The young man looked bad. His face was pasty and blue underneath his tan and he stood with his eyes down and knees stiff, as though he found it a lot of work to stand up.

Those unhappy eyes raised up in anger at Donncha's short "God to you." He waited, but the groom said nothing more, only standing with the saddle and waiting. Seosamh did not notice that Donncha's color and attitude were no brighter than his own. "Aren't you going to say you're sorry for the loss of my father, man?"

Donncha's weariness hardened. He put the saddle down over the top bar of the little garden fence. "I myself have lost so much with the passing of Anraí Ó Reachtaire, lad, that I'm beyond offering consolation to . . . to others."

"You've lost more than you think, boyo." Seosamh met Donncha's gaze with difficulty and squinting, but he met it. "Boys to shovel manure are cheap and plentiful." As Donncha continued to stare, he added, "My name is Ó Reachtaire, and I come into this estate of my father's, as you'd know if ever you had a thought in your head."

Donncha MacSiadhail had several thoughts at that moment, passing in quick succession. So this was to be the rest of it: after the burying. Well, perhaps. "It could be your mother who has been left that money, Joe-ín."

Strife lent to Seosamh's face a normal amount of color. "You'll leave my mother out of this, MacSiadhail. She won't stand against her only son."

These words somehow restored Donncha's usual ironic complacence. It occurred to him that there was a great amount of manure that needed shoveling this day, and no cheap and plentiful boys nearby to do it. "If that's the way it is, Joe-ín, then good luck to you. I hope you remember where the manure forks are kept." He yawned, stuffed his hands in his pockets, and started walking down the drive in the sunshine.

"Wait." Seosamh followed after. "Where's my mother?"

Donncha's face went wide in wonder. "Surely she's still at the church or resting in the house of a friend in town. Didn't you leave her back there?"

Seosamh didn't answer this. "I ... thought she was ... Never mind, though. Just tell me where you've put the grey horse that won the race."

Now the wonder turned to enlightenment. Donncha grinned like a trap. "You'll have to whistle pretty before you find that animal, Seosamh. He certainly isn't here."

Seosamh was not prepared to accept such an answer, for he had already sold the horse and was carrying the deposit in his trouser pockets. He grabbed Donncha by the sleeve and turned him.

"You won't find him," said Donncha with admirable patience. "That horse never belonged to Anraí at all, and he didn't say that it did. It was a lending and has returned to its home now."

"Lie!" shouted Seosamh. "It's a lie and you're a thief! I'll have you in the gaol cell, a MhicShiadhail, before nightfall."

Donncha was too tired to keep his patience at this. He took a swing at Seosamh, which was too weak and off center to have connected, except that Seosamh himself was weak and off center enough to flinch into it. He staggered backward and howled. Donncha, who had never been much for hitting people, stood slump shouldered and waited for Seosamh to hit back.

Seosamh did hit back, and in the hand with which he hit was a five-pound fishing weight. Had Donncha taken the blow squarely on the temple, as it was aimed, he likely would have joined Anraí in the stony soil. But Donncha had blocked with his hand, and the loaded fist only clipped him over the eyebrow. He went down and stayed down.

When he awoke, the shadows had all moved and the birds had stopped their early singing. Both Seosamh and the black stallion were gone, as well as Anraí's exhibition saddle and bridle.

Donncha crawled into his nest of hay, though the stalls were foul and the water needed changing. His eyes were crossed from the blow and he kept retching the breakfast he hadn't taken.

At least he wouldn't have to lunge the black stallion, he thought, and fell out of consciousness again.

Within sixty minutes it was known by Maurice the hosteler that Seosamh Ó Reachtaire had taken possession of his father's stable and accused Donncha MacSiadhail of stealing the race winner. Within ninety minutes most of Carraroe had the news.

Ó Flaithearta, the grocer, told the wife of Diarmuid Ó Cadhain, who told the postmaster and the Protestant rector besides. Morrie of the *Dreoilín* told Máire Standún as she took the household's fish off the boat, and though both of them had other things to worry about, they spared a bit for Áine NíAnluain and the unfortunate Donncha.

Máire walked home with the gleaming silver pollack in a basket, and her heart was pounding. Ruairí was gone. Gone. Gone with Anraí Ó Reachtaire, and Donncha, poor lad, would suffer for it, if Seosamh had his way. *She* would suffer for it, though not as badly as she might have, had she been weaker.

She came into her own kitchen and found her sister sitting at the table, an untasted cup of tea before her and a sour look on her face. "So you've already heard," said Máire, putting the fish into cold water to await dinner.

"Heard what?" Eibhlín lifted her pretty face to Máire, and it looked as though she'd been crying.

"About Seosamh, Anraí's son, coming into the farm at his father's death. And claiming Donncha had stolen . . . a horse from his father."

Máire, who had no more compunction about repeating gossip than any other resident of Carraroe, had to repeat it all twice. Then she was certain there were tears in her sister's eyes, and she remembered Eibhlín had slept through breakfast. "Eibhlín! What on earth is the matter today?"

Eibhlín flinched, and when Máire took her hand, it was very cold. "I have such a headache. And my eyes and nose burn," Eibhlín said, and she stirred her cooling tea.

"You'd best go to bed," said Máire. "For the summer is a bad time to be sick."

At those words Eibhlín's small features twisted out of shape, for she was suffering, too.

The news that passed through Carraroe, like water down the throat to the belly and into the limbs, had missed one particular limb: the rectory of the priest, where Áine sat with Nóra, the housekeeper, praying, napping, drinking tea, and receiving visitors, all in preparation for the official wake that would be held tonight.

In the winter a man might lay out for three days, but this was midsummer, and besides, Áine hadn't the strength to endure such a stretch of formalized grief.

Anraí's death, however terrible, had not been so unexpected to his wife. She had had him forty years and so had no cause for complaint. Seventy was an old age for a horseman. For a fisherman, it would have been exceptional.

Not one of the many callers at the rectory this fine afternoon spoke a word about Seosamh's accusation. Most assumed she knew, but whether or no, it wasn't the sort of talk that fit in with such a call.

Donncha did not come to tell his side of the story, for he had to watch the horses. He wondered if he would be arrested for this "crime" and who would tend the place if he were dragged off. But no one came. No one.

Blondell heard about the accusation after his very late breakfast, from one of his stableboys who had been sent on an errand to the town, and upon hearing, he became too angry to speak. His son was angry, too, and each of them held his anger in private, for each had a reason to disbelieve Seosamh Ó Reachtaire's story that he could not reveal, and though the reasons were different, father and son behaved in much the same way, and they kept their secrets faithfully. They dropped all business for the day and walked out in the park together.

Because Knockduff was too far for people to go on foot, Anraí's wake was held in Carraroe. The coffin, which was not of deal but good, planed oak, was taken from the church to Maurice's hostelry, for that had the largest room in the town in which whiskey might be poured. And there was whiskey enough, for a large bottle of aged liquor from Dublin sat on one end of the black bar, and a keg of something that never saw a government inspector was hoisted up to the other.

The men stood as thickly as on the best of ordinary nights, and they were only half the population, for the women who normally did not frequent Maurice's hostelry called it instead "the wake house," and they came anyway. Between the two pillars of whiskey along the bar lay babies in ranks in their white woolen blankets, and the children fell asleep on the wall benches or under them. Maurice sat at a table like one of his own customers, for he was taking no profit from this biggest crush of the year, no profit but in the material for stories. He watched the cloud of tobacco smoke on the ceiling fill and sink, until by ten-thirty it had reached the level of the window, after which it leaked out into the evening.

There were the ones who came to the wake for the thoughtfulness of showing, such as Blondell and the priest Ó Murchú and the priest from Ros an Mhíl. And there were the ones who sat out the wake, which was almost everyone else. They would be in the room with the coffin or in the connecting room all night, escaping only to breathe air.

Áine did not sit by the coffin, for she was ready to let the old body go, after the day and the previous night of watching. She sat in the dim light of the far parlor, where the women gathered around her, along with such older men as had known Anraí and herself when young. They said a rosary and then broke to drink tea or whiskey, and then another rosary. There ought to have been a third, but no one remembered to begin it, and by that hour of the night all the memories of seventy years were released, back to the stories of Anraí's childhood as youngest of twelve on Inchamacinna Island.

These had suffered the common dispersal. Four had gone to the sea, three to America, and two to England. Two others had gone to their graves early, and only Anraí had gone to the horses. It was noted that the passion for horses was born into a man, not sprung out of convenience or through the blood of his parents, for there had been no horsemen among the Ó Reachtaires of Inchamacinna. And look at young Tim Ó Cadhain, surrounded by Diarmuid's fine herd, with a calling for the priesthood so strong in him he was in the seminary by age thirteen. And then, there was Seosamh . . .

It had been great fun, remembered old Mícheál Ó Ceallaigh, for his brothers and sisters and cousins to sit on Anraí, who was small and as a child would fling himself upon his oppressors in rages where he felt no pain. So belligerent had he

been, in fact, that one was *forced* to sit on him until the fit
was over.

Áine could not deny it. "But there's no one who's tried that
in the last sixty years and got away with it," she added, in her
protectiveness feeling just a bit like flinging herself upon
Mícheál. And the old man shook his head. "Anraí has done
his own share of sitting on people, I think. Though he was a
true friend."

"A true and loyal friend," added three voices together, and
there was a raising of glasses all around.

Áine did not raise her empty teacup. "His loyalty was to
his horses, first, and his rages all on their behalf." She said
this because she still possessed the right to criticize, and felt a
responsibility to keep the wake realistic.

And she sighed, her mind back on the dozen Ó Reachtaires.
The sea took the four and did not give one to old age. Not
one. England gave back one, when she had become too old
to work, but Anraí had been the last one living.

She had given him no children. Except, of course, Seosamh.

Even in the long, talking hours of the wake, Áine did not
learn what Seosamh had done to Donncha, for that conversation remained in the room with the pipe smoke, and the door
was kept closed.

Máire Standún was at the wake, representing her small
tribe. She sat in the same room as Áine, but because of her
lack of seniority or connection to the Ó Reachtaires, on a
bench at the other side. Many young women in her situation
had brought candles and knitting or spinning gear, but Máire
had brought only a book. She read very well by dim light,
and all assumed it was a prayerbook.

She was not used to being up all night, but rather only half
the night, and that in the evening. So Morrie of the *Dreoilín*
found her nodded over her pages when he came at dawn,
and he closed the book upon her hands.

"A Mháirín, open your eyes," he said. Not whispering, for
a whisper carries in a crowded room.

Her heavy brown eyes opened very wide and quickly and her
whole body tensed. "What, Morrie?"

"There was a boat in by moonlight, to tell me that the

English Major Hous is on the road from Galway. With soldiers in wagons."

She took a very guarded breath and glanced up at the ceiling. She was surprised to see a grey light filling the spaces between the rafters. All around her were others that hadn't kept the "wake," and some kind heart had stuffed a roll of knitting behind Áine's head as she lay sleeping against the high back of the enclosed bench.

"So what will you do?"

"In ten minutes I won't be here," he said calmly. Máire looked straight into Morrie's face. The man looked half asleep, but his eyes were glistening. "Perhaps you should come, too."

She grimaced. "I'm in no danger, Morrie. It's Tadhg Ó Murchú who must go, for if someone has betrayed us at all, he's put his head in a noose."

"But he won't. I've been there at his window already. He says he has a funeral this morning, and likely the soldiers mean nothing."

"English soldiers don't travel under moonlight for nothing," answered Máire. "Did he suggest you stay, too, since the soldiers 'mean nothing'?"

Morrie smiled grimly. "He didn't. And I must go, a Mháirín. My own head is in a noose, and it won't help his at all that way." Máire put her hand upon his and squeezed it, regardless whether anyone was looking. Morrie was gone, and so, in five minutes, was Máire.

A morning wind was coming up. After the fug of the hostelry, the eastern glow was dazzling and it was bitter cold. Máire's eyes were red from tobacco fumes from the bar as she paced the dead and empty street.

They would come and get him and take him away. Perhaps they were already here, but no—she turned in a circle on the gravel—no troop of British soldiers would enter Carraroe unknown, not even at dawn, with most of the population at a wake. But soon. It was not so far to Galway City, and no boat went much faster than a slow wain.

They would take him away, and he'd be shamed in front of the strangers and abjured by his own church, and then they'd hang him for sedition. For sedition: that rock of honesty and devotion to his people. And he wouldn't lift a hand to stop them. Like Christ.

But this was Ó Murchú, and he knew he wasn't Christ. He'd be scandalized at the thought. And he was always a canny man. Máire leaned against the grocer's wall, not caring if the whitewash came off. She felt a strong desire to throw stones at his window. To hiss at him. To shake him.

And here came the priest down the street toward the hostelry now.

Ó Murchú could not miss her. She was the only dark thing on this pale landscape of greys. She hurried toward him, but he didn't move a foot to join her.

"It will be an early funeral," he said, though looking into her face he knew very well she had not come to talk about the funeral.

"Get *out* of here while you can!" Her voice cracked.

Very quietly he said, "Morrie can go. Even you can go if you feel the need, Máire, for your time is your own. But I cannot go without giving up all, for if I run away from my duties here there will be no doubt in the world that I am afraid of this Major Hous."

"You should be afraid of him. We don't know what that man Grover found out, but I'd be willing to bet it was near everything. Or why would he then disappear between morning and night like that?"

Ó Murchú looked away. "I'm not worried about Grover. I don't think his disappearance is connected."

Out of the corner of his eye, Ó Murchú saw Maurice appear in his doorway, his dark hair rumpled over his ears. He was yawning. Immediately the priest turned and went to him, leaving Máire shivering alone in the street.

Her anger and her worry fought for the upper hand. The man was fey, fairy touched, and would go to his doom with a complacent smile. Fool!

The thought of fairy and of fool met in her mind. "Ruairí," she whispered. "You might have been of some use, for once." In another moment the idea possessed her. She blundered between the hostelry and the next house and came out of the yards and over a series of low and broken walls until she was on the point of land above the bay.

"Ruairí MacEibhir!" she screamed into the wind. "You said you loved me! You called me your queen of heaven, which is blasphemy, and now you are gone!" Her words were gone, too, eaten by the roaring air.

Freezing, buffeted on the face and arms, she sank down on the naked stone promontory. For a moment her mind was black.

Then Máire knew how she was to summon this spirit. She knew as though she had been told. Kneeling, she put one hand on the cold, mica-flecked rock, and the other she raised, palm open, fingers spread, against the wind. She lost her shawl to the wind, and it hung from her by only one corner which was caught in her waistband. Her hair snapped free of its ribbon tie and whipped everywhere in its black mass.

"Son of the granite, son of the wind, return to me at my call. I am Máire Iníon Chaitlín, daughter of your distant kinsman and half blood to you, and by your oaths I command you."

The wind came up screaming and Máire slipped on the stone. The wind was a blur in her eyes and *he* was a white blur in her eyes and he was pulling her to her feet, standing between her and the wind. His face was as pleasant and as foolish as always.

"A Mháire, a Mháirín, Empress of my Heart, all you had to do was to call me! To come to you I do not need to be tied and dragged."

She groaned and he kissed her once, impulsively. "A Mháire, what is it? You are distracted."

"You . . . you were gone," she began.

"I was, certainly. But not for long. And did that alone destroy your peace, darling?"

"We need you," she said, in a childish voice, and then tears started in her eyes. "There are soldiers coming for Tadhg Ó Murchú."

His brown eyes blinked twice, taking this in. "So. I see," he said, and with odd dignity he released her arms.

"And he is your friend, isn't he?" Máire asked, for she thought he might refuse to help.

"Oh, he is." Ruairí stepped lightly off the stone and lifted her after him. He was still blinking rapidly, and he stared widely all around at the stones and the sedges and the stripe of foaming water on the shore.

"I've gone the distance, in these few days," he murmured.

Seosamh came to the hostelry soon after Máire had left it, and it seemed to him that all desires would be granted to a man who was up so early and about his ends.

People were leaving to tidy up for the funeral, which would be very soon now. Seosamh cut in between Siobhán NíCeallaigh and her husband as they stood at the doorway, feeling the brightness of the morning on their faces.

Inside was a smell of cold ham and cooked eggs, which woke his stomach roughly. There was his mother, in the parlor that didn't possess a bar. Her face was red and shiny, and she still dabbed under her ears with the towel Maurice had put at her disposal when he had heated water for her in the kitchen. She was all dark from the neck down, for she had borrowed a black blouse from a cousin of hers. Sitting next to her was Tadhg Ó Murchú, adding the black severity of his cassock to her mourning. His foot was up on the bench, with the endless-seeming row of cassock buttons running beside his shin, and he had his knee braced against his hands.

Both of them looked up, and the priest's round face did not alter its calm, closed expression. But Áine stepped toward him.

"Ah, a Sheosaimh! You are making it to the funeral after all. You have even borrowed a good suit for it."

Seosamh put his hands in his pockets as she hugged him. "Of course I am, Mother. I would have been at the wake, too, but . . . I wasn't well."

"That's a shame," she said, releasing him. She didn't question him further as to his illness, but she smiled very sadly. She glanced away from him, down at the black, water-ringed table, where a pair of dark gloves were hiding under her white missal.

They were going to walk out, he saw, and his moment would be lost. He couldn't wait until the funeral and the burying were over.

"Mother, I think Donncha has stolen one of Father's horses."

Áine dropped the gloves again. "Donncha did what?"

"Stole the grey horse that won the race. It isn't to be found at the stables, and he won't admit it even belonged to Father."

"The grey horse! Oh, Sheosaimh. Donncha didn't steal that

fellow. He was telling the strict truth. That horse never was Anraí's." Áine's face was almost merry as she looked at her son, and she hid her mouth behind her hand. "The horse more belongs to Father Ó Murchú here."

The priest took his cue blandly, but promised himself a short lecture to Áine on the nature of truth. "He was only lent me, for a while, in order that I might put him to work. I had no idea he was a racehorse. What is it you want of him, a Sheosaimh?"

Seosamh leaned against the doorjamb, to keep from falling. Part of the money he had taken for the horse was in his pocket, but the rest of it was on his back, in the form of shirt and coat. He realized that some answer was expected of him.

"I only felt it my job to keep track of the property. To keep things safe."

Áine's smile faded. Hesitantly she said, "Your father left a will, you know. He made it in Clifden last week, before the race."

Seosamh straightened himself. "Oh, I know well the old man left everything to you. That's not an issue with me. But someone has to . . ."

"He didn't leave it to me, a Sheosaimh." Áine looked at him and then out the door, where the light was growing. "He . . . thought that since the stables have always operated so near to the wind, as it were, that any change might drive us out of the business completely. So he left the place to the grooms—Donncha and Ruairí—with instructions to take care of me. And I'm sure they will admirably, a Sheosaimh, for what else have they been doing all along but taking care of Anraí and myself?"

His ears filled with the ringing of shock or sickness. His belly seemed to favor sickness. "Donncha? And the other one . . ."

Now Áine's face drew in pain, watching him. "But son, you know while I have a roof over my head, I will take care of . . ."

Seosamh had staggered through the doorway, and he leaned his arm against the wall of the hostelry in the position taken by many men before him, men who had drunk too much and eaten too little. But then his body seemed to change its mind, and instead of vomiting he took off running down the street, past the weary procession of mourners leaving the wake, and the decorous procession of those who had already changed for the funeral.

Past the wagon of the Ó Cadhains he ran, and that numerous clan stared down at him silently, knowing who he was. He almost knocked down Seán Standún, who was still very delicate about his feet and who had come to the funeral on the arm of his youngest daughter. She cried out as he blundered by, perhaps in anger.

He was out of the town and out of breath, but he didn't stop to recover.

A few miles along, just north of Lochán an Bhuilín, he came face to face with the soldiers.

CHAPTER SIXTEEN

Stolen Away by the Fairies

"But if he refuses to be saved, my darling, then what am I to do about it? What is it the part of a friend to do? It was Tadhg Ó Murchú himself who stopped me from coming to your rescue in your battle with the bailiff."

Máire crouched down to be out of the sea wind. "You were going to rescue me?"

"To stand by you, at any rate. Though as it turns out, you didn't need me. And that's what the man said, that you'd do better by yourself."

"He did?" A very young and boyish smile lit her dark face. "Well, God bless him for it. And you, for your desire to help. But it was only for my sake, wasn't it? You told me you don't care for the Irish people."

Ruairí didn't miss the smile, nor the fact that it came with the mention of Ó Murchú's sentiments. He squatted down beside her and did not touch. "It was for you, certainly. But I would do it again without you, a Mháirín, for the people of this parish have become as sacred to me as my own kin."

"Is that the truth?" Máire's brown eyes were startling and wide in the early light. Ruairí swallowed and looked away. "It's true enough, lass. It's a geis on me now, that their labors should be mine."

She put her hand upon his shoulder. "But I don't want to waste time talking about that," he said, and slid it off again. "Let's be about this rescue."

*   *   *

It had not seemed to Máire that much time had passed while she stood by the noise of the ocean, but evidently the funeral had begun. The street was empty except for the sound of the church organ. The two of them came out from between the buildings into brightness. It would not stay cold, today.

"He cannot flee, for that would be to betray his priesthood. But, of course, if they catch him the bishop won't have two thoughts about casting him out, either. What we must do . . ."

"It's too late," whispered Ruairí, for his good ears had caught a sound along the road, and in another moment Máire, too, could hear the beat of feet moving together.

Major Hous came down the street with his coat open and his hat under his arm, more weary than the soldiers who marched behind him. They had traveled from Galway seated on benches, while he had ridden. He approached the rectory and then paused, listening to the organ. At last he directed his men toward the church itself.

There was no one at all in the street except a girl standing by a grey pony, and he wondered if this emptiness was because there had been word of his coming or just another example of the indolence of the Irish. As he trotted closer he saw that it was a fair-sized horse, but its pony face and the unusual size of the girl had conspired to trick his eye.

His mount, though it had walked through the night, grew very nervous and shied away from the pair. Hous sent his lieutenant and five men around to the back of the building, while a dozen more walked up the worn steps, their rifles pointed up at the sky.

A shriek greeted the arrival of the soldiers, and Father Ó Murchú glanced up, though not in great surprise. ". . . that a man with failings—and that is every one of us here—can still be a holy man and the beloved child of God."

It was a sound statement and showed some insight, but none of the congregation was listening. They were on their feet and staring at the rifles in the doorway and at the ordinary male faces, set in watchfulness, that the stained glass of the windows converted into demons.

Áine, mystified, moved from her front pew to stand in

front of the coffin. Her white missal shone in her black, gloved hands.

Major Hous entered the church then, alone of the company. Father Ó Murchú addressed him from the pulpit in English. "Are you going to interrupt this funeral, Officer?"

Hous felt the eyes of all these dowdy, poor people on him. He returned their stares with a certain coldness. "I wouldn't think of it."

Ó Murchú's gaze was not cold, but neither did it give anything away. He continued to look at, and through, the major as he spoke, though he was not speaking to him. ". . . For the first thing we learn in our catechism is that God is our Father and He knows us. Not content to have only created us, body and soul, He sent His Son, who is One with Him, down to be one with us, and there is nothing of your pain here that He does not know and feel: neither the wind that cracks your faces nor the rain that rots the bedding away. In the night He is with you in the darkness, and in the day digging in the garden, and always on the ocean, where you have no promise of return. He was with Anraí Ó Reachtaire on the day of his birth, and I am certain He is with him now. And I am certain He is with us in this church, as we mourn Anraí and honor him and release him in our hearts, to go back to his Father at last."

Tadhg Ó Murchú was a good speaker but not a loud one, and it was all he could do to drag the heads of the assembly back to face him as he finished his sermon. But he worked at it powerfully, for he wanted them to remember.

He stepped down from the lectern, and a few of the soldiers, perhaps Nonconformists, took a step through the doorway, only to be restrained by Major Hous, who was raised Church of England and knew what a mass was. For the long offertory they stood there, almost at attention, blocking the increasing daylight out of the doorway.

Hous wondered, as he listened to the stream of Latin, whether perhaps the priest was giving the congregation instructions for a concerted attack upon the soldiery. Though their own language seemed to Hous made up only of sounds of complaint and throat clearings, still he knew many of them spoke Latin. Or worse, French. There were over a hundred people here, and the women as rough as the men, he had no doubt. But two dozen regulars were a match for any hundred peasants.

The communion was very slow, as it seemed that every pew would empty out its contents to the altar rail; and to slow things down even further, the two altar boys who aided the priest had been frightened into clumsiness.

There was noise in the street; his men had evidently found something to laugh about. He spared a moment to look, though the service was almost done.

The girl they had encountered on the street had now led her horse by the forelock to the foot of the church steps, where it was clowning for the men. It was a silly-looking beast, lop eared and with a hanging head, and at her command it put the most unlikely expressions on its face. It could cross its ears.

The girl herself was heavy eyed and with lips that promised something. Hous wondered if she was looking for trade and would carry her advances even into the church. He decided to put a stop to that, but as he opened his mouth the girl lost her hold on the horse's forelock.

"Oh, dear!" she said, in English, and the horse stepped up to the door.

First it pushed one trooper aside and tried to stick its head between the man's coat and his shirt. "Hand-raised and spoiled," said the major. He pushed at the animal's hip and received a stinging tail across the face.

"Prick it with a knife!" The major was spitting horse hairs as three right hands reached to do his bidding. In another moment the horse had exploded, shrieking, toward the nave of the church.

"Now you've done it," said the girl very flatly.

"Ite, missa est," Ó Murchú had said. "Go, the mass is over." The congregation was in its mumbled reply when the horse screamed. Every one of them turned and every mouth was open as they watched the race winner of two days before charge down the central aisle snapping its teeth. The stallion looked neither right nor left, but came at the priest like a devil unleashed, took him by the throat, shook him, hauled him over the altar rail, and dragged him toward the small, side door.

At first it was thought the man was dead, for the assault

was horrible and straight for the throat, but then Ó Murchú, too, was screaming, though his words were lost to most amid the horse's violence.

There were soldiers at that door, of course, but very few of them had ever in their careers gone to battle against a raging stallion, and had very little idea how to go about it. Nor were they sure whether they were now to take the Popish priest, rescue him, or merely watch him torn asunder.

Out in the yard the beast shook poor Ó Murchú again, so that the priest's head and arms were entangled in the long chasuble he wore, and then with a gesture more like a fox's than a horse's, it flung the man over its back and went galloping down the road, with its burden flopping and bellowing on top.

The major's own horse had been left with his batman, but when he ran to it, it was dragging the soldier by the length of its rein and could not be mounted. He commandeered the Hackney horse out of the shafts of Ó Cadhain's wagon and slashed the lines to riding length with his saber. "Keep them in the church!" he shouted behind him.

Riding that high-stepping horse in its blindered bridle, bareback, he came out of the town of Carraroe to find an empty road and no sight or sound of a horse over all the treeless landscape. Since he could not convince the beast to leap the embankment, he kicked it north along the road until he had disappeared as completely as the stallion and the priest.

The parishioners were still in the church, every man jack of them, held at prayer by riflepoint. Neither did they look eager to leave, for in that one space Major Hous witnessed more upturned eyes and crossings of self than he had encountered in all his previous career in Ireland. He noted the faces, from the ancient with the stick by the doorway to the bereaved widow in her black lace.

"Where's the girl? The girl that started all this."

His lieutenant dipped his eyebrows in thought.

"I told you to keep them in the church!" said Hous.

"She . . . she wasn't ever in the church, sir. After the horse went mad, I don't think any of us saw her again."

Hous strode down the aisle, his boots making a racket, and

stopped at the widow. "Who was the girl at the church door?"

Áine stood in her dignity. "I didn't see anyone in the door but soldiers."

For a moment Hous was angry, but he glanced behind him and saw that she was speaking the truth; no one in the church could have seen down the steps and past his men.

"Who owns that horse?"

Áine smiled, as she had for Seosamh. "Many would have liked to. My old man, for one of them. But no one owns him. Though sometimes he is friendly, he is not tame."

Major Hous smiled along with her, grimly. "I agree with you there."

No one had an explanation to offer better than that simple one offered by the major's eyes. Knife pricks had set off the spoiled, untrained beast, and it had gone for the man in its path as a fox goes for a goose. Old Colm Ó Baoill, who rarely strayed from the stoop of his cottage for anything less important than a funeral, had a variant upon this: that it had been a fairy horse and had stolen the priest away. This was offered in Irish and translated, with much reddening and apology, by a shamefaced grandson.

Major Hous thanked the old man but preferred his own explanation. He sent his men out to comb the stone hills and the boulders of the peninsula, to find the remains of the brutalized Ó Murchú.

It was a fool's errand; it took all the day, and half of the men ruined their trousers in the bogs.

It was not too far from Casla, that poultry house where Toby Blondell had not been desperate enough to linger on the day when he ran away. The desperation of a man may exceed that of a boy, or perhaps Tadhg Ó Murchú had grown up with chickens. He made no complaint about his lodging.

That is not to say he made no complaint. For thirty minutes Ruairí MacEibhir had squatted in the other open corner of the hovel and listened to his faults itemized. The fairy was a swaggering, intrusive, and unintelligent lout. His life was utter selfishness and his soul as dumb as that of a

beast. He had thrust his way into the Catholic Church with
no more sense of his own actions than a cow lapping the holy
water font. And he had now capped his life of thoughtless-
ness with the mortal sin of sacrilege against the sacrament of
the mass, which was all Ó Murchú's fault, he had to admit,
for allowing this camel his head in the church door to begin
with.

Ruairí listened without much attempt to interrupt, for his
few minutes of roaring rage, though purely theatrical, had
taken all fight out of him, and his flight up from Carraroe to
the crossroad had been at full speed. Besides, he had his ear
pressed against the woven screen of the window, listening.

Through the half light he noticed something, and he put
up a finger. "You have blood on your neck," he said to
Ó Murchú.

The priest slapped his hand to the spot. "If I do, who's to
blame for that, you renegade?"

And Ruairí grinned toothily. "Better a little pinch now than
the rope's pinch down the road."

On Ó Murchú's lap was the seam-ripped and tooth-torn
funeral chasuble. His head drooped over it, and he sighed. "I
was prepared for that. To run is to bring shame both to my
vocation and my convictions."

"Hear me, Tadhg Ó Murchú. You didn't run; you were
dragged out by the throat by a murdering mad beast. Your
bishop will be very pleased to have a dead priest instead of a
priest in the dock. Your friends in France and in America,
from all I hear, will be glad enough for your living presence
among them."

Ó Murchú said nothing.

"And Máire Standún, I think, will be glad for you to get
safe away."

The priest's eyes flickered left and right in the light of the
willow screen. "I imagine she will; why not? Is she a part of
your bloody scheme, Ruairí?" He did not seem pleased with
the idea.

"It is the work of her hand only," answered Ruairí. He also
did not seem pleased. "And she is climbing the hill to us this
moment."

*   *   *

Máire came up with a bale of fleeces on her back. Hers was not a fast progress, and because the weight was on her shoulders, she tended to wobble. In the shadow of the poultry house she put down her burden and then disappeared into the hole in the roof, amid a protest of hens.

"So you're the author of this comedy, I hear."

She peered around her. "In some ways I am. Don't be sullen, a Thadhg. What was done fulfills all your stipulations . . ."

"I know. It'll make the pope *and* the queen very happy."

"And you too, I hope," said Máire.

The dark man and the dark woman confronted each other, hardly able to see. Ó Murchú didn't answer, and the air began to crackle with their suppressed feeling.

Ruairí shoved past her and worked his head and shoulders through the hole. It was a difficult job.

Máire found him by feel. "Where are you going, Ruairí? I brought your supper in with me. It's in my lap."

"I'm not . . . I have somewhere to be," he called down through the slats.

She took the canvas of his trousers in her two hands and pulled. She was a strong woman. "What do you mean, you have somewhere to be? What sort of appointment would take you away in the middle of all this?"

"Don't go yet," said Ó Murchú, and in his voice was authority.

Ruairí MacEibhir hovered over them, half crouching, his hair in the slats where the chickens had messed. "I *will* go, though. There is no reason I should be here with the two of you." He glanced over at Ó Murchú, grimacing for the dirt in his face. "I will return for you tonight, and we'll have you in Clare by tomorrow at the same time."

Máire was not oblivious. "What does the man mean: he won't be here with the two of us? Does he think we're sweethearts?"

"I do think that, and it is true." He pulled upward, and she pulled down with doubled strength. Ruairí came down heavily half on her lap and half on the cake, ham, and potatoes. He rose again and hit his head against the roof.

"Well, can you deny it, woman? It seemed to me that if the soldiers took him, you'd die on the spot. And you, Priest of the Parish no longer, what is there to keep you away now, from this woman who is worth so much more than I?"

Máire gave an astounded snort. And Ó Murchú, speaking calmly with his face as closed and secret as ever, said, "I told you once, Fairy Man, that if I broke my vows, it would not be for Máire Standún."

"Of course not!" added Máire, explaining the obvious. "There has been nothing like that at all. You, Ruairí MacEibhir, are as bad as any of the nasty-minded old women in the parish."

He heard her, but didn't take his eyes off Ó Murchú. "Well, then. If you want nothing of this woman, and I am too dangerous a swain, is this treasure to be left gathering dust?"

"What do you mean, you are too dangerous a swain? Did . . . did he"—and she pointed at the priest through the darkness—"did he tell you to stop courting me, Ruairí?"

"He did, and wisely. I killed a man, a Mháire. I killed the man Grover."

"Good for you!"

"A Mháire NíStandún!" shouted Ó Murchú. "You are a bloodier heathen than he is!"

Ruairí tried to explain. "I shouldn't have done it, for I had taken a vow against that. I broke his back as I would kill a rabbit, and it is probably for that reason the soldiers marched into the church this morning."

"Don't take away all my credit," murmured Ó Murchú. "They knew what they were about, if they went for Morrie, too."

Máire settled against the filthy wall. "I'm learning a lot today," she said. "And you're more of a fool than I took you to be. But what other husband is there for a nationalist wife than a dangerous one, even if he is a fool?"

"But it could be that you would be left . . ." Ruairí stopped in the middle of his phrase. "A Mháirín, I'm not one for cutting my own throat. If you are saying you'll have me . . ."

"I'm not saying all that," she answered. "I have questions in my mind, but neither my father nor this priest here nor even you, laddie, is the one to decide whether I'll marry and who I'll marry."

Ruairí sat up and struck his head on a perch, which broke.

But Máire glanced uncertainly from him to the priest. "I'd like you to close your ears, Tadhg."

"I'm not likely to repeat what I hear," he said, laughing. "I've had practice in that before now." But he lowered his head and put his index fingers in his ears.

This method was not proof against hearing, he found, even when he ground his teeth to help. He heard the word "mare," and then Ruairí answered very clearly, "Well, I do have a great respect for them, darling, but . . ." And then the fairy was laughing very coarsely, and Máire said nothing at all.

The voices went on for a long time, and when they lost their urgent up-and-down-ness, Ó Murchú got tired of having his fingers in his ears. Unobtrusively he lay his hands over the mangled chasuble on his lap.

It was Ruairí, speaking: ". . . and the mare is out of Tim Ó Cadhain's best blood mare and by Anraí's black. But *her* baby is by my own black king, and it will be a filly. She's the very horse for you: Anraí paid Diarmuid for her already, though she's not even a swelling in her mother's belly."

He sounded very confident, as though the matter was decided between them.

"Hers is the blood of all the good horses in Connemara— those that are really horses, my love, not púca fairies—and she will be the foundation of our stable."

"You're going too fast," answered Máire. "I haven't said I will. This is not the time to be discussing affairs of the heart, with the soldiers getting lost in every combe and Tadhg, here . . ."

Shifting uneasily, Ó Murchú put his second fingers into his ears. They worked better.

He almost fell asleep from the weariness of being bruised, bloodied, and hauled over the hills, but a sound roused him. Ó Murchú raised his eyes in time to see Máire's full petticoat disappearing through the roof. She put her face in again and winked and whispered, "Tonight."

He was left alone with the hens all afternoon, and they shared the very nice funeral supper that Áine had ordered, Maurice prepared, Máire carried, and Ruairí sat upon.

Two days went by. Ruairí MacEibhir came back from Clare very tired, only to find Donncha in worse condition than

Ruairí. The horsemen worked together for a week of long hours, repairing the neglect caused by three days of upset.

The soldiers were gone, and Major Hous had become reduced to one of Maurice's stories: a small part of the large story that was the great race and its tragedy, and the other tragedy or miracle that had happened at the funeral. The major's name was remembered, however, for he had had the boldness to ride off on Ó Cadhain's bone-jarring Hackney, though he hadn't gained anything by it but barstool fame.

Ruairí was in Carraroe often, and each time he looked happier, sleepier, and broader about the shoulders. He called upon Máire at the back door of her house, according to approved custom.

On a day of clouds a week after the funeral of Anraí, it was Seán Standún who opened the door and who closed it after Ruairí.

The fair man stood like a razor. "My daughter," he said, "tells me that she is with child by you."

Ruairí's eyes opened wider. "She does? Then she must know very little about the act of engendering. I had thought Máire raised chickens, at least."

Standún didn't move. In his hand he held his polished walking stick, which he no longer needed. He held it very tightly. "It is not Máire we're talking about."

Now there was a ring of white around each of Ruairí's eyes. "Eibhlín? She is *very* ignorant, then. Or does me more honor than I deserve, in that case. Bring her here to me."

Seán Standún hesitated, fingering the stick, but at last he called her name. He had to call twice.

Eibhlín slid into the room, looking pale, pretty, and very frightened. She stood behind her father.

"Now why would you tell your father I have trifled with you, woman? You know very well I have courted your sister to distraction since I came here."

Standún moved, so that he himself could look at the girl's face. She backed against the wall. "You told me you were just sporting with her"—her voice was high and small—"that it was me you loved. You told me . . ."

"I told you to behave yourself, and I told you nothing else!" He did not move toward her or threaten her. In fact,

Ruairí seemed to take the accusation as a backhanded compliment, ineptly conferred. "And I notice it's only since I came into half of Anraí Ó Reachtaire's property that you see fit to throw this at me, girl, yet by looking at you I guess you have been carrying for two months or more. Wasn't I the father till now?"

Again Standún stepped between them. "How do you know how far along she is, if you're not the father?"

Baldly Ruairí answered, "I know something about breeding, both horse and human. An old monk could see she's carrying." He looked to Eibhlín again. "I told you, when I found you hiding in the ditch, waiting for your lover, that a foal needs no father, but a baby . . ."

"Hiding in the ditch!" Standún had a long neck, and now all the tendons stood out from it. "Waiting for whom?"

He shouted this question at Ruairí, who was listening to the sound of footsteps on the stairs. "You'll have to get that from the girl, Seán. It's not my place to tell you."

Eibhlín was backed against the wall, looking very sick. She made a sudden spring for the doorway, only to slam into Máire, who was coming into the room. The dark woman's much longer arms held her pinned. "Did she accuse you, Ruairí? Did she really? I wondered if that was her little game."

Eibhlín struggled and cried, childlike, but Máire would not release her. "Then, as she is such a weasel, I will tell you who she was meeting at night."

"Don't talk!" cried Eibhlín. "Or . . . I'll tell them where you went at night, almost every night . . ."

Standún's face went sick, white, and angry.

"Where I went? I went riding, is where I went. Twice or three times, Eibhlín." She turned to face Seán Standún. "With this man here, who knows what respect is due to a woman.

"Eibhlín's beau was Seosamh Ó Reachtaire, who ran away after knocking Donncha MacSiadhail senseless, leaving bills behind him and Diarmuid Ó Cadhain claiming to have bought from him a horse that doesn't exist."

She let her sister go, but as her father followed after, livid faced and cursing, Máire blocked the door. "Let her be. You won't do that innocent babe a harm, Father. Not this time."

"Damn bastard!"

"Another damn bastard," she corrected him. "But this one won't have the misfortune to be raised here, with you and that word in your mouth." She glanced at Ruairí. "That is, if my man is willing to take it into the grand house I have waiting, and to raise it among our own."

Ruairí could hardly speak. "Whatever the queen of heaven says." And in sudden enlightenment he added, "We will raise the baby in Áine's name. And Anraí's."

Máire's grin matched his, and the joy of their understanding sent him skipping from foot to foot.

"Oh, that's a fine idea, Ruairí. Very clever."

EPILOGUE

A Visit to the Land of His Ancestors

Nineteen forty-three was a year in which the coastal people of Connemara and the islanders to the south pulled many things out of the water: wreckage of British ships, German submarines, and airplanes of all nationalities. According to old custom, the fishermen did their best by the survivors they encountered, and did very well, too, by the goods that washed ashore.

Occasionally, a German submarine would surface near one of the Galway hookers or even the canvas curraghs of the minor fishermen and ask if there were fresh fish for sale. In the rest of Ireland, such an event would have made people nervous, but Connemara fishermen had lived on the edge of disaster for hundreds of years. Besides, the pay was in good Irish punts.

It was not a matter of international diplomacy but one of land taxes that brought Aengas Theodore Ó Baoill (called Teddy, by his friends) from Galway down the Coast Road. He was not quite a tax collector, but he heralded the approach of the man who had the black authority of the tax collector. He hated his job and was good at it.

A family consisting of three brothers and their elderly mother and father had made some money with a horse business and a good amount of land, until the death of a business partner. After this they had dispersed their stock and sold most of the property. Since then, income seemed to have

dwindled terribly, and in the past two years there had been
no tax report at all from the MacEibhirs.

On the drizzling drive past Salthill and into the landscape
of boulders, Ó Baoill felt his own sort of Ireland—the Ireland that was nervous, that read all the war news—falling
away from him into the inscrutable stolidity of Connemara. That man with the cart there, hauling turf in the
rain—what if Ó Baoill were to ask him about events in the
Asian theater? He would assume it to be located in Dublin, or
even Galway, like the Abbey Theatre, and would explain that
he hadn't the money for such things as theaters.

Ó Baoill had had five years of night study on the subjects
of Irish archeology, anthropology, and of course, Irish history, as well as one very small and careful course on Catholic
theology—whatever had been needed to advance with the
government. These studies had left him with a very sour taste
in his mouth regarding ancient Ireland, and the opinion that,
if it took all the bright men in modern Ireland half their
working lives to maintain a few peasants in their state of
artifactual, anachronistic ignorance, then that state of ignorance was too dearly bought.

Yet it was his job to go into this parish and find out
things without disturbing the status quo or leaving the people
feeling their own government as one more outside oppressor.

Ó Baoill could do that, thanks partly to the Cois Fhairrge
dialect bequeathed to him by his grandfather, who had moved
from the area to work in Cork. This dialect he could don like
a pair of overalls and take off again in converse with educated
men of school Gaelic. He had also inherited the round face
and small features of his grandfather, whom he had disliked.
Ó Baoill could slide into a neighborhood of the west without
raising an insular, anaphylactic response from the natives,
and he could find things out. It invariably cost Inland Reve-
nue more money to send him out than his researches produced.

At the base of Knockduff he found no stable at all, but
only the Ursuline school, which had settled into two old
barns and a house. There was a lot of building going on, and
no hope in any of it for an Irish tax collector. One of the
sisters pointed him south around the mountain, where the
MacEibhir house itself was located, but after two hours of

slow driving and hard peering out the rainy windshield, he had not located it. He drove on to town.

Mr. Ó Baoill did not like Carraroe, which seemed to him half slum and half museum. He did not like the bars he sat in that evening, nor the Smithy's and Guinness that swelled his bladder and promised him a bad mouth in the morning. But he stared at the dirty wall with as bovine an eye as he could command and he brought the conversation insistently around to horses.

His daughter, he said, had a pony out of a mare raised at a farm out here. Good jumper, lots of ribbons. No, it wasn't one of Ó Cadhain's lot. Another name. Odd name. MacEibhir—Granite's son—were there any others like her still on the hills, he wanted to know.

The men in the Brown Pot stared at each other like so many owls. MacEibhir's stock. They nodded wisely. Good stock. Old stock. Too bad it was failing, now with the pony registry coming so strong and ponies starting to be worth something again. Ó Cadhain had some of the old ones. There were a few still breeding in Ros an Mhíl. Professor Blondell had had a MacEibhir pony stallion kept at his place for years, though it had rattled alone in the old stables and had little enough work, except for breeding mares at a few shillings a service. Did Teddy know that the stable under Knockduff was now a girl's school? They had two ponies, it was remembered, but no one could recall whether they were of the true MacEibhir breeding. Likely they wouldn't sell, anyway.

Was it drink that did the business in, asked Ó Baoill, feeling himself on familiar territory. The muffled laughter that spread up and down the bar warned him he had made a mistake. He cursed into his beer and went passive, giving the conversation time to recover its rhythm.

The recovery took twenty minutes and went by way of brags about how much a man could drink and not show it, how queerly he could show it if it came to that, and how visitors crumpled before decent poitín, and at last someone explained to Ó Baoill how much whiskey had been wasted, trying to touch the heads of old Ruairí MacEibhir and his sons, inside the walls of this very hostelry.

Ó Baoill sighed in relief as the name came up again, and to reward himself for his patience, he ordered a supper of ham

and an egg. Now that conversation had gone in a circle and
returned to the MacEibhirs, he would have to inject the
subject no more. It would float on its own.

There had been five in the family, counting the mother,
who was rightfully a Stanton. Teddy Ó Baoill listened and
nodded as he was told all the information he already knew:
that the boys were called Anraí, young Ruairí, and Tadhg;
that they had come with a good ten years between the first
and second, and five between the second and third, which
was strange out of one woman; and that they had never
seemed to lack for anything, though horses were a chancy
occupation. Of course they'd had old Donncha to help them:
a sad fellow with no family of his own.

Ruairí's children, on the other hand, had stayed close, all
horse-mad together. There was a framed picture behind the
bar which the bartender pulled off the wall for inspection,
leaving a rectangle of clean wallpaper behind it. It was a
photograph of three dark shapes on stocky white horses,
which were all up on their hind legs in a line. It was a very
poor photo, in which the horses showed far more clearly
than the boys, and it took Ó Baoill's next-stool neighbor to
point out to him that none of the ponies had bridle or tack of
any kind.

Did they compete in horse sports, then? They did not,
much. One man in a heavy geansaí remembered wrestling
with Tadhg MacEibhir as a growing boy, and being thrown
by him. They "helped out" in the parish in their casual way.
So did everyone.

Did they have children of their own? Not a one of them.
None married. Now, there were no horses on the mountain.
No MacEibhirs, either.

It was now eleven o'clock, and Ó Baoill was tired and too
full in the stomach. He dared ask it; where did they all go,
these people? Wasn't there one of them left, to help him find
the right pony?

Great silence. Silence of chickens with the hawk overhead.
Silence of stones. Ó Baoill heard the wind against the hostelry
door and the rain against the window.

The fisherman spoke for the entire bar. "Louis Ó Cadhain
is a good hand with a pony. But as for Ruairí and his people
. . . we don't know a thing."

And that was it. Neither more evenings, more beer, nor more bars could change that answer. The men of Carraroe didn't know a thing, and Ó Baoill cursed their unconquerable ignorance.

Four days passed and Ó Baoill had a bad head, caused by exposure more to tobacco smoke than to beer, and he entertained the possibility that the missing family had been kidnapped by the Germans. Or perhaps they were in the pay of the Germans and had fled to escape exposure. Perhaps all the parish was in the pay of the Germans. Or perhaps it was the British navy that had spirited them away, though that seemed less likely on the face of it. Most likely, though, they were all still here and delinquent in their tax, and the men at the bars simply didn't want to tell Teddy Ó Baoill. What a shame.

He could not find a photograph of the MacEibhir family any better than the one on the barroom wall, except for one candid shot of Máire, the mother, taken in her middle years. She was large boned and just a touch heavy, and she seemed to be considering slapping the camera out of the photographer's hand.

But Ó Baoill had come prepared with the information that the child of Máire Stanton's sister had been raised by the MacEibhir family. Áine Ó Reachtaire had subsequently emigrated to America; she was still alive in Chicago. He would very much like to have called her on the telephone, saving some days, but what with the difficulty of using the transatlantic cable during wartime he merely returned to Galway and wrote to the woman, not mentioning taxes but only that the government was concerned about the family's disappearance. Could she supply information or, failing that, pictures of the parties involved?

In due time, Mrs. Persky née Ó Reachtaire sent to Mr. Ó Baoill a snapshot of a drawing she had done as a young woman, as well as advice to the government not to worry about her family, but rather to spend their monies on the children's schools.

Ó Baoill thought of the stable filled with little girls and nuns, and laughed at how pleased Mrs. Persky must be at that.

He did not gain much from the sketch. It was not a drawing of talent, for all the people in it, mother, father, and children, looked much the same age, and the eyes were most unrealistically done.

Another week passed while Ó Baoill sat and thought, before he made a phone call from his office to that very same Professor Blondell who had once kept a pony stallion in his stable. Ó Baoill explained that there was some concern over the disappearance of an entire family from the county in that mysterious manner. He did not mention anything about taxes. He drove down the long, bad road to see the professor that same day.

Blondell's big house had suffered little change in sixty years, but the stone stables had been sold and transmuted into two neat family dwellings, with children on the stoops. As Ó Baoill's car eased past them, the children rose up and ran inside: not out of fear of Teddy Ó Baoill, but because it had started to rain.

Blondell was a lean-faced, hawk-nosed gentleman of some seventy years, whose field seemed to be Irish history. By the plaques on the library wall, Ó Baoill also picked up that the professor's affiliation was with Trinity College. Ó Baoill found himself inhibited by a respect learned through years of night classes, and he was a touch sullen because of it.

But Blondell had a most engaging smile and was not at all haughty. He kept the battered flat saddle of his childhood on a stand by his desk, and he explained how he slipped his day's mail through the stirrups: near side incoming and offside outgoing. He invited Ó Baoill to tea.

He was very willing to talk about Ruairí MacEibhir, whom he had known since his own childhood. He had watched Ruairí's boys grow and had been a sort of unofficial godfather to them.

Ó Baoill knew why Blondell had to be "unofficial" as a godfather. His vowels, as well as his name, shouted Church of Ireland. He returned the old professor's smile, knowing this.

The family were always good sorts, said Blondell. Not clever. Not precisely clever. Good sorts. Ruairí had taught him how to ride. He had taught him Gaelic.

Ó Baoill did not ask the man to speak Gaelic.

They had always talked about traveling, Blondell told

Ó Baoill, as he fed him a good-sized tea with cold ham and hot sausage, and they both looked out at the rain from the east-facing window. They had talked about travel in the vague, enthusiastic way people will who have never traveled. When the kids were grown, they had said they would all go somewhere. Blondell looked out the window, while Ó Baoill looked at Blondell.

"I don't even know," said the professor carefully "in which direction they went: north, south . . ."

"Hardly to the Riviera."

Blondell shot a glance back at Ó Baoill. "No. Hardly the Riviera." He was of Ó Baoill's sort: the sort that read the war news daily.

Blondell guessed his friends to be still in Ireland. He was sure they were out for pleasure.

True, they were a bit old for starting. Certainly Máire was eighty, but in strong health. Ruairí's age he couldn't state precisely; he'd always been grey. The boys never seemed to grow up.

It didn't surprise Blondell they had left without saying good-bye to anyone. He would have liked them to take leave of him, but he wasn't surprised that they didn't. It did surprise him that anyone had reported them as missing. It would surprise Blondell inutterably to find their disappearance had anything to do with the war.

On the phone, Ó Baoill hadn't precisely said that he thought the disappearance was related to the European war. Nor did he now take the opportunity to correct Professor Blondell's misconception. He sighed and scratched his nose.

"They left things undone," was what he said.

"Nothing important." Blondell's was the peculiar stare of a man trying to be understood in many ways at once. With his raptorial nose, it was daunting. Ó Baoill thought briefly that if this man wanted to, he could make a student feel as flat as a cowpat.

"Though they are here among us in the twentieth century, my friends were not of us. If we expect such as they to follow our rules, we will only be disappointed."

That again, thought Ó Baoill. What had he expected out of an historian? Let a poor, English-speaking man of Drogheda

run away from his taxes and see who makes apologies for
him.

For a moment Ó Baoill sat in anger, and then that melted
before the knowledge that this man here, who so valued the
Gaelic primitivism, did so because he was not a Gael. In that
knowledge, Ó Baoill was able to smile and shake Blondell's
hand at parting.

"Ruairí MacEibhir was like a second father to me," added
Blondell, with the same careful, almost secretive intensity he
had shown whenever speaking of the horse trainer.

Ó Baoill considered the size of the house around him, and
the quality of Blondell's tweeds and vowels, and he chuckled
to himself. A second father.

Carrying a map drawn for him by Blondell, Ó Baoill finally
found the house against the side of Knockduff: the house that
the family had deserted. It was imposing in its size. But it
was certainly not what one would call a manor house; it was
the work of a man with more energy than education. It was
of rough stone, and had a vague resemblance to a Norman
castle, or perhaps to the fort at Dun Aengus. It swelled
outward from the stone of the mountain itself which was its
north wall. Only the roof seemed professionally done.

Perhaps it would go to Áine Ó Reachtaire or to some distant
Stanton relation. Or perhaps all of it would come to the
government for charges. If that happened, for once his recov-
eries would be larger than his salary.

At the door he found a wreath of weeds, now very sodden,
which had collapsed against the jamb, proving that though the
door wasn't locked, it had not been used in some time. And
there was a red ribbon with three sticks tied into it on the
stoop, and a bowl of milk, well diluted with rain. (It seemed
that this year it would rain all spring and summer and into
the autumn, too.) More peasant piseógí to encumber Ó Baoill's
work. He went in.

The place was empty of furniture. Ó Baoill went to the
kitchen to find the cupboards bare. He stood in the kitchen,
away from the rain, and let his attention wander over the
faded, much-repaired murals on the walls, while he considered his drive back to Galway over the bad roads. The
paintings were very naive; they made him laugh. A bridge. A

Chinese girl. An umbrella. Ó Baoill had left his umbrella somewhere, perhaps at Blondell's.

Ó Baoill went home feeling very depressed and feeling that more than enough had been done in this instance. He wrote out a short report, in which he recommended having the house at Knockduff checked for structural stability before they considered taking it in lieu of land taxes. It might not be saleable.

Ruairí MacEibhir and his family were most probably still in Ireland, he wrote, because without some sort of passport they could not enter any neighboring country, not with the war. It was possible they were to be found in Mayo or Cork or Dublin, like so many dispossessed Connemara men.

And if they were not found roaming, by the census or the parish or the police, then the missing people would eventually turn up again amid the bog and stone of their home. People like MacEibhir do come back.

Ó Baoill's understanding was flawed and his reasoning biased by a desire to be finished with his fruitless task. But despite all this, his conclusion was correct. People like MacEibhir do come back. Again and again.

THE UNFORGETTABLE FANTASY NOVELS OF
R. A. MacAvoy

☐ TEA WITH THE BLACK DRAGON (25403-0 • $2.95) "A refreshing change from the more familiar epic or heroic fantasy. I recommend it highly."—*San Francisco Chronicle*

☐ TWISTING THE ROPE (26026-X • $3.50) The Black Dragon is back! "Wow! MacAvoy's done it again." —Anne McCaffrey

☐ DAMIANO (25347-6 • $2.95) "A treasurable read. MacAvoy is undeniably a writer to watch for."—Anne McCaffrey

☐ DAMIANO'S LUTE (25977-6 • $2.95) "This is fantasy at its highest point."—Andre Norton

☐ RAPHAEL (25978-4 • $2.95) "This sequel to DAMIANO and DAMIANO'S LUTE concludes a remarkable trilogy full of warmth, gentle humor and MacAvoy's undeniable charm."—*Library Journal*

☐ THE BOOK OF KELLS (25260-7 • $3.50) "Strongly recommended to all. The strength of the novel lies in the credibility of both setting and character." —*Fantasy Review*

Buy these titles wherever Bantam Spectra Books are sold, or use the handy coupon below for ordering:

Bantam Books, Inc., Dept. SF8, 414 East Golf Road, Des Plaines, Ill. 60016

Please send me the books I have checked above. I am enclosing $_____ (Please add $1.50 to cover postage and handling). Send check or money order—no cash or C.O.D.s please.

Mr/Ms _____

Address _____

City/State _____ Zip _____

SF8—5/87

Please allow four to six weeks for delivery. This offer expires 11/87. Prices and availability subject to change without notice.